storm

surge
rene gu

eridge

Tyndale House Publishers, Inc.,
Carol Stream, Illinois

For Ron and Barb,
I'm so thankful to know you both.

Visit Tyndale's exciting Web site at www.tyndale.com

TYNDALE is a registered trademark of Tyndale House Publishers, Inc.

Tyndale's quill logo is a trademark of Tyndale House Publishers, Inc.

Storm Surge

Designed by Dean H. Renninger
Edited by Lorie Popp

This novel is a work of fiction. Names, characters, places, and incidents are either the product of the author's imagination or are used fictitiously. Any resemblance to actual events, locales, organizations, or persons, living or dead, is entirely coincidental and beyond the intent of either the author or the publisher.

Library of Congress Cataloging-in-Publication Data

Gutteridge, Rene.
Storm surge : sequel to the Splitting Storm / Rene Gutteridge.
  p. cm.
  ISBN-13: 978-0-8423-8766-8 (isbn-13 : pbk. : alk. paper)
  ISBN-10: 0-8423-8766-8 (isbn-10 : pbk. : alk. paper)
  1. Government investigators—Fiction.   2. Arson investigation—Fiction.   3. Death row inmates—Fiction.   I. Title.
  PS3557.U887S763 2005
  813'.6—dc22   2005022827

Printed in the United States of America

10 09 08 07 06 05
 7   6   5   4   3   2   1

prologue

S top talking so loud."

"I feel like I'm going to vomit."

"Take a deep breath. I'm not going to be able to help you unless I understand what the matter is."

"You're acting like you don't know."

"Shhh. Talk quieter."

"Don't you know?"

"Know what?"

"He's a . . . a . . ."

"Who?"

"You know who."

"You're scaring me, man."

"You should be scared, Jefferson. We should be."

"Come over here. Shhh. Quieter. Around this tree. Now. Tell me."

"You haven't noticed how crazy he's been acting?"

"Are you talking about—?"

"Don't say his name!"

"Shhh!"

"Just don't say his name. He knows things. He knows a lot of things, things he shouldn't."

"What kinds of things? What?"

"He knows things about me. He told me so."

"What kinds of things?"

"Things that shouldn't be spoken of."

"Tell me."

"It doesn't matter. He knows things about you too."

"Now you're talking crazy."

"I think there's something wrong with him. He's making stupid decisions. Anyone can see that."

"We have to trust him."

"No, we don't have to trust him. We don't. I don't."

"What are you saying?"

"Let's speak to . . ."

"To who?"

"Shhh."

"What?"

"Shut up. He's—"

"What the—?"

"Sir!"

chapter one

through the window of a second-story room in the Dallas courthouse, Sammy Earle studied a cluster of green oak leaves refusing to turn their natural orange color and drop to the ground. Spread against the grass below was a fiery lake, circling the tree with near precision, untouched by children wading through it.

"It's time," said Doyle Clarkson from the doorway. In the past week, the man who had promised him freedom a year ago had grown distant, fashioning a stoic face whenever they met. Sammy had hired Doyle Clarkson because of his famed reputation as a criminal defense attorney. It had cost him every dime he had.

Three days ago, Doyle had come to the jail, dressed down in a casual silk shirt and dark khakis. Sammy could barely look at him. He knew every trick in the book. Doyle's choice of dress was meant to make Sammy forget about his high price tag, forget that what had already cost him so much was probably going to cost him even more.

"You should prepare for whatever happens," Doyle had said. It was not the first indication Doyle had given that he was slowly growing hopeless.

Sammy no longer owned a home or a car. He'd kept

1

three good suits and some stock. So by "prepare" Sammy could only assume that Doyle was talking in a spiritual sense.

Sammy fingered the brown handkerchief that poked from the breast pocket of his suit. Turning, he met Doyle's eyes. The man was striking, with shiny silver hair, transparent gray eyes, and a natural tan to his skin. He'd always looked good on TV.

Doyle smiled meekly. Next to him was Maureen, his lovely assistant, carrying a hard, leather briefcase by her side. She'd chosen a conservative navy suit. Maureen avoided Sammy's eyes. From the beginning, he'd sensed that she never believed in his innocence. It hadn't mattered much. She was simply eye candy.

Doyle said to Maureen, "Tell the others we'll be out shortly," and then he approached Sammy. "How are you feeling?"

"I don't understand this," Sammy whispered. It was all he could say. His knees felt weak, as if they were barely able to hold the weight that had piled onto his shoulders.

For weeks and weeks, he'd held his head high, believing in the justice system that he had worshiped for decades. Even the statistics were in his favor. The chances of a white, upper-class male being wrongly convicted of a crime were nearly zero. Yet it had happened.

It had been one nightmarish day after another. Doyle and his team had combed the evidence, assuring Sammy that it was at best circumstantial. The trial was complicated. His ex-girlfriend, Taylor Franks, had tried to set him up, faking a kidnapping to try to bring him down. Unfortunately, that had brought out some less-than-pleasant facts about him, including how he'd maliciously ruined her credit. That despicable relationship was probably going to cost him his life.

He'd spent hours in jail, lying flat on his back, staring at a musty, stale ceiling, trying to figure out how it all connected. The assistant DA who was working the supposed kidnapping case had been murdered. That night Sammy had been beckoned to his house by a strange note. His fingerprints were everywhere. His footprint was on a patch of dirt. He immediately became the one and only suspect.

Even Doyle had expressed problems with Sammy's theory that he'd been set up. The note that had summoned him to ADA Stephen Fiscall's house, the note that Sammy said proved he was set up, was the prosecution's weapon, showing motive. The ex-girlfriend who started the whole fiasco with the stunt she pulled was the prosecution's star witness—pretty, vulnerable, and full of seedy details about what kind of man Sammy Earle was.

So the prosecution had connected the dots—too easily, Sammy thought—one by one. Taylor Franks was so "scared" of what a horrible person Sammy Earle was that she faked her own kidnapping. Sammy, afraid of information that the DA had learned about the kidnapping case and that he was about to become the primary suspect, murdered the DA.

"Quite sloppily murdered the DA," Sammy had pointed out to Doyle at one of their first meetings. "Don't you think," Sammy said, "that if I was going to murder a district attorney, being a criminal defense lawyer myself, I might be more careful about it?"

Doyle had agreed, though he thought the prosecution would probably try to show Sammy as a drunk, erratic man with an infamous temper. And to their credit, they painted that portrait nicely.

The irony had never been lost on Sammy Earle. He'd defended many criminals whose money and fame sometimes were an asset and sometimes a detriment. He'd stared across the table at high-powered people. Once in a while he'd had to prepare them for the fact that all their money and connections and fame were not going to get them out of the trouble they'd caused. More often than not, Sammy would smile and shake their hands, graciously accepting the hefty pats on the back and the occasional, sentient hug. He'd seen grown men cry when their verdicts were read.

But he'd always failed to grapple the emotionality of the entire judicial process from the point of view of a defendant.

"Sam, you look sick. Are you okay?"

With those few words, Sammy began weeping. Uncontrollable bursts of sorrow and dismay seized every muscle in his body, and he collapsed into a nearby chair, hiding his face with his hands, slumping to try to hide his soul.

He heard Doyle walk to the door and close it softly.

"I'm innocent!" Sammy wailed. "This can't be happening! I'm innocent! I'm innocent!"

Doyle stood several feet away, wordlessly expressing his horror. His calm demeanor turned rigid, and through teary eyes Sammy could see Doyle contemplating how he was going to get his client to the courtroom to hear his sentence.

The word *guilty* had nearly collapsed him days before. Doyle's finely rehearsed speech to Sammy about getting his things in order had not helped his confidence, though Doyle had ended the short meeting with a thumbs-up and a wink, gestures he was known for. Every newspaper picture or piece of video of the man always showed his famous, politician-style wave or that stupid duet of winking and thumbing it. The public ate it up.

No matter what the outcome was today, Sammy knew

the drill. Doyle would walk down the front steps of the courthouse, greet the reporters, and tell the world that he will fight for Samuel Earle.

But the money had run out. And if he was going to face the death penalty, it wasn't going to be with Doyle Clarkson. It was going to be with a public defender with an alcohol problem to rival his.

He could really use a drink right now.

"Sam, stand up," Doyle instructed.

Sammy pathetically obeyed, his shoulders slouched as he drew his frame erect.

Doyle slid his hands across Sammy's shoulders, from both sides of his neck and out, as if he could flick away the enormous burden Sammy was about to face. "It is in the judge's hands now," Doyle said, adjusting Sammy's brown handkerchief.

Sammy knew he admired the color choice. Doyle's own handkerchief was a muted burgundy. Not so long ago, Sammy really believed that the color of a suit and the style of hair made a difference in how the jury perceived you. But walking into that courtroom in a few minutes, he might as well be naked, because that's how he felt.

"There's nothing else we can do except hope for the best."

Sammy stared out the window again. The cluster of leaves was still clinging for dear life, as if believing it had a chance against Old Man Winter.

"It'll be okay," Doyle said softly.

Sammy looked at him. For the first time, he heard compassion and genuine concern.

Sammy walked to the door. Doyle opened it for him. That gesture might be the last nice thing done for him. If ordered to be executed, he would have ten years of worthless appeals processes . . . ten years of wretched existence before dying an honorless death. If sentenced to life, he was sure he would serve out his sentence wishing he were dead.

His bones quivered.

The legal team that had failed so miserably stood in the hallway, stealing glances as Sammy walked past. It felt as if he were walking on the air, weightless and numb. The shiny, fluorescent-lit hallway stretched before him like an endless tunnel. Around him, the conversations muddled against the fearful and desperate screams that filled his head.

How could a man walk to his own death? Is that the last decent thing a criminal could do? Carry himself to his own death?

But he was no criminal. Not a saint, by any means. But not a murderer. *Not a murderer.*

Somebody, somewhere, was a murderer. The problem was, Sammy had made so many enemies in his lifetime that he could not even begin to guess who might've done it.

But whoever it was, he was out there enjoying the land of the free.

chapter two

nbelievable," Mick Kline whispered, raising his Canon to eye level and clicking pictures as fast as his shutter would handle it.

"You've got the best seat in the house," Jack Graff said.

"How long have you been doing this?"

"Flying helicopters or chasing tornadoes?" Graff asked.

"Both."

"Flying helicopters for twenty years. Used to do that LA gig. Worked for a studio. Took famous people here and there. Paid well, but pretty boring. Then I took this job for a little more excitement, covering the news, you know. I'm from California, so I had no idea part of my job description would be chasing these storms." Graff grinned as he turned a knob with his right hand and adjusted something above that. "I fell in love with it during the first one. There's nothing like it in the world."

Mick studied the storm. "This one's setting up to be big."

Graff radioed the chief meteorologist at the station and gave him his location. Dale Drear was known for his precise weather-predicting skills and love for interrupting prime-time television to track a storm. Depending on the show he was interrupting, he could cause quite a bit of hate mail to come in.

Over another frequency, a helicopter pilot from a rival TV station reported his location to Graff.

"That's Tim Sewell. He's been chasing these things for thirty years. But he has an obsession with telling me his location, like we might bump each other out of the sky or something. Could happen, but I don't need a location report every fifteen minutes."

Mick took a moment to look around him. It had been years since he'd been in a helicopter, and never to chase a storm. He hadn't stopped smiling since they got into the air two hours ago to watch the thing develop from the Oklahoma-Texas border.

Below, a tiny town, four square miles wide, settled itself quietly between the green pastures. The sun's light bounced off the enormous thunderhead to its west, spilling golden rays on top of the rooftops.

"I heard you were at the May 3rd storm in Oklahoma," Graff said.

"One of my pictures was used in *Newsweek*."

"That must've been quite a sight. I have a buddy who flies for one of the news stations there. He chased that tornado clear across the state. How long did it stay on the ground? A few hours?"

Mick nodded.

"He said he saw it come into Oklahoma City as an F5. He was taking pictures, and the next thing he knew, half the city was blown away. Those were some of the most amazing photos I've ever seen. Entire suburban neighborhoods completely gone."

"I hid underneath an overpass with a family. They had two small kids with them. It was terrifying. The noise that thing made was something I'll never forget."

"Wasn't it about a mile wide too?"

"Yeah. Enormous. That tornado was a freak of nature."

"Speaking of tornadoes, looks like we've got a wall cloud," Graff said and radioed the station. The small Doppler-radar screen he had crammed among the other equipment in the cockpit confirmed what they were seeing.

"Jack, we're going to break into programming in about three minutes and put you on live, okay?" said Dale Drear.

"Ten-four." Graff turned to look out the window. "That's one huge wall cloud. And it's coming together quickly." He glanced down at the town below. "Odell should be safe. But everything south and west is going to get hammered. Look at that wall of rain."

Mick could smell it. Solid and dark, it created a misty curtain against the western horizon.

Drear reported on hail and the size of the rotation inside the wall cloud.

"We're going to move another quarter of a mile out," Graff said into his radio. "I don't want to get sucked into this thing." He maneuvered the camera. "I love this new camera. It makes me look like I'm right on top of the tornado. People actually think I fly that close!"

Mick laughed. "If only we could."

They were about a mile east of the storm. The wall cloud had lowered significantly in just a matter of seconds, and this was not lost on Drear, whose voice crackled through the radio. "Jack? You seeing this?"

"Yep."

"Next time we go to you, it'll be live. The sirens are going off in Vernon." Behind Dale's voice was the chaotic sound of the newsroom coming alive.

"Here we go." Graff smiled. "You got your storm!"

Mick couldn't believe his luck. It was September, when the Texas plains would usually produce a pretty good storm or two, but rarely a storm of this magnitude. Those usually came in April, May, or June. And he'd never chased one in a helicopter. He was actually eye level with the wall cloud. He could see the rotation swirling the thick green clouds.

His concern focused on the people below. People weren't on the lookout for deadly storms in September. Though Vernon had tornado sirens, the small towns surrounding it probably did not.

"We have a visual on fingers," Graff said into his radio.

The ghostlike clouds, dipping toward the earth like long, bony fingers, were the first indication that the wall cloud was probably going to drop a tornado. Storm chasers in their cars were yelling out wind speed and direction through their radios. Mick could see one of their vans below.

"There," Graff said.

"The hook." Mick raised his camera and began shooting again. Dipping below the wall cloud was a large hook, which was the tornado emerging.

"This thing is lowering fast!" Drear was saying, presumably to a live audience. In his voice was a strained urgency. "Get underground now. Get to your safe shelter. Children, if you are home alone, go to your storm shelter or to an interior bathtub or closet. Get blankets and helmets if you have them. Whatever you do, do *not* run outside to look at this. Get inside your homes now, unless you live in a mobile home. If so, you need to get out of your mobile home immediately and go to a stable structure. If there is not a stable structure, try to find a nearby ditch. . . ."

The tornado had now straightened into a sharp cone shape and looked to be about two hundred yards from the ground. A large cloud of dust swirled below it. But there was no debris. Yet.

Adrenaline rushed through Mick as he took pictures. He listened to Graff skillfully explain their location.

"Dale, we look to be about ten miles south of Odell and about five miles west of Vernon. This tornado is lowering very rapidly, and it looks like it's right on top of Highway 287, just west of Highway 283."

"Jack, we're confirming that location by radar. Doppler is indicating wind speeds topping one hundred and ten miles an hour. Has it touched down yet?"

"Not that I can tell," Graff said. "It's hovering right above but will probably drop any second now."

"We have debris!" said a storm chaser on the ground.

"Confirmed," said Graff. "We have debris."

Mick watched the large debris cloud swallow the view of the ground below.

"Dale, we are tracking a southeasterly movement. It will be crossing Highway 287, possibly a mile and a half before Junction 283, in about two minutes."

"Folks, if you are in your car on Highway 287, you need to get out of the way of this storm. An underpass is not the safest place to be, but if that's all you have, get there. Do not stay in your car. If you are anywhere east of this storm, hurry and get out of the way. If you are headed west or south on either of these highways, turn around now."

Mick had forgotten to continue to take pictures. He raised his camera and clicked a few shots of the tornado, which looked to be an F3. It was white in its center, ghostly gray toward the edges, set against a dark blue wall of rain. Lightning speared from the sky at an alarming rate.

Graff noticed it too. "Dale, we need to make folks aware of the lightning situation out of this storm."

"Jack, we confirm that. The hook echo on this is very impressive."

"It's turning," Mick said, pointing toward the tornado. "Look at that. It's going to travel right down the highway."

Graff glanced nervously at Mick and nodded. "Dale, are you seeing this? Can you confirm that the tornado has turned and is taking an easterly direction?"

There was an eerie pause over the radio.

A storm chaser on the ground confirmed he was seeing the same thing and that it was traveling straight down the highway.

"Folks, listen up. This tornado is tracking easterly right on course with Highway 287. If you are on this road, get off now."

"Do you have a mile marker?" Graff asked one of the storm chasers on the ground.

One storm chaser thought it might be at marker 114, but he couldn't confirm it.

Graff said, "It looks to be about a mile from the junction."

Mick gasped. "Look at all those cars!"

A line of cars had stopped on the highway, trying to turn around but were now in gridlock.

"God, help them," Mick mumbled. His camera dropped to his lap.

"C'mon!" Graff roared. "Get out of the way! Get out of your cars. Run!"

"Oh no . . ."

They watched two cars thrown off the highway. Other drivers panicked, driving down the median and into the ditch and even out into the pastures.

"It's turning again!" Mick pointed through the windshield. "South."

Graff was talking with other storm chasers through the radio and nodded. He switched frequencies. "Dale, it's moving south off the highway. We may have some casualties on 287. We need emergency personnel."

"What's that town down there?" Mick asked. "Is that Vernon?"

"No. That's Lockett. Dale?"

"Yes, Jack, I'm here."

"The tornado just shifted, headed southeasterly, on course for Lockett."

"Okay, we're confirming that by radar."

"Does Lockett have tornado sirens?" Mick asked.

Jack didn't look at Mick. "Probably not. Maybe they'll notice the helicopter and commotion. Hopefully the sheriff's department is on its way."

The twister danced across the flat plains, tearing up a few trees as the tip snaked along the dirt. Graff held his position over Lockett. The town looked peaceful, oblivious to the monster swirling toward it.

Below, a sheriff's car raced toward the town with its lights on.

"Please turn," Mick said. "Come on. Turn. Turn it, God."

"Jack? What's the position?" Dale asked.

"About half a mile northwest of Lockett, headed directly toward it."

"We're confirming that."

Graff swallowed. "This is going to be a disaster." He aimed his TV camera directly on the town.

In the distance, the tornado roared furiously. Mick could see what looked like a barn roof circling around and around, plus tree limbs and other things he couldn't identify.

Graff cursed as they watched the twister scoot toward the outer edges of the town. Trailer parks and small wooden homes lined the streets. A solitary stoplight swung in the wind on Main Street. He moved the helicopter south, and they both watched helplessly as the twister tore through the middle of the town. The debris cloud was so thick there wasn't much to watch except wood and roofs and trees being sucked up into the core.

Graff switched to a private frequency and got Dale. "The entire town is hit. I think it swallowed the whole thing up."

Mick could hear Dale sigh heavily and swear. "It's lifting," Mick said, motioning to the hook.

Within a matter of seconds, the entire tornado vanished into thin air.

"Thank God," Graff said. "I'm going to help look for survivors, Dale."

"Go ahead," Dale said. "We'll track the storm from the ground. It's pretty small in diameter, moving at about fifty. You'll be of good service there. Thanks for your help, Jack. See you back at the station."

"Pick up that camera of yours," Graff told Mick. "People need to see what a twister can do."

Mick nodded, took a deep breath, and waited for Graff to circle back around the tail end of the storm. When the rain cleared they hovered above the town. Graff started lowering his copter and was now talking to the sheriff's department on the radio. With their eagle-eye view, they could hopefully spot survivors or people trapped underneath the rubble.

Leaning against the window, Mick looked down. People swarmed the streets, running in all directions, pointing and shouting in panic. And then he saw a family of four sitting in a white porcelain bathtub, the only thing left of their house, which had been stripped bare from its foundation. The father's shirt was ripped off—one sleeve was left on his arm. A small boy trembled next to his mother, who was holding a baby swaddled in blankets. The boy looked up at Mick, big tears rolling down his bloody face.

Mick started to raise his camera, then put it down. "Let's get this thing set down. They need help down there."

chapter three

h ey, my man!" A wide grin stretched across Reggie Moore's face as he leaned back in his chair and extended his arms over his head.

"What time did you get in?" Mick asked, dumping his FBI files on his desk, which sat across from Reggie's. Reggie had been out of their Dallas office all day, tracking down some final documentation on the RICO case they were about to make an arrest in. This late afternoon was the first time the partners had seen each other all day.

"Too early." Reggie yawned. "But we're so close on this case, I wanted to try to get a head start."

"I hope nothing goes wrong. You know how we have that curse."

Reggie groaned. They referred to it as "the curse" because of how many times yearlong-or-plus investigations of theirs had bottomed out at the last minute. The most recent was an eighteen-month investigation into a national bank scam that ended with the police accidentally destroying crucial evidence when they sank the boat the suspect was on.

Though the curse had emerged in reality only five times, they'd had many more close calls. It was a sickening feeling to lose a case after working on it for months and months. They started a tradition of eating Tex-Mex after a bad day at work, except Mick had sworn off eating out with

Reggie now that Reggie was on a combination of the South Beach and Atkins Diets.

The last time they'd gone out to eat, Reggie had actually tried to order a cheese enchilada without the tortilla. The waiter politely explained that there was no way to cook the enchilada without the tortilla wrapped around it. So Reggie had ordered the full enchilada, and when it had come, he unwrapped it, scraped the chili sauce onto the cheese, and simply ate melted cheese. Paid eight bucks for it.

Mick was beginning to conclude that Reggie simply liked the challenge of finding alternate ways to eat regular food. However, Mick had to admit that Reggie was looking really good these days.

"I've got Lamberson scheduled to be tailed on Thursday morning," Reggie said. "So what'd you do this weekend?"

"You hear about that big storm up by the Oklahoma border?"

"Yeah. You chase it?"

Mick smiled. "By helicopter."

"No kidding!" Reggie chuckled. "You're going all high-tech now."

"It was amazing, man. To look across at the wall cloud, eye level . . . words don't describe it."

"That hit a small town, didn't it?"

"Yeah. Lockett."

Reggie shook his head. "Well, I guess that is enough excitement for one weekend, eh?" He raised an eyebrow. "No hot dates?"

Reggie and his wife, Marnie, had decided it was their life mission to make sure Mick didn't end up single his whole life, as if that might be a horrible thing. He'd actually come to terms with living alone. His luck had been so bad in the romance area that he was pretty sure it was meant to be.

Though that little theory had been rocked ever so

slightly yesterday when he'd received a call from Faith Kemper, a woman he'd met a year and a half ago while he was investigating the death of his brother, Aaron. They'd had a strong connection, though their lives were both so full of grief at the time, there wasn't much room left for love.

Faith was coming into town tonight. She had called to see if he was free for dinner. It had shaken him up a bit. He'd thought about Faith off and on over the past months but had written her off as one more lost love.

"Brother, where are you?"

Mick looked up, staring into Reggie's concerned face. "You okay?"

"Yeah. Just tired. Spent all Saturday night helping those tornado victims."

Reggie glanced at his watch. "Well, go home. I've got to wait here anyway until I get that phone call about the Caymans. Besides, Marnie's got some women's thing going. I'm looking for any excuse to stay out of the house."

"Okay, okay, you've forced me. I'm going." He slapped Reggie's hand and grabbed his bag. He had a hot date with a bunch of pictures he'd dropped off to be developed. Whether or not his meeting with Faith tonight was a date was still in question.

Mick decided not to immerse himself in his pictures until he'd straightened up his apartment. More than a couple of weeks had passed since he'd cleaned, so he vacuumed and dumped his dirty clothes into a laundry basket in his closet. He ran his hand along certain pieces of furniture that looked a little dusty and might be noticed by a woman.

He took a quick shower but was out of aftershave. A little gel in his hair wouldn't hurt, he decided, but at the end of it all, he looked a little gooey. After running some water through his hair, he then looked wet and gooey. So a ball cap it was.

He checked his watch. Faith said she'd be at his apartment around six, so he had thirty minutes. He went downstairs to pick up his mail. Two bills and . . . another letter. He recognized the writing.

He rushed back upstairs and opened the letter. It was exactly like the first two: a newspaper headline, cut out, with a single letter highlighted in yellow. The envelope was addressed to him, with no return address. All three had been sent from Dallas.

The letter highlighted was *T*. The other two had been an *A* and an *S*. He took the others out of the drawer he'd stuck them in and examined every detail. He wasn't sure if the headlines meant something or not. The one with the *A* highlighted read "Insurance Commissioner under Scrutiny." The one with the *S* read "Crime Rate Drops." The new headline read "Fall Hurricane Season Predicted to Be Harsh."

Mick threw the headlines on the coffee table and fell back into the couch. He'd received the first one about eight days ago and the second one on Friday. Monday had brought the third one. He'd not told anyone about them yet. He wasn't sure what there was to say. Mysterious notes with highlighted letters? A certain practical joke.

A knock at the door caused him to jump. Faith was early, which didn't surprise him. She had seemed like a woman who had it together before her husband was murdered. He hoped she was able to get on with her life now that his killer was behind bars.

He opened the door and couldn't hide his surprise. "Jenny?"

Aaron's widow, Jenny, cocked her head. She looked as beautiful as ever. "You look like you just saw a ghost. Are you okay?" she asked.

"Um . . . yeah . . . what are you doing here?"

"Is this a bad time?"

"No . . . yeah . . . I mean, no, of course not. Please come in."

Jenny eyed him as she walked past. When she entered the living room, she turned around. "What's up? Do you have a hot date or something?"

"What makes you think that?"

"Hello? Not a stitch of clothes on the floor." She noticed the small desk in the corner. "Did you *dust*?"

"It's not what you think."

She circled him. "Well, surely you wouldn't be going on a date with a ball cap on." She looked down at the coffee table and the newspaper headlines. "What're these?"

"Just some work stuff." He snatched them up and threw them in the drawer. "So, what brings you by?"

She didn't look convinced but sat down on the couch. "Did you see this?" She handed him the newspaper she had tucked underneath her arm. The headline read: "Dallas Lawyer Out of Appeals."

Mick sat next to her while he scanned the article. Sammy Earle had murdered an assistant DA ten years ago when the DA suspected he had information linking Sammy to a kidnapping that had ended up being a hoax . . . a hoax that had nearly cost Mick his life.

"Doesn't bring back good memories, does it?" Jenny said.

"He still claims it was a setup?"

"Aaron followed this case for years. According to the press, Earle never wavered from that claim. The evidence against him tells another story, though. You don't follow it?"

"Not really. I'll see a headline here or there, but for me it was over a long time ago."

"The execution date is coming up."

"You came by just to tell me about this?"

"No." She sighed. "Thursday . . ."

"I know. Aaron's birthday."

"It's been a year and a half, and it still kicks me in the gut."

"A year and a half is not a long time." Faith Kemper could tell her that. She had still been suffering two years after her husband's murder.

Jenny swiped at her tears. "I feel like all I do is come over here and cry." She laughed at herself. "I really did want to show you this article, though. I don't know why. It was just a curious case back then, and it still seems to be. Earle has been writing letters and petitioning and doing everything he can to save his own life, but it doesn't look like it's going to work."

"Not much does when you murder a DA. It's kind of like killing a cop."

Jenny nodded and looked down.

Aaron's killer, who'd shot him because of a traffic ticket, received life in prison ten months ago. He'd avoided the death penalty by arguing that the murder was not premeditated. Whatever the case, a fine man was dead because of it. The best man Mick had ever known.

Mick watched the minute hand tick toward the six. The last thing he wanted was Jenny and Faith in the same room together. Things were complicated enough without them meeting. He'd had strong feelings for both of them. He'd always loved Jenny, even after reconciling with his brother and realizing Aaron and Jenny were meant for each other. And Faith was a woman who'd drawn him in quickly but had more mending to do.

His head was spinning at the thought of these two cordially shaking hands. He hopped off the couch, much to Jenny's surprise. "Well, listen, let's plan for dinner Thursday."

Jenny slowly stood, a small smile creeping onto her lips. "You *do* have a date."

"No, I—"

She cut him off. "It's none of my business. I won't pry." She patted his arm and grinned. "But I'd lose the ball cap if I were you." She flicked it off with her finger and studied his hair. "Maybe the hat's not such a bad idea."

Mick grumbled and scooped the hat off the floor. "It's not a date. Now get outta here."

Jenny laughed all the way to the door. "You used gel, my friend. I wasn't born yesterday." She opened the door and closed it gently behind her. He could still hear her laughing.

Through the dark third-story window, Joel Lamberson watched with great interest the man getting out of his Cadillac, which sat alone in the vast parking lot. The man was large, not just fat but tall, with a big head of fluffy white hair. He chewed on a cigar as he lifted himself out of the driver's seat, hanging a hand over the top of the open door for leverage.

The man shut the door and looked around, peering into the darkness, using his thumbs to tuck in the shirt that had slipped out over his big belly. A large, silver belt buckle glinted in the parking-lot lights. He wore an expensive suit that fit poorly, making him look common if not cheap. His large mouth and thick lips turned the unlit cigar over like a cow chews cud.

"There's nobody here, you fool," Joel mumbled, stepping back from the window as the man turned his attention toward the building. But the man never looked up, never suspected somebody might be waiting for him.

But somebody *was* waiting for him.

Joel paced the small office, gearing himself up for a fight. This wasn't going to be pretty. He would argue calmly, as if he had the upper hand. It was going to be a psychological showdown.

From the hall, he could hear the old elevator come to life and descend to the passenger waiting on the first floor. Joel kept the lights off. He wanted the element of surprise. He just hoped the old man didn't fall over dead from a heart attack. The man was used to being in control, giving the orders.

Now Joel would be giving the orders. He brushed his hair off his sweaty forehead and waited in the shadows, listening to the elevator.

The quiet *ding* made Joel's heart flutter the exact way it had four years earlier when he'd realized how rich he could become. The elevator doors swooshed open, and heavy, padded footsteps neared. Joel stood by the tall, metal file cabinet, his fingers clutching the skin in the palm of his hand. He took a deep, trembling breath.

The office door swung open, and he heard the man grumbling about the light switch. His body took up nearly the entire doorway. After a few seconds, he found it and the office glowed with white light.

Joel felt naked and exposed, but he held himself steady, waiting for the man to look in his direction.

At first he didn't. He messed around with some things in his jacket pocket. Joel noticed his hands. Much more feminine than fit him. His fingers were slender and smooth, with groomed nails. It was a weird contrast to the scruffy male body that they were attached to.

And then Joel was staring into his eyes.

The man gasped and stumbled backward, dropping the keys that he'd so diligently searched for moments before. "Joel!"

Joel had imagined this moment over and over for days,

but he had not realized how good he would feel when he saw the shock in his eyes.

"What are you doing here? You about gave me a heart attack!"

"You haven't been returning my phone calls."

"I told you the less contact we have, the better." He bent with great effort and grabbed the keys off the floor. He studied Joel from across the room. "You don't want this thing to blow up in our faces, do you?"

"I just wanted a simple phone call returned. Don't you believe that I am an important part of all this?"

"Of course I do." The man then noticed the file cabinet Joel was standing by. "What do you think you're doing?"

"Just came to talk," Joel said mildly, even sticking a hand in his pocket with ease. He was really impressing himself. This once lanky, shy teenager had come a long way.

"What do you want to talk about?"

"My cut."

The man rolled his eyes and groaned. "Not this again. You are a greedy man. Are you forgetting where you came from, Joel? Forgetting who is giving you the chance to become very rich? Patience. Patience. I always say it. You never listen."

The fatherly tone did not appease Joel. "I want more. I deserve it. My work has been spotless."

The man smiled. "Yes. You've done good work. So far. But it looks to me like you're getting a little ahead of yourself. We haven't finished our task now, have we?"

"Maybe I have."

The man walked over to the file cabinet. He glanced sideways at Joel. "Just shut up. Don't ruin this thing now, when we're so close. Just shut your mouth and do what I say."

The large man unlocked the cabinet and pulled the top

drawer out. He flipped his fingers through the folders and stopped. He opened the folder that his fingers held. It was empty. "What the—?" He turned to Joel, who had now walked a few feet away.

"I'm not playing games," Joel said, though nervousness had crept into his voice. "There is a lot at stake here, Ira. More than money. A woman too."

The man cursed. "Where are those papers?"

"Maybe now you'll listen." Joel smiled.

chapter four

maybe it wasn't a date, but it felt like a date. Even with three layers of two different kinds of deodorant, Mick still felt a teasing threat of moisture trying to break through the skin of his armpits.

Faith sat across from him at the restaurant, seemingly oblivious. She was as beautiful as ever. She'd cut her white blonde hair, and it rested neatly on top of her shoulders. She laughed as she told stories of Bea, her beloved grandmother. When Mick had seen Faith last, she still hadn't told Bea that Paul, Faith's husband, had been murdered.

"She took it as I expected," Faith said as the desserts arrived. "It broke her heart. And she couldn't believe the measures I took to keep it from her. Then I got a lecture about all the grief she'd had in her life, including two still-born children. She slapped my hand and told me she was a tough old broad and not to keep things from her anymore. Can you imagine what she was like in her younger years?"

"I loved that lady the first time I met her," Mick said.

"So what about you?" she asked, pointing her fork at Mick. "So far you've been asking all the questions. How are you doing?"

"Great. Work is going well. We're getting ready to make a big arrest this week on a RICO case we've been working for over a year."

"What's a RICO case?"

"Racketeer Influenced and Corrupt Organizations Act."

"I have no idea what that means, but it sounds exciting!" Faith said. "You still enjoy working for the FBI?"

Mick nodded. "It's interesting work. There's something unexpected waiting for me every day."

"Are you still chasing your storms?"

"Yeah."

"I can't look at a thunderstorm without thinking of you."

A quiet easiness settled between them. Mick studied Faith as she took a small bite of her cheesecake. He'd lost his appetite as soon as they'd sat down to eat. The strong feelings for her that surged back as soon as he saw her again amazed him. He'd almost forgotten them, but here they were, as if they'd never gone away.

When it came to love, he was the first to admit he had problems with denial.

"How are you doing with Aaron's death?"

"Okay."

She smiled. "That's what I used to say. It seemed to placate people. *Okay* was the perfect word, insinuating you're going to make it, but you've definitely seen better days."

"Well, I don't know that I've put that much thought into it. But it's the truth. I'm learning to live with it."

"It's been over three years for me. The pain is dulling. Truthfully, I never thought it would. I drive two hours to go to church with Bea every Sunday at the nursing home. There's this old guy who preaches like he's twenty years old. All the residents love him. I do too."

"I'm glad. You look great. There's peace in your eyes."

Faith shook her head. "There you go again, trying to get the subject off yourself. Not going to happen," she said, waving her finger.

"I'm honestly not that exciting." Mick laughed. "I spend my free time chasing storms."

"Not women?"

"Not these days." He sighed. "I'm too old and too straight for that anymore."

"Mick, you don't give yourself enough credit."

"Single life isn't that bad. For one, I get to leave the toilet seat up."

"You're hilarious," Faith mused. "Come on. Spill the beans. When's the last time you went on a date?"

Rolling his eyes, Mick intentionally stuffed his mouth with his dessert and shrugged playfully as he chewed.

"Mick! You're not getting off that easily. The last time we talked, you'd lost the love of your life. What was her name again?"

Mick swallowed. "You know I'd rather be eating pig intestines right now than talking about this, don't you?"

She grinned. "Yeah. But I like to see you blush."

He was doing plenty of that. He could feel the heat rushing up his neck.

"Jenny," she suddenly said. "That's it, right? Jenny. The woman you lost to another 'better' man, as you put it."

"Can we switch topics if I promise the next topic will be just as tantalizing and interesting?"

"Hmmm. It's going to have to be awfully fascinating to beat the look on your face five seconds ago." She smiled. "All right. Change gears."

"Wallace Bledsoe."

Faith leaned back in her chair, obviously surprised. "Whew. That is quite a subject change."

"You okay to talk about it?"

"Sure," she said. "What do you want to know?"

"Have you been following what's happened to him?"

"Well, there was the trial. He pleaded guilty to murdering Paul and the others. But the man was clearly insane. Everyone in the court, including the judge and jury, could plainly see it. Dr. Grenard testified. Did you know that?"

Mick shook his head. Abigail Grenard was the bureau psychologist who'd helped crack the case against Wallace and who'd tested Mick's patience when he was sent for evaluation after Aaron was murdered. He still had a good rapport with her, even though every other agent trembled at the idea of having to walk into her office.

"Anyway, Wallace was sentenced to a mental hospital. He's never allowed to leave."

"I did hear that."

"So what do you want to know about him?"

"I'm not sure. I've just been . . ."

"What?" Across the table, the candlelight flickered against her skin. Her blue eyes waited expectantly.

"I've been receiving some strange letters in the mail."

"Letters?"

"Not letters as in written notes. But letters, like from the alphabet."

"I'm not following."

"I'm not sure I am either. They're headlines out of a newspaper, with one letter highlighted in each one."

"Are you serious? That's weird."

"There's been an *S*, *A*, and *T*. *Sat*. That doesn't make much sense."

"Have you told your supervisors at work?"

"No. Tom's been out of town until today. It's too early to tell what this is. It may just be a practical joke."

"Some joke. You think Wallace is behind it?"

"I'm not sure. I know Wallace is really disturbed, but I don't know how accountable he holds me to his capture. His mail would be screened, I'm assuming, at a mental hospital."

"I don't know." Faith sighed. "I don't know much about that. You've made a lot of enemies throughout the years. Aren't you concerned?"

"I'll get concerned when a letter arrives with a bomb strapped to it." He smiled.

"That would creep me out."

Mick wasn't too far from being creeped out either. He was hoping it was Marnie spelling out the name of a blind date she wanted to set him up with.

His cell phone rang. It was a high-tech satellite phone that Reggie had hooked him up with. Reggie had even set the ring tone so any time he called, it played the theme to *Star Wars*.

Faith looked amused.

"Sorry, it's my partner. I need to take this real quick."

"No problem."

"Hello?"

"Mick, it's Reg. Where are you?"

"Uh . . ." Mick glanced across the table. "Where are you?"

"I'm standing in front of a burning building."

"Why?"

"Are you in the mood for Tex-Mex?"

Surrounded by a horde of emergency vehicles, a five-story, flat-roofed building smoldered against the streams of water the firefighters were dousing it with. On the west side of the building, a section of pea green paint was left, and its design was a clear indication of seventies architecture. About 25 percent of the building was gone.

Mick glanced at Faith, who was staring at the building. "I'm so sorry about this."

"You said someone you know is dead in that building?"

31

"Reggie thinks it's one of the guys we've been watching on the RICO case, a guy we were about to arrest. But that would be impossible."

"Why?"

"Because it would mean I have the worst luck in the world."

Mick stepped out of his truck and saw Reggie rushing toward him through the chaos of emergency personnel. As he drew closer, Mick saw a conflicted expression cross Reggie's face when he noticed Faith. He knew Reggie was curious about the lovely lady by his side, but more important things were on his mind.

Reggie nodded politely at Faith and then pulled Mick aside.

"Are you sure it's Joel Lamberson?"

"There was the gold ring on his finger, and even though he was badly burned, I could still make out his features."

A pungent odor surrounded Reggie, and the smoke in the air caused Mick to cough. "This is unbelievable. Anybody else in there?"

"No. A janitor arrived to find the building burning and called 911."

The medical examiner's truck pulled up, and the two men who hopped out were greeted by two other men in ATF jackets.

"Why is ATF here?" ATF stood for the Bureau of Alcohol, Tobacco, and Firearms, but Mick and Reggie liked to joke that it stood for the Bureau of Always Ticking off the FBI.

Reggie appeared out of breath, as if he didn't have enough in him to explain that part. "Apparently they've been investigating an arsonist. They seem to think this may fit the profile of the guy they're after."

Mick folded his arms in front of his chest and eyed

Reggie. "So what you're telling me is that this is going to be an ATF investigation because it's possibly the work of an arsonist, and we're going to have to break the news to them that the FBI is now going to be involved?"

"Yeah, that's pretty much it."

"Have you called Tom?"

"I was hoping you'd want to do that."

Mick sighed and looked over at Faith, trying to smile. "It'll be just a second," he called to her over the noise.

"No problem." She smiled back.

"Are you on a date, dude?" Reggie asked.

"That is the least of your concerns right now. Who's the guy in charge here?"

"Well, that's the other thing. It's not a guy. It's a—"

Suddenly over the emergency noise came the sound of a large motorcycle. Everyone turned as a Harley-Davidson rolled into the parking lot, the rider wearing a black helmet with a black-tinted visor. The sea of people parted as the rider came through and then killed the engine.

"—woman," Reggie finished.

"What?"

"The person in charge of the investigation is a woman."

"And she wouldn't happen to ride a Harley, would she?"

"That's the rumor." Reggie glanced worriedly toward the rider as she swung her leg off the bike and removed her helmet. Then he looked at Mick. "Apparently she's quite a legend. And not necessarily in the Joan of Arc sort of way."

Mick and Reggie watched as the woman started shouting orders. Men scurried in all directions, or at least acted as if they were trying to do something important. Reggie and Mick glanced at each other. Reggie was rubbing his temples.

"I'll handle this. You look like you could use a break," Mick offered.

Reggie nodded. "I feel like my head's going to explode.
That smell gets to me every time."

"Do me a favor, will you? Go introduce yourself to
Faith over there and see if you can arrange a ride back to
my apartment for her. Her car is there. But give me a
second to explain everything."

Mick walked back to Faith, who was still standing by his
truck and watching the scene.

"I'm sorry," Mick said as he approached. "I'm going to
have to stay."

"It's okay. Really."

"It was great seeing you again."

She smiled, that easy warmth glowing in her eyes.
"We'll see each other again, Mick. I think you're going to
be someone who will be in my life for a long time." She
kissed him on the cheek and then noticed Reggie.

"That's my partner," Mick explained. "He offered to
arrange a ride back to your car."

"Thank you. That is so kind."

Reggie approached and stuck out his hand. "I'm Reggie."

"Faith."

Mick slapped Reggie on the back. "Take good care of
her."

"I will, brother."

Mick started walking toward the woman whom all the
movement seemed to be centered around. She was backlit,
so he couldn't see much more than her stance, which
looked like it was meant to be intimidating.

He cleared his throat.

She turned, her sleek ponytail swinging like a little
girl's. But her countenance was anything but charming and
cute. On top of deep-set brown eyes and tanned skin was a
cold expression. Her lips were full but pressed into a thin,
determined line, set straight across her face.

"I'm Special Agent Mick Kline. I'm with the—"

"Federal Bureau of Incompetency, I know." She turned back around to face the building.

Mick stepped up beside her. She certainly wasn't winning points with her tact.

She continued to stare at the building. "What are you doing here?"

"The body found in the building is a guy we've been watching for months on an embezzlement case. The Securities and Exchange Commission alerted us to him about a year ago."

The woman hardly acknowledged that Mick was talking. Instead, her attention seemed to be on the medical examiner's team rolling a gurney into the building. Her hands were clasped behind her back, and her feet were spread apart in a military fashion, yet Mick couldn't help but notice the French manicure and mauve lipstick.

"I'm sorry. I didn't catch your name," Mick said.

"Senior Special Agent and Lead Investigator Libby Lancaster."

Mick paused, suppressing a smile. "I'm horrible with names, especially long ones, so can I just call you Libby?"

"Funny," she said without a hint of emotion. "Agent Lancaster will do. What are you doing standing around here? Shouldn't you be up there examining your evidence?"

"Just wanted to check in with you first, since you're in charge."

Libby glanced at him, obviously surprised by the statement. She eyed him for any hint of sarcasm. Mick held a steady expression. "Never thought I'd hear a bureau agent say that."

"I'm not here to interfere with your arson investigation. Though I'd happily receive any information you'd like to give me about it, since I seem to be involved now."

Libby shouted to one of her agents, directing him to do something in regard to the phone lines on the other side of the building. Then she said to Mick, "This is the fourth fire of a large building like this in eight months. All have been at least four stories or more. The one before this was only two weeks ago.

"This is the first one with a fatality. Like this one, the rest were started at night." She checked her watch, as if noting something, and walked away, throwing her ATF jacket over her shoulder to reveal a modern black pantsuit. She beelined to another ATF agent, then disappeared behind a fire truck.

Mick turned to look at the building. Gray ribbons of smoke slithered into the dark sky and veiled the stars that could normally be seen twinkling above. He mentally prepared himself. The smell was already making him sick.

i n a small cement room, Sammy Earle waited. A rectangular window—no more than a foot and a half high
and three feet wide—framed an ink black sky and two
distant, twinkling stars.

This room was notably unusual. The chairs and table
were wooden, not metal. The door was painted red.
Screwed into the cement wall was a cheaply framed print
of the *The Last Supper*. It was the only thing in the room
to look at, so Sammy studied it. Truthfully, the picture
appeared flat and lifeless, with feminine-looking men leaning in awkward directions. Yet he was drawn into it. It was
something about the eyes of Jesus.

He'd tried religion before—not that anybody would
believe that, but it was true. In his early twenties he'd dated
a Catholic woman who insisted they attend mass, so he
faithfully did. He'd been fascinated with the liturgy. He had
a great sense of peace watching the priest in his virtuous-
ness. Sammy thought it strange how he'd been comforted
by the idea that a man could sit at a small window and
pardon him of his many sins.

As much as he'd been comforted by the idea that the
priest was pardoning his sins, he never really believed it.
Because at the end of the day, the man who sat behind the
screen was just a man like him, and Sammy still always felt
guilty.

He could hear footsteps approaching down the hall. He knew them to be the footsteps of Warden Byron McAubrey. He was the only one who wore shoes expensive enough to make that kind of tapping noise against the tile. Sammy'd had very little contact with the warden in his years here on death row. His impressions of the man came more from the other prisoners.

The warden was tall and lanky, with a balding head, round, scholarly glasses, and small ears that stuck out a little too far on either side of his bony skull. He didn't look like a warden to Sammy. He looked academic, like he should be teaching something important at some lofty university. When he spoke, it was slowly, in a polished Southern accent. Every day he wore a white starched shirt and a dark tie. He never wore short sleeves, even though the prison tended to get warm in the summer. McAubrey took a lot of pride in his job, and for some strange reason, that comforted Sammy.

Sammy's appointment with the warden had been postponed from earlier in the day. One of the prisoners had committed suicide this afternoon, and it had put the entire prison in lockdown.

The door opened and the warden walked in, greeting Sammy with a professional smile—impersonal but polite. "Mr. Earle. Good evening. I'm sorry for the delay. My day is tied up tomorrow with meetings, so thank you for meeting me at this hour."

Sammy nodded. He hadn't been given a choice, but why not pretend that he had? For ten years, his whole life had been stripped of every normal thing, like changing a meeting time.

The warden, sitting across from him, continued talking. ". . . decide if you want a clemency hearing. It is completely up to you, and we can arrange it."

"No."

"You're sure?"

"Yes." Sammy had very little control over his situation now—in fact, he was sure this would be one of his last decisions—but to stand before the clemency board and beg for his life seemed contrary to the man he once was. Maybe there was very little of that man left, but he had to hold on to what he could for dignity's sake.

Mr. McAubrey had a neatly organized brown folder laid out in front of them on the table, and he was jotting notes. Sammy wondered what the folder held. Was it just his life since coming to the prison? Or did it contain everything about him? It seemed so thin. Perhaps it was only the last ten years.

Mr. McAubrey was looking at him, waiting for his attention. Then he said, "We've got some difficult issues to talk about, Mr. Earle. You're going to have to start thinking about some things."

"Can you call me Sammy?"

Mr. McAubrey paused, then nodded with a short smile. "Of course."

"Thank you."

The warden flipped to the next page in the folder. "We're going to need to take your measurements for the garments you'll be wearing for the execution." His eyes appeared intensely passionate.

It made Sammy want to cry. Nobody had looked at him like that in many years. "Okay."

"Do you have any family that will be taking care of your funeral arrangements, Sammy?"

"No."

"Would you like your ashes scattered in any particular place?"

"No."

"Is there someone you would like to have your belongings?"

His belongings consisted of his Rolex watch, gold cuff links, and leather shoes that back in the day had cost him three hundred dollars. "Yes."

Mr. McAubrey looked up. "Who is that?"

"My former secretary, JoAnne Meeler."

"Do you have an address?"

"No."

"Okay, we'll try to get in contact with her." He smiled.

"She hated my guts."

"I see."

"But she took care of me. I never knew why. But she did. She was a kind woman."

Mr. McAubrey wrote in his folder and said, "Chaplain Barber will come by to see you."

"No need."

"You're sure?"

"Yes."

"We can provide a Bible for you if you'd like."

"No."

Mr. McAubrey seemed disappointed, and he stared at Sammy as if hoping he might change his mind. "Sammy," he finally said, "you've made decisions in your life that have brought you to this point. But there are still decisions to be made that will take you to the next point in life."

"I don't believe in an afterlife."

Mr. McAubrey leaned forward, his face tight with concern. "Whether or not you believe in it is inconsequential, Sammy. It's there." He leaned back in his chair and spoke in a fatherly way. "I've witnessed fifty-seven executions. And I suppose I've seen everything there is to see when it comes to death. Whether you're dying of cancer or by execution, if you're lucky enough to know the time when you'll die, you should seize that opportunity. Many men have died on the very day they were celebrating life. They never had a chance—or never took it—to contemplate the afterlife. You have been given that chance. Don't squander it."

Sammy blinked. He stared at the table but couldn't find any words.

The warden continued. "We'd like to know what your requests will be for your last supper. Our chef is prepared to make anything you like."

"I haven't thought about it."

"We can give you a few days on that."

"No. I can tell you now."

"Okay." Mr. McAubrey looked up, holding his pen, ready to write down the request.

Sammy took a moment to think. "I'll have the Reuben—double the Thousand Island dressing, half the sauerkraut. I'd like french fries with the spicy salt on them, a salad—ranch dressing on the side—and a large Coke." He ordered it just like he used to at the first-floor deli in his old office building. "And make it quick. I've only got twenty-seven days." Sammy smiled at his own joke. He used to say he only had fifteen minutes. He had hardly ever taken the time to sit down and enjoy the sandwich. There was always work to be done.

Mr. McAubrey smiled too. "Got it. Now, you'll have phone calls you can make. You'll want to decide who that will be."

"I need to give that some thought."

"Sure."

"Mr. McAubrey?"

"Yes?"

"You're a really nice man."

The warden adjusted his glasses and looked embarrassed by the statement, though he grinned at Sammy as if he were an old friend. "I could say the same about you, Sammy."

Sammy shook his head. He wasn't nice. Just desperate and humiliated. His old ways were gone because they were no longer useful to him.

"Will there be a—" Sammy found the word stuck to his tongue—"pill?"

"A pill?"

"Something to settle my nerves? Do you give something to help me before the execution?"

"No."

"I don't know how . . ."

"Of all the executions, Sammy, only one prisoner had to be dragged into the execution chamber." Mr. McAubrey nodded. "When it's time, you'll be ready."

Sammy didn't feel assured. He couldn't imagine the day. He'd tried over and over again, but he couldn't actually visualize himself walking in there.

"We'll get all of this processed," Mr. McAubrey said as he stood. "There will be some paperwork for you to fill out in about a week. And you think about seeing Chaplain Barber. I think it would be a mistake not to talk with him."

He smiled once more at Sammy, the same smile he'd come in with. It wasn't that the man had turned cold. In fact, what Sammy sensed more than anything was Mr. McAubrey's own preparation of emotions for the execution. It was as if he had to step back and distance himself.

He looked back once at Sammy before leaving the room. His eyes indicated that Sammy was very much a human being worth respecting.

Long ago, though, Sammy had stopped feeling worthy of any respect or dignity. He looked years older than he was. His hair was nearly all white now, his face a woven mess of wrinkles and strain. He'd gained twenty pounds in prison because he ate some form of potatoes with every meal. Why would McAubrey, assuming Sammy murdered a DA, treat him as an equal?

The guard entered to get him, and within seconds, Sammy felt small and unworthy once again.

Mick followed a firefighter up the stairs to the third story. When he opened the door, it was as if all light were swallowed up. He'd never seen anything as dark in his life. Fortunately in his career in the FBI, he'd never had to deal with many fires. Mick took the handkerchief the fireman had given him and placed it over his mouth.

"Down the hall it's not quite as bad," the firefighter said. "You'll be able to breathe a little easier."

Mick nodded as the fireman waved the beam of his flashlight back and forth across the floor. Ahead, he could see more flashlight beams bouncing off the wet walls and hear a few muddled voices. The smell could hardly be tolerated. It was acrid, as if he were walking through mounds of burned garbage. A suffocating heat like that of a steam bath made it even harder to breathe.

The firefighter motioned that the office was up ahead. He stepped aside and Mick entered. Five people were moving around, including a medical-examiner photographer, who was using a special camera equipped with a flash that would be able to cut into the blackness. The medical examiner was busy taking notes over the half-charred body, which lay crooked on the floor.

Mick held in his stomach muscles. It was a disgusting sight.

He decided he wasn't going to get to the body anytime soon, so he walked around the office, seeing if he could garner any clues. The ceiling and walls and part of the

floor were burned. The desk that sat in the middle was
black with soot but didn't look burned. Black fire marks
streaked the side of a metal filing cabinet that the body lay
next to.

Mick scanned the room through the small amount of
light, trying to find anything that would help him understand why their suspect had ended up dead in a building he
seemed to have no business in.

He'd noted the office directory when he walked into the
building. It housed several small businesses, including a
chiropractor, an insurance company, and a temp agency.

This office gave no indication to its use, not even a suite
number. He also noticed there was no computer or fax
machine, and it appeared unusually tidy, like it was hardly
ever used.

He borrowed some gloves from the medical examiner
and opened the file cabinet. Flipping through the files, he
spotted a lot of empty folders, but their bottoms were bulging like they'd recently held quite a bit of paper.

"Lucky you."

Mick turned around to find Agent Lancaster standing
behind him. She was looking at the body next to them as if
it were an interesting piece of art.

"Why's that?" he asked.

She watched him close the file cabinet, likely making
sure he wasn't removing any evidence. Then, looking at the
body again, she said, "He's lying on his right hand."

"Why does that make me lucky?"

"The extremities always burn first, which makes it very
hard to fingerprint most burn victims. But his fingerprints
were saved because his hand is underneath him. Good
break for you. Maybe it will keep you from botching your
own investigation."

"You hate the FBI. I got it the first time."

"I don't hate you at all. Unless, of course, you're involved in my investigation." She turned away from the body and faced Mick. "Why don't you tell me who this guy is and why you're investigating him?"

"We've been watching him for several months in connection with an embezzlement scheme. He was the accountant for a company we were alerted to by the Securities and Exchange Commission. In the company's last filing the commission saw some cash-flow thing that looked a little suspicious. We were getting ready to call our dead guy here before the grand jury. Now I guess we're back to square one."

"Dead guy have a name?"

"Joel Lamberson."

"Interesting. So you've been watching him, but you have no idea why he might be in this building?"

"We were going to begin a tail on him this week and probably make an arrest soon."

The medical examiner's team rolled the body into a bag, zipped it, and lifted it onto a gurney.

Mick found a more interesting spot on the smoky carpet to look at.

"Your suspect was dead before the fire," she said with a tinge of boredom in her voice. "There were no blisters on his body. When a body burns after it's already dead, the skin doesn't blister. It cooks like a roast in the oven; it just browns." She followed the body out into the hallway.

Mick walked to the door. "Hey, Agent Lancaster?"

"What?"

"You don't happen to know the average rushing yards per game for the Cowboys last year, do you?"

Her eyebrow popped up with curiosity. "Why?"

"Just wanted to make sure you weren't an expert on

everything," Mick said with a smile, hoping to lighten this lady up.

"Two hundred and thirteen yards." She continued down the dark hallway guided by a single flashlight.

chapter six

all three men stood in Tom Bixby's small, crowded office. Mick and Tom held Styrofoam cups of coffee, and Reggie had his forty-eight-ounce mug. But nobody was drinking coffee. In fact, Mick and Reggie stood next to each other watching several emotions roll across their supervisor's face like the ground rolling in an earthquake.

Tom rubbed his eyes and pinched the bridge of his nose. "I don't know what's more frustrating—our suspect dead or the idea that we have to partner with the ATF." He looked at Mick. "So they're investigating this as part of a serial arson case?"

Mick nodded.

"What information did you glean last night?"

"Not much. Everyone there was real touchy about the FBI showing up. I didn't want to raise a stink, so I figured I'd let the . . . um . . . smoke clear and find out all I could this morning. All I know is that this is the fourth building in about eight months, all large buildings, all started at night. The last two have been two weeks apart."

"Has ATF identified any relationship between the properties being burned, or did our suspect just strip his gears and decide one morning to go out and start some fires?"

"Don't know anything about that yet."

Tom sipped his black coffee before heading to the other

side of his desk. "Okay, well, let's find out all we can. I don't want to appear heavy-handed with the ATF, but I'm not going to let their arson investigation get in the way of all we've worked for here."

"What are the chances the two are related?" Reggie asked.

"I think the chances are good," Mick said.

Tom nodded. "I think we're getting ready to see an entirely new side to this case. Reggie, make sure we've filed everything we need to file. Get the names of all ATF agents working on their side of this thing so we can add them to the grand jury 6(e) list in the event we have to share parts of the investigative file with them. Also, get someone started on identifying the ownership of the buildings that have been burned. Find out when they were purchased, how much they paid for them, who the real-estate broker was, who originally built the buildings, who the past owners were. I want to know everything possible so we can maintain an upper hand in the event we have to turn this into a task-force case."

Tom took a breath. "Reggie, I also want you to get started on the paperwork we need to send back to head-quarters for approval of a joint task-force investigation and make sure we have all our reports up-to-date. Mick, get in touch with the lead investigator for ATF and make sure you're in the way over there at the scene, but make nice so they don't freeze us out. We're probably going to need them on this one."

Reggie chuckled.

Tom looked at him. "Something funny?"

"Sorry," Reggie said. "It's just that Mick is . . . well, he's kind of scared of her."

"I'm not either."

"Scared of whom?"

"The special agent. What's her name?"

Mick sighed. "Lancaster."

"Yeah, that's it."

"You're scared of her?" Tom asked Mick.

"I'm not *scared* of her."

"She is kind of scary." Reggie smiled.

"She's just . . . she's . . ."

"She's what? Got a third eye?" Tom asked.

"She rides a Harley," Mick explained.

"And knows football stats," Reggie added.

"Her tongue could cut through metal."

Tom glanced back and forth at his men. "So what you're saying is that this lady is tougher than you."

Mick and Reggie both shrugged. It couldn't be disputed.

Tom shook his head. "As if we don't have enough problems. Just promise me you'll handle her, Kline."

"It'll be fine."

"Good. I want to be kept up-to-date."

Reggie nodded and walked out.

Mick stayed. "One more thing."

"What?"

"I'm getting these weird notes through the mail to my house. They're newspaper clippings with one letter highlighted out of each headline."

Tom's eyebrow rose in concern.

"I'm not worried, just going through protocol."

"How many have you received?"

"Three. No clue what it means."

Tom seemed disturbed, as if this particular detail was going to send him back for his fourth cup of coffee and his eighth cigarette and possibly up the flight of stairs to Dr. Grenard, the in-house shrink. "Okay, thanks for telling me. Isn't there a form or something we fill out for that sort of thing?"

"I'll take care of it," Mick said, smiling.

Tom nodded, then went back to the mound of paperwork on his desk.

Outside Tom's office, Mick found Reggie smiling at him from across his desk. "Very funny," Mick said.

"Couldn't resist. And she *is* scary!" Reggie laughed.

"Well, why not mention I brought a date too?"

This caused Reggie to laugh even harder. "So it was a date!"

Mick fell into his chair and rubbed his temples. "At this point in my life, my friend, I think it was what they call a sympathy dinner. Women feel sorry for me. They think that I'm old and lonely, so even though they don't want to commit to a relationship, they're willing to keep me company."

Reggie shook his head as the chuckling died down. "Dude, you are not old. Marnie's been talking about this lady from her workout place. . . ."

Mick waved his hands. "No, no, no. No more blind dates."

"Brother, where are you going to meet ladies, huh? You don't go out. You don't do anything on the weekend except go to church. The only other thing that gets you out of the house are storms that have the potential to escort you straight out of the dating scene and into your grave. I mean, give yourself a shot."

"Reg, as much as I appreciate your interest in my lack of a love life, I think I can handle it."

"You know what your problem is? I think you're too complicated. You need a woman who can love you and who you can love. In my opinion, there's no such thing as a perfect match or a perfect mate. You either choose to love the person or you don't. Find a woman you think is hot, and in your case probably religious, and go for it."

"It's that simple, is it?"

"I think so. That's how I met Marnie. Saw her at party. Went over and talked to her. Thought she was cool. Dated her. Then made sure I married her."

Mick sighed. "Yeah, well, as much as I'd love to sit here and talk about lovely women, I'm afraid I have a date with Aphrodite's wicked stepsister."

Mick stood by his truck and quietly observed Agent Lancaster. She was probably five foot eight, but the way she carried herself made her appear even taller. Her thin frame stood steady. At the moment she was leaning over a set of blueprints rolled out on a makeshift table, having trouble holding down the pages because of the wind. As she scraped her hair out of her face in frustration, Mick approached and put his hand down on the corner of the blueprint.

She looked up. "Agent Kline." She glanced at her watch and straightened. "A little late in the morning, isn't it? I figured I would've been beating you away with a stick at sunrise."

"Had some business at the office."

Agent Lancaster smiled for the first time since they'd met last night. But Mick didn't know why. Something had amused her, though.

"Have you concluded that this is your arsonist?"

She placed a folder on the blueprints to hold them down and then walked over to a watercooler. Mick followed. She sipped her water and stared at the burned-out building, now fully visible in the morning light. It was charred on the top and sides. Yellow crime-scene tape tied to signs and trees surrounded the morbid scene. Mick watched ATF agents and firefighters duck under the tape as they came and went from the building.

"Last night, did you notice something odd about the file cabinet?" she asked.

"The file cabinet?"

"The one that your suspect was lying by?"

"I noticed there seemed to be documents missing."

"But what I found strange was that the drawer was not pulled open. And there were no documents on the desk or on top of the filing cabinet. That's strange because normally when a fire is set to destroy documents, the file drawer will be open so the fire can reach it. But you say documents appear to be missing anyway."

Agent Lancaster seemed to be thinking out loud, so Mick remained quiet. He liked the passion in her eyes. He could hear the delight in her voice at the idea that this was going to be a little more complicated than she'd anticipated. She added, "You have no idea how many criminals we've caught simply because they thought a book would burn in a fire. Books and large masses of paper actually have a hard time being engulfed by flames."

"Interesting."

Agent Lancaster shrugged; her mind appeared to be tracing various scenarios. "We're still not sure how this fire was set."

"So you're not sure if it's linked to the other fires?"

"I'm not ready to pack up and get out of your neatly gelled hair yet, Agent Kline." She glanced at his head. "No gel today?"

Mick ran his fingers through his hair. What was it with women and their gel comments?

"Anyway, we do know where the fire started—in the office next to the one that contained Mr. Lamberson. Whoever set this fire didn't take into account the firewall, which delayed the fire by several minutes. I would assume the intention was to make the fire look accidental by starting it somewhere other than where the body was found, so it looked like he was trapped. Unfortunately for the arsonist, Mr. Lamberson is speaking from the grave. Got word this morning that he was strangled."

Mick took out his notepad and jotted down notes. "Witnesses?"

"No one other than the janitor, who called the fire in. But he did not see anyone in the building or leaving it." She paused. "Are you a patient man?"

"Sure," Mick said.

"Good. Because arson investigations are complex. They take a lot of time and effort and patience to piece together."

"As opposed to RICO cases, which are just insanely simple."

"Don't rush me on this, and I'll make sure you have the evidence you need."

"Any connection to the other buildings?"

She smiled a little. "You work mostly white-collar crime, don't you, Kline?"

"Yeah, so?"

"Don't see much action in the field, do you?"

"What's your point?"

"No point. Just trying to figure out how much patience I'm going to have to have with you."

Mick couldn't help an escaping laugh. "Okay. Sure."

She handed him a card. "Meet me at my office at seven tonight. I'll give you more details then."

"Why then?"

"Because it's bad for my reputation to be seen talking with you." Another small smile crossed her lips.

Mick sensed he was dealing with a smart, savvy, mischievous woman. "As much as I'd like to make this easy for you, I've got a job to do concerning Lamberson. I need to know why he was here and why he was killed and by whom."

Another ATF agent approached, hardly acknowledging Mick. "Libby, I found a—"

"Agent Stewart, this is Special Agent Mick Kline from the bureau."

Stewart's mouth hung open midsentence. He promptly shut it and nodded cordially. He then looked at Lancaster. "Can I see you for a moment?"

She grinned, a grin that spoke of her confidence that her words had done their job . . . keeping Stewart from saying anything he shouldn't. "Sure. I'll be with you in a moment." Stewart backed away a few feet, and Lancaster said, "I want to know what you have on Lamberson."

"Then I guess we'll see what cards we can trade tonight."

"I guess so. Don't be late." She joined Stewart and they walked off.

Mick sighed and returned to the office that had held Lamberson a few hours ago. The smell, though somewhat diminished, still burned inside his nostrils. He wondered how firefighters ever got used to it. He took the stairs the ATF agent had led him up the night before and found the office area relatively quiet. A couple of forensics technicians were examining the room, so Mick went to the office where they thought the fire started. The black, shadowlike patterns on the wall showed how it had resisted the flames and climbed into the ceiling, buying Lamberson several minutes to escape had he not been dead first.

A block of streaming light from the window glowed throughout the dark room, making it easier to see the remarkably neat and unused office. He carefully pulled out the desk drawers, which were filled with nothing more than supplies. Mick picked up a half-melted stapler off the desk and pried it open. There were no staples inside.

One badly burned picture of the mountains hung lop-sidedly on the far wall, but other than that, there was no decor. Unlike the other room, there wasn't even a file cabinet.

Hearing the techs walk down the hall, Mick went to the office where Lamberson had been found. An eerie outline showed where his body had kept the fire and smoke from damaging the floor. He studied the position of the outline. Lamberson had been found on his back, with his right arm pinned beneath him. He was probably strangled from behind. The killer probably let him fall to the floor, where he collapsed just like they found him.

Mick walked around the small office once more, then moved to the far end of the hallway. From a window, he looked out from the east side of the building. Below, Agent Lancaster was talking with other agents. They seemed to be observing a pile of lumber and construction materials with great interest. Lancaster was gesturing and looking very lively as other agents took notes and talked with one another. Mick wondered why a pile of lumber would draw such attention.

He heard footsteps behind him and turned to find a tall, hunched janitor with gray frizzy hair slowly walking the hallway, the whites of his eyes visible as he observed the destruction. He was fumbling with his keys as he approached a small closet opposite the offices.

"Excuse me," Mick said.

The man looked up.

Mick walked toward him. "Can I speak with you? I'm with the FBI."

"Sure," he mumbled, "but I already talked to the folks downstairs. I'm just getting my stuff. I buy all these clean-ing supplies myself. Gonna have to get another job now, I guess. No use in cleaning this building."

"I'm sorry to hear that," Mick said.

"I learned a long time ago that there ain't much peace in this world. So what'd you want to ask me?"

"You're the one who saw the fire last night and called the police?"

"That's right."

Mick gestured at the office doors. "Ever see anyone come in and out of these offices?"

"No, sir."

"You have a key?"

"No. Since I been here, I never cleaned them. Not supposed to. They're always locked anyway."

"Do you know who occupies these offices?"

"Nope."

"Thanks." So whoever set the fire in the office next door had a key to get in. Mick just had to figure out who that was.

The janitor opened his closet.

"Any supplies missing?"

The janitor shook his head. "Everything's here."

the medical examiner's room was cold and stale except for "I Heard It Through The Grapevine" playing over the intercom. Dr. Lee Pai, a young-looking man for his position as head of the ME's office, was busy jotting down notes and bobbing his head to the tune when Mick walked in.

"Special Agent Mick Kline."

Dr. Pai managed a cordial smile. "The ATF is thorough, aren't you? You had men out here all morning."

"I'm not with ATF. I'm with the FBI." Mick nodded toward a table with a body lying underneath an off-white sheet. "That's my suspect."

"That's the fat guy who dropped dead of a heart attack while line dancing with a woman who wasn't his wife at a bar last night."

"Oh. I'm looking for the dead guy who was supposed to look like he died by fire but was actually strangled."

"One room over. Come with me."

Mick followed Dr. Pai, trying to ignore the sickening smells that floated around him. He'd already seen the body once, and that would probably give him nightly disturbing images for months and months to come.

Mick had always wondered what kind of person would want to work in a funeral home, and being an ME didn't seem that different, except there was a lot more science behind it. Strangely, the MEs always looked so normal.

Three Dog Night's "Joy to the World" was now playing, and Dr. Pai was bobbing his head up and down again.

"You like *The Big Chill?*" Mick asked, hoping the chit-chat would keep his mind off the saw sitting on the table to the right.

"Oh yeah!" Dr. Pai said. "One of my favorites. JoBeth Williams is hot!"

Mick suppressed a smile. He would've thought Dr. Pai might be more inclined to the Glenn Close types of the world.

"So," Dr. Pai said, "you're here about this fellow." He gestured to the white sheet, which Mick noticed right away was draped across a much smaller man than the one in the other room.

"You've identified him?"

"He had no identification on him, but we got a thumbprint and matched it to a guy named Joel Lamberson, thanks to a DUI charge four years ago. His wife had reported him missing early this morning."

Mick knew that Joel and his wife, Anita, had two teenage daughters. They lived well in a four-thousand-square-foot house that seemed disproportionate to how much Mr. Lamberson had been making as an accountant. This was just one of the details the bureau had been gathering for a while now in hopes of nailing Lamberson on an embezzlement scheme.

"Anyway," Dr. Pai said as he flipped open the chart he was holding, "the guy was definitely strangled, and I can say with almost 100 percent assurance that it was with a small rope. By the way the muscles in the neck are bruised all the way around, it's apparent that . . ." Dr. Pai set down his folder. "Well, here, let me show you—"

"Oh no, that's okay," Mick said quickly. Dr. Pai's fingers were just about to pull the sheet off Lamberson. "Um, I don't really need to . . ."

Dr. Pai smiled. "Not a field agent, eh?"

"As a matter of fact, no, but I've already seen the body once. Don't need to see it again."

Dr. Pai nodded. "No need to explain. I've had plenty of tough cops in here puking all over the place. I keep a bucket in the corner now." He jabbed his thumb over his shoulder.

Sure enough, a blue bucket sat nonchalantly in the corner.

"Was there anything else on Mr. Lamberson? Keys, maybe?"

"No."

"I wonder how he got to the building. There were no cars in the parking lot."

"According to his wife, his car is missing. Also, we did find a good amount of alcohol in his system."

Mick took out his pad and jotted down notes. "Any signs that he struggled?"

"He had a blow to the head, indicating he was probably struck first, which knocked him down, and then strangled. The blow to the head didn't kill him, though. It did little more than bruise him."

"What more can you tell me about the wife's reaction? I don't want her to know the FBI is involved."

"She was shocked. She said he was going out to get a few things at the store. Said he does that a lot, goes to those twenty-four-hour grocers and looks at car magazines or something. Yeah, right. Car magazines. He then comes home with the groceries. She said she got worried when he hadn't returned after three hours."

The door to the room opened. An attractive woman

with curly red hair and beautiful skin acknowledged Mick with a warm smile. "I'm sorry to interrupt."

"Not at all. Come on in. Carla, this is Mick Kline from the FBI. This is Carla Howard, my assistant."

Mick shook her hand, which was soft but strong. Their eyes met. She had amazing hazel eyes and not a stitch of makeup on. Mick's heart thumped approvingly in his chest.

"Hi," she said.

"Nice to meet you."

Mick let go of her hand and wished that Reggie were here now, so he would see that he didn't have to be set up on blind dates to meet women. In fact, Mick was thinking this was a woman he could easily ask out. He checked her ring finger. *No ring! Aha!*

"I won't keep you," she said, smiling at Mick and then looking at Dr. Pai. "I just needed to know how you want me to open up the skull in room 3. Also, do you want me to keep the liver intact?"

Mick sighed. Some things were just not meant to be.

Mick pulled into a parking space at his apartment and got out of his truck, stretching his arms toward the sky. It had been a long day. He'd hardly seen Reggie at all, which always put him in a bad mood. He checked his watch. He had an hour before he was to meet Libby Lancaster. The thought of wading through that woman's personality caused him to think about calling in sick.

He opened his mailbox, apprehensive he might find another mysterious letter inside. To his surprise, there was no mail. Another tenant walked up and opened his mailbox, sliding out a slew of junk mail. Mick stared into his empty box. He could not remember a time when he hadn't had at least a flyer in his box.

Walking upstairs, he pushed his key into the lock, turned it, and realized immediately that it was already unlocked. He stepped back and gathered himself. Listening carefully, he thought he heard footsteps inside.

As he pushed the door open, ready to tackle the intruder, he heard a scream and found himself staring at Jenny. She was doubled over laughing hysterically. "You scared the daylights out of me!"

"What are you doing here?" Mick asked as he shut the front door. After Aaron died, Mick had given Jenny a key to his apartment for safekeeping and in case she ever needed anything.

She went to the kitchen and opened the oven. A wonderful smell drifted out. "I've been wanting to make that baked chicken casserole Aaron loved so much. But it feeds an army." She looked at him and smiled. "I thought you might enjoy a home-cooked meal. I left a message at your office. You didn't get it?"

"I've hardly been in today."

"Playing hooky?"

He laughed. "I wish."

"Looks like the casserole is about done. You have time to eat?"

"I've got a meeting in about an hour."

"Good. Plenty of time to eat, then." Jenny pulled the casserole out of the oven. "Your mail's over there."

Mick threw his keys on the table and walked over to the pile of mail. Sifting through it, he noticed a handwritten envelope similar to the other three he'd received. He turned his back to Jenny, who was busy tossing a salad, and opened the envelope. Inside, a newspaper headline read "Park to Reopen." There were two highlighted letters: *P* and *O*. He tucked the article back into the envelope.

"I miss those small things," Jenny said from the kitchen. "Getting the mail for Aaron."

Mick joined her. "This smells great. You're nice to come over and cook for me."

She did it from time to time or brought Chinese food over and they'd watch a movie. For years he'd been trying to hush his feelings for Jenny that liked to whisper to him when he was alone. He'd fallen in love with Jenny years and years ago, before he'd turned his life around. He'd treated her poorly, playing those silly games people play. She, in turn, met his brother and fell in love with him. They married and then Aaron was murdered. But no matter how hard he tried to deny it, Mick was beginning to realize he would always have feelings for this woman. These days, though, she was finally starting to feel a little more like a sister-in-law. Maybe that hole was closing ever so slowly.

He watched her set the table and wondered what it would be like to come home to such a lovely woman every night . . . to have dinners cooked . . . to have a hand stroke his cheek and ask about his day . . . to have little ones embrace his neck. He'd been a bachelor for so long that the idea of it all seemed fanciful and surreal.

"How was your day?" she asked, gesturing for him to sit at the table. She brought him a drink and served the casserole.

"It was a little out of the norm."

"I'll bless the food, and then I want to hear about it." She bowed her head and thanked the Lord.

Mick did too. He didn't pray or eat like this often enough. Most of the time he ate frozen dinners in front of the television.

"So what happened?" she asked.

"Had to go to the medical examiner's office. One of our suspects died in a fire."

Jenny made a face. "That doesn't sound pleasant."

"Let me ask you something. Do you think I'm too picky?"

She looked at his plate. "Well, you're eating it, aren't you?"

"Not the food. Are you kidding? I'll eat nearly anything as long as it has been cooked to the right temperature or refrigerated properly."

"You're not talking about your fear of food? Because that's always such a fascinating topic."

"Women."

"Oh! Even better!"

"Reggie thinks I'm too complicated. He says I just need to find a beautiful woman and marry her."

Jenny chewed while she contemplated. "Well, I don't know that I would agree with Reggie. I mean, there has to be chemistry. Just because a woman is beautiful doesn't mean she's the right one for you."

"Exactly. For instance, it wouldn't be wrong for me to think a woman is attractive but then decide not to ask her out because she saws people's heads open all day. Is that wrong?"

Jenny blinked from across the table. "I'm not following."

Mick waved his fork. "Never mind. You know, I think that I'm one of those rare people in life who is meant to be single. There's nothing wrong with being single, right?"

"Mick," Jenny said, smiling, "you just haven't found the right woman yet."

"Not true," he said. "I have found the right woman several times, but apparently I wasn't the right man at the right time."

"Whatever the case may be, you'll find the person for you. She may be right in front of you, and you don't know it!" She poured dressing on her salad.

"So how was your day?"

"Weird." She set down her fork, which Mick knew from experience was not a good sign from a woman. It meant a serious conversation was about to take place.

"Weird?" He gobbled down a few bites just in case he was going to have to set his fork down and pay heavy attention.

She sighed. "I hate to even bring it up, Mick. You've got a lot on your plate, a lot to worry about with work, and this is only going to be one more thing. But I can't shake this feeling."

"What feeling?"

She rose and went to her purse on the counter. She pulled out an envelope and handed it to Mick. Inside was a handwritten letter without an addressee.

I am about to die. But I am innocent. I am writing this to anyone who may be able to help me. My lawyers are all out of tricks. But someone out there knows the truth. I did not kill Stephen Fiscall. Somebody set me up. Somebody wanted me to rot in a prison cell. Out there somewhere is the real killer. I will probably still be executed, but I need someone out there to know that somebody got away with murder. Two murders. My death included. Please do all you can to find the truth.

Sammy Earle
Attorney-at-law

Mick couldn't hold in his surprise. He let out a short laugh and looked up at Jenny, who shrugged. "I know," she said. "That's why I had to show it to you."

Mick flipped the envelope over. It was addressed to

Aaron. "That's strange. Why would it be addressed to Aaron?"

"It was sent to our old address and forwarded to me. I guess Mr. Earle didn't know Aaron died."

"He must be going through the names of people who worked the case. Maybe he got the names off court documents."

"I don't know."

"When did this letter arrive?"

"Today."

Mick reread it and folded it up. "Can I keep this?"

"Sure. I don't know what to make of it. I mean, the evidence so clearly shows that Earle murdered that DA. Remember? They not only had his prints, but they had motive too."

"You're talking about that letter they found at his house, indicating the DA had some information on Earle."

"If I remember right. It's been ten years ago. But I've been reading some of the newspaper articles about the case since his execution date is coming up."

Mick leaned back into his chair and stared at the ceiling.

"You okay?" Jenny asked.

"Yeah." He sighed. "It doesn't seem like that long ago to me. Can ten years have passed? What an awful time. Those are some of the worst memories of my life. Running from the police. Trying to make it without food or water. Then getting food poisoning because I had to eat out of a Dumpster."

"Do you think about it much? Other than when you refrigerate your raisins?"

"No." Mick's appetite waned, so he pushed his plate away and wiped his mouth. He rose to refill his tea. "It just reminds me of Aaron. It reminds me of bad times and good times. That was the point when I stopped being so angry at my brother. The guy literally saved my life." He leaned against the fridge. "But you already know that."

Jenny turned around in her chair to look at him. "Aaron was a good man. He did more on this earth in his short life than most people do their whole lives."

"Maybe I'll do some checking into the case. There's got to be a reason Earle sent this to Aaron."

"A couple of years after the case, Aaron continued to look into things. He never talked much about it, and I only knew of it because he kept a big box of stuff about the case in the attic."

"What do you mean? What kind of stuff?"

"I don't know. I never went through it. But I know there was something about the case that fascinated him. He kept going through information, making phone calls. I'm not really sure when he stopped. And I don't know what he was looking for."

"Do you still have that box?"

"Maybe. I have some stuff in storage. You want me to check?"

"Definitely."

chapter eight

the Santa Fe Building glowed against the last light of evening. The twenty-story building had five tall, arched windows at the front and a copper-covered mansard topping off the twentieth floor. It had once been used as the headquarters of the Gulf, Colorado, and Santa Fe Railway Company. It had a nice twenties historical flair about it, though it was crowded between two newer buildings.

Mick took the elevator to the third floor, went through security, and then was led back to Agent Lancaster's office. The receptionist announced Mick's arrival as formally as if he were a diplomat.

Agent Lancaster looked up from her mound of paperwork and offered a polite smile. "Agent Kline, right on time. Come on in."

Mick walked in and took a seat across from her meticulously organized desk. Several large shelves circled her desk, which faced the door—as any good law-enforcement officer knows is always smart. One entire wall of her office was windows, giving a beautiful view of downtown Dallas.

"Just a second," she murmured and immersed herself in her work again.

Mick got comfortable, folding his hands in his lap and crossing his legs, while glancing around her office to see what made this woman tick. On one side of her desk was an eight-by-ten picture of Libby standing next to a handsome man, and in front of them were two blond children. They all appeared very happy. That was a side he had yet to see of this agent, but then again, he hadn't known her very long. Still, she didn't seem very maternal.

There were some medals and plaques on the other side of her desk, but he couldn't tell what they were for. Meanest ATF Agent of the Year, perhaps? He chuckled to himself at that thought, then found her staring at him.

"You okay?" she asked, stern faced.

Mick nodded and stopped smiling.

She sighed and stood, stretching her arms above her head. "What a day, and it's not going to end until late tonight." She slipped off her suit coat, revealing a sleeveless black shell underneath. When she turned to hang it on a coatrack beside her desk, Mick noticed a large burn scar stretching from her shoulder to below her elbow. It wrapped all the way around her right arm.

As she turned back around, Mick asked, "What happened there?"

She glanced at the scar, as if she was hardly aware it was there. "Long time ago. Firefighting days."

"You were a firefighter?"

"Yeah. Seven years." She opened one of her desk drawers and pulled out a bologna sandwich. "Sorry. Forgot to bring my lunch to the site and haven't eaten since late last night. Do you mind?"

"No," Mick said, staring at the mayo peeking out from the two slices of bread. "That's been in your desk all day? Not in the fridge?"

"Yeah. Why? You want some?"

Mick shook his head.

Libby took a bite and studied Mick with curiosity. "Something wrong?"

"Um . . ."

"Spit it out, Kline."

"You might want to do the same thing."

"What?"

"Unrefrigerated mayonnaise and deli meat are breeding grounds for bacteria."

Lancaster stopped midchew and was staring, dumbfounded, at Mick. She finally swallowed and started laughing. "Kline, you have got to be kidding me."

"I'm not."

"No, I guess you're not. But don't you have more to worry about than me getting food poisoning?"

Mick shrugged. "What can I say? It's a hobby."

Libby took a big bite of her sandwich and chewed vigorously. After swallowing she said, "I've seen worse things than a little food poisoning."

"I haven't," Mick said with a shaky smile. He looked over at the picture. "What a nice-looking family you have."

Libby turned around. "Oh, that's my twin sister, Lacey, and her husband, who likes to sit around and try to impress me with his knowledge of weapons."

"Cute kids," Mick said.

Libby shrugged. "They're okay. Spoiled rotten, but what can you do?"

Mick felt like he'd been sitting in her office for hours.

She retrieved a bag of chips next. "So," she said between bites, "here we are."

"Here we are."

"I guess you want some information from me?"

"That would be nice."

She shoved her food aside and found a folder on the opposite end of her desk.

While she was flipping through it, Mick said, "I want you to know that we're willing to cooperate as much as we can with this investigation. We're not as interested in the arson as we are in the man who died. Maybe they're linked, maybe not, but we hope this will be a good working relationship."

Libby laughed. "Kline, you're a real piece of work. Haven't you been in this business long enough to know the drill? Of course everyone says that. Every bureau makes the same claims when we have to work together. We smile, we shake hands, and we come across as cooperative and responsible. We assure each other that when we get any new piece of information, 'We'll let you know.'

"But the reality is that we all go back to our offices and pinch the bridges of our noses and curse the fact that we have to work with one another. You know I'm going to sit in here and tell you that I'm being forthright, when the reality is that I'm not going to tell you everything I know. And vice versa. So let's not kid each other here and pretend that this is going to be easy-breezy. You and I both know that right now we're each other's worst nightmare."

Mick found his mouth hanging open. *He* was a real piece of work?

"What?" she said, grabbing a chip. "I'm a straight shooter. I don't know how else to be."

Mick studied her. Without that belligerent attitude, she was actually a very attractive lady and very ladylike. A tiny diamond cross hung from her neck, and she wore a couple of gold rings and a dainty bracelet. Her skin was smooth, dotted with a few freckles. A light pink lipstick colored her lips.

"Look," Mick said, breaking the silence, "I'm very aware of how things work. But I meant what I said. You may be a straight shooter, but I'm honest. I'm not here to make your life miserable. I want to make this investigation go as smoothly as possible."

"I find most men are intimidated by me."

"Well—" Mick smiled—"the lipstick and mascara are a bit deceiving."

She pulled out some papers from the folder. "All right. Four fires over eight months, two of them two weeks apart. We suspect that the arson is insurance motivated, but we haven't been able to prove that yet, because we can't find documents supporting our theory that there are at least one or more shelter companies."

"You're sure these fires are all connected?"

Libby seemed to grapple with something. Then she said, "The first three fires had the exact same signature. They were all set using matches and gasoline, from the inside of the building at several spots. In the first building, we found evidence that the electrical wiring had been tampered with, but apparently that did not cause the fire."

"Indicating someone tried to start it by making it look like an electrical fire, failed, then just torched the place."

"That's the theory."

"You said the first three buildings. What about the fourth?"

Another pause. "The signature changed."

"Really?"

"The fire was set from the inside, with something other than gasoline, though we're not sure what. We've sent it to the lab. No matches were found. Of course, now we have a dead guy too."

"I wish I knew why Lamberson was there. Now that he's dead, there's the potential that our entire RICO case is out the window."

"And maybe somebody knew that."

"We've been careful. Nobody knew he was being watched."

Lancaster shrugged, as if she weren't willing to believe it.

"Tell me about your fascination with the lumber."

"What lumber?"

"You and your agents were huddled around a pile of lumber on the side of the building this morning."

"Observant."

"What's it mean?"

"It gives us a stronger indication that this is insurance fraud. Two of the four buildings had building materials on the premises. As you know, when a building burns down, it's hard to prove whether or not construction was really going on. They had receipts showing they'd paid a construction company to do the renovations. The paper trail was very precise. But now they get double the money . . . for the loss of the building and for the loss of construction materials. Plus the value of the building goes up because of the supposed renovations."

Mick nodded. It was a classic insurance-fraud scheme but very hard to prove if you can't find the arsonist. And now they seemed to have a serial arsonist on their hands. "So you think the lumber was there as a setup?"

"To me it shows that the building was being set up to be torched. Since the entire building didn't burn this time, we know there were no renovations going on."

"I spoke to the janitor, who said he had no cleaning agents missing."

Lancaster nodded. "Yep."

Lancaster's cell phone rang to the tune of "As Time Goes By," adding to the complexity of the woman sitting across from him. *She's a romantic too?*

She snatched it up. "Lancaster . . . where? . . ." She shut her phone. "We've got another fire, twenty blocks away. Let's go."

Lancaster gasped as they pulled around the corner. A five-story building was partly engulfed in flames. She hopped out of her car, and Mick followed her.

The fire chief greeted her. "It's abandoned, but we think there may be a couple of street people in there," he yelled over the chaos. "We thought we heard screaming. But it could've been an alley cat."

Mick realized this was at least a three-alarm fire. The buildings nearby were in danger of catching on fire too. A stiff breeze was adding to the problem. Even several yards back, the heat choked him.

"Where are the other trucks?" Libby yelled back.

Mick looked around. There were only two trucks. One truck sprayed water on the burning building, the other on the building next door.

"There was an accident. The trucks collided at an intersection when an SUV ran a stoplight. I've called for backup, but there was a big wreck on I-35 so we've got a delay."

"How many men do you have in there?"

"Two teams of two."

Libby turned back to the fire, her wide eyes reflecting the enormous flames. She cautiously stepped forward, examining the building. "This one's abandoned," Libby said to herself. "So why this one?"

Mick stepped up beside her but couldn't offer any explanation. He watched her gaze roam the building and the premises. Something caught her attention, and she walked over to a metal sign that was turned facedown, about twenty yards from the building.

Mick followed her. A heap of junk was scattered around it. "What's wrong?"

"Help me lift this up," she instructed. They pulled it off

73

the ground. She scraped her hand across the front of it, and chunks of dried mud fell off. Her eyes widened with fear. "Oh no."

"What?" Mick looked at the sign through the light the fire was providing. He could see part of a word but wasn't sure why Libby was so upset.

Libby whirled back toward the fire trucks, then bolted toward the chief. "Chief! Get your men out! Get them out!"

Mick tried to knock off a little more mud, and then his heart stopped. He couldn't make out all the words but he saw enough: *paint factory*. Though abandoned, there could possibly still be chemicals in there.

He dropped the sign, turned, and heard Libby still yelling.

The chief had his radio out. Mick could hear him shouting, "Get out! Get out!" and see him shake his head as if he couldn't get a response. He watched one of the guys on the ladders who was spraying the roof. He could see terror in his eyes as he heard the message coming over his radio. The firefighter started to climb down.

Mick looked back at the chief, whose frantic face made Mick run toward him, hoping he could do something to help. As he approached, he didn't see Libby.

"I can't get them to respond!" the chief was shouting to no one in particular.

"Where's Libby?" Mick hollered.

"Who?"

"Agent Lancaster? Where is she?"

The chief's vacant eyes told Mick he had no idea.

Mick raced toward the building and saw her. She'd grabbed a firefighter's bunker coat and a mask off one of the trucks. She was running straight for the front entrance. In the distance, Mick could hear sirens approaching.

"Libby! Wait!" Mick yelled. "Wait! The backup is here!"

But she disappeared into the dark entrance. Above, the flames roared from some of the windows and the roof.

"What is she doing?" the chief cried.

"I'll get her! Backup is here!" Mick took off toward the front of the building. If he could just get to her before she got too far into the building, he could convince her to let the arriving firefighters go in. "Libby!"

Then he heard it—a strange, deep, vacuumlike sound that actually pulled him toward the building for a second and then a sound so loud his eardrums vibrated in pain. He didn't have time to do anything but realize he was airborne, blown back from the building and now arching upward. It felt like two gigantic hands of a bully had pushed him back-ward.

In another second, he was flat against the cement in front of one of the large wheels of the fire truck. He'd hit the windshield of the truck and slid down. He cried out, his entire left side racked in pain. He rolled over and tried to get to his knees, but his body collapsed. He turned his head and looked at the gigantic fireball that floated above the building. He heard screaming. His eyes watered from the ashy particles floating through the air.

The pain seemed to center itself in his left arm. He tried to struggle to his knees again, but the earth spun, and he fell over. Grabbing the bumper of the fire truck, he managed to sit up. "Libby!"

The sirens faded, and the bright orange flames dulled and blurred in front of him. He tried to keep his eyes open, but they stung and watered so badly they automatically closed.

And his arm stopped hurting.

chapter nine

h ow's that?" the nurse asked as she pinned the sling, causing Mick's left arm to rest tightly against his torso.

"It feels tight."

"That's good. You'll want to keep it that way until you get the cast. Take the anti-inflammatory pills to get the swelling down, and you should be good to go on the cast tomorrow. And here're some pain pills. By your pale complexion, looks like you're going to need these too. One pill every four hours. Not any more. Got it?"

Mick nodded as she placed the instructions and pills into a bag.

"Somebody will be in here to check you out in a moment."

Mick couldn't get comfortable on the small, emergency-room hospital bed. His arm throbbed with pain, and his mind couldn't leave the horrible scene behind. Why would Libby do something so stupid?

The curtain flew back and Reggie appeared, a mixture of energy, relief, and burden scrambled over his features. "She's okay."

"Thank God. I can't believe it."

"Apparently she has a bad concussion, so they're admit-ting her, and she's got some pretty bad cuts. I didn't get to see her, just talked to one of the agents."

"What about the firefighters?"

"Two were already out of the building. They'd gone out the back entrance. One of the other two is dead, and one is in critical condition. They flew him to the burn unit."

Mick rubbed his eyes. He never could get over the emotion of hearing about the death of a firefighter. He finally said, "Do they know yet if anyone was in the building?"

"They don't think there was anybody there. It was probably just a cat screaming."

Mick shook his head and stared at the white tile his feet dangled above.

"You okay?" Reggie asked.

"Yeah. Do me a favor. Get back out to the scene. Make sure you're in the way."

Reggie nodded. "Don't worry, though. Tom's already got guys out there."

"I know. But I want you out there. Now it's personal, and I don't want anything left undone."

"Go home and take care of yourself. We can handle it."

A nurse walked in with a mound of paperwork and a clipboard. "I hope you're right-handed."

Peering through the small window in the door, Mick watched as Libby lay in bed and stared out the dark window of her hospital room. A sheet and blanket covered most of her body, which was propped up by two pillows. An IV ran into her bruised arm. Her face looked the same as her arm.

He opened the door and she turned her head. When she realized who it was, she grinned, the first time he'd seen a genuine emotion cross her face.

He grinned back. "How are you feeling?" He pulled up the small stool that sat by the bed.

"Like I got thrown across the universe and landed on a pile of rocks."

"You look that way too."

She touched her face. "Twenty-eight stitches all over the place, and don't ask me where because I don't even know. I think I have some underneath my chin." She touched it lightly with a finger, then looked at his arm. "Broken?"

"Yeah. Will get the cast tomorrow."

"You were running after me. That's what they told me."

"Yeah."

"That was a stupid thing to do. Me, I mean. I should've never run into that building. It was instinct. I lost my sense of judgment. One man died anyway. And it sounds like another one probably wishes he were dead." Libby's voice quivered.

"It was a brave thing you did. I'm just glad you're going to be all right."

"They tell me I may be here a couple of days. Means they're going to hand over the investigation to Goober."

Mick laughed. "You have pet names for everyone you like?"

"That's his real name. No lie. Agent Toby Guber. And he's not a goober—he's a moron."

"Why don't you have any visitors from work?"

"They all wanted to hang around here and feel sorry for me. I sent them back into the field. I'm going to catch this person if it's the last thing I do. Now it's personal."

Mick smiled.

"So," she said, "we didn't get to finish our conversation at the office. I wish I had my notes here. I can't remember what we covered."

"Agent, I'm not here to grill you for information. I came to make sure you're okay."

"Oh." She looked down, seemingly interested in some fuzz on the blanket. "I'm fine."

"Yeah, you look fine."

She met his eyes. "I'm really okay. They're only keeping me here as a precaution and so they can make an extra three thousand dollars. I got knocked out. They're acting like I lost my head and they had to reattach it."

"So you truly are an expert on everything, including the medical field."

"I know me, and I know I'm okay. I'm just a little dizzy." She smirked. "Why do you think I'm an expert on everything?"

"Because you can quote football statistics off the top of your head. That's a sure sign of a genius, right?"

She laughed. "Oh yeah. That. I forgot about that."

"You're a football fan?"

"Yes. But you surprise me, Kline."

"Why's that?"

"I figured you would've checked your facts."

"What facts?"

A sly smile slid across her lips. "I made it up, Kline. I picked a number that sounded right and threw it out there with a confident nod. You totally bought it!"

"Oh."

"Look, don't take it hard. I'm just the type of person who would check something like that. I don't trust anybody except my priest."

"Your priest?" Mick asked.

"Don't bust my chops. I'm religious, and I know it's not hip to be religious these days. But if you ask me, we'd be a lot better off—this country—if everybody would get their lazy—" She cleared her throat. "Anyway, if everybody would get into a pew and listen to a few pointers from God."

"I agree."

"Don't patronize me."

"I'm not." Mick laughed. "I agree."

She eyed him curiously. "Really?"

"I go to church myself."

She seemed surprised, then shrugged it off. Her hands slowly made their way to her head, and she grimaced.

"What's wrong?" Mick asked.

"Just a bad headache. Hit my skull against a slab of concrete. I guess that's what you would expect, right? A headache." She grimaced again.

"You want me to get a nurse?"

"No. It'll pass. They've got me on enough pain meds to make me hear weird things—like you go to church."

"I'll let you rest."

"Thanks." She settled back into her pillows. "Take care of yourself. Get that inflammation down so you can get your cast on."

"I'll be in touch."

"I'm sure you will, Kline."

Mick laughed as he walked out the door. "And I was worried about you getting food poisoning."

Mick groaned and tried to get comfortable on the couch. Even with the pain medication, his arm continued to throb uncontrollably through the night. He got maybe an hour of sleep on the couch, with pillows propped all around him.

When he heard a knock at the front door, he called, "It's open!"

Jenny rushed straight to him, her mouth open dramatically. "Why didn't you call me last night? I could've come to help!"

"That's why I didn't call you," Mick said. "You'd worry all night. I knew you were off work today, so I figured I'd call this morning and you could drive me to the doc since I can't drive until I get the cast on."

"What happened?"

"Did you hear about that big fire last night?"

"I saw it on the news."

"That's what happened. I was there with ATF when the whole building exploded into a gigantic fireball."

"You're lucky it wasn't worse than a broken bone. The other firefighter died this morning."

Mick felt the emotions rush back.

"Here, let me fix you some coffee." She went to the kitchen and poured the water into the pot. Then she said, "Oh, I almost forgot. I found that box of stuff Aaron had kept on the Earle case." She walked outside, where it was still sitting next to the front door, and brought it in. "It's pretty heavy. He had a lot of information here. I don't know what most of it means, though." Jenny set the box on the floor by the couch.

Mick sat up, using his good arm to finger through the papers. He took out handfuls of paper and set them across his coffee table. "A lot of court documents."

Jenny nodded from the kitchen, where she was making him scrambled eggs.

"Looks like a case history on Sammy Earle too."

"I noticed that."

Mick scanned the papers, trying to find anything that might be significant. When he lifted the last documents from the box, he saw a book at the bottom. He picked it up. "That's weird."

"What?"

"*The Count of Monte Cristo.* Did Aaron like this book?"

"I've never heard him mention it before. I read it in high school."

"Me too." Mick flipped through it. Some random

passages were highlighted, but other than that, it didn't look like it had been read. He found another document, the autopsy report on ADA Stephen Fiscall. Mick could see where Aaron had made notes.

"This seems so odd," Mick finally said, joining Jenny in the kitchen, where she offered him his plate of eggs. "Why would Aaron be interested in this case after it was all over and there was a conviction?"

"I don't know. He didn't want to talk about what happened. He was just so glad to have you back."

"These eggs are good."

"It'll help the queasiness from the painkillers."

Mick hadn't realized how hungry he was. He hadn't eaten anything since eating a couple of crackers and orange juice at the hospital last night.

Jenny checked her watch. "Aren't you supposed to be at the doctor at ten?"

"Yeah."

"Well, eat up. We need to leave here in about ten minutes."

"Oh, let 'em wait. You know how long we have to wait when we're on time. These eggs are too good to rush."

"That was a mistake," Mick conceded after he and Jenny had been waiting for over an hour and a half in the waiting room of the doctor's office. The nurse had informed them that since they were late, they'd have to wait for another opening where they could slide him in. "Sorry."

Jenny smiled. "It's okay. All I had planned was going to the grocery store and the library."

A nurse finally called them back into a small room. "The doctor will be with you in a moment," she said and shut the door behind her.

"And a 'moment' in medical lingo means slightly less than the length of eternity," Mick said.

Jenny laughed. "Doctors. Can't live with 'em. Could die without 'em."

"So, you had a boring day at the library planned, eh?"

"I wouldn't say boring. I love reading."

"Well, how'd you like to go to the state prison with me?"

Her eyes widened. "Really?"

"Yeah. Let's go pay Sammy Earle a visit, see what this letter is about."

An excited grin burst onto Jenny's face. "That sounds fun . . . kind of."

"Better than sitting around feeling sorry for myself. Tom said I had to take two days of medical leave, so why not make it interesting."

"You're just like Aaron. He could never sit still. On a Saturday, I'd lie on the couch and read a book, maybe watch a movie. Aaron would build a deck!"

"We get that from Mom."

"Your mom! We should call her, tell her what happened."

"Oh no. Absolutely not. She'll be calling and worrying and sending truckloads of Campbell's soup. Let a few days pass and then we'll let her know."

The doctor came in, a young guy who looked straight out of medical school. "Hello, Mr. Kline. I'm Doctor Blane." They shook hands. "And you must be Mrs. Kline."

Jenny nodded but added, "Just not his Mrs. Kline."

Looking confused, the doctor asked Mick to sit on the table, and then he gently unwrapped the sling. "How's it feel?"

"Hurts like crazy."

"I received the X-rays this morning from the hospital.

Luckily, we have a clean break, so we'll put the cast on and see where we are in about four weeks."

"Sounds good. I guess I better get used to taking a bath with my arm out of the water, right?"

"Actually, that's from the old days," the doctor said. "Casts are now waterproof, so you can go swimming if you like."

"Medical advancements never cease to amaze old fogies like me," Mick said.

Jenny laughed.

They watched as the doctor tenderly wrapped an Ace bandage from above Mick's wrist to three inches above his elbow. Then he applied another wrap, which he wet with water, around it. It dried almost instantly. "All right. You're good to go. We'll see you back in four weeks," the doctor said before he left.

Jenny added, "I hope you live that long, being from the 'old days' and all."

Mick elbowed her in the ribs.

chapter ten

jenny pulled the car into the visitors' parking area at the state pen.

Mick laughed, then groaned. "Don't make me laugh! It hurts too bad!"

"What are you laughing at?"

"You! You look like you're on the adventure of a life-time."

She shot him a look. "True, most of my days are not spent talking to dangerous criminals. But I'm not scared."

Mick got out of the car and walked beside her as they went through the front doors. After security, they signed in at the visitors' area and waited to be called back.

"Will we get to talk through the glass with one of those phones?" Jenny asked.

"Doubt it. Since Earle is scheduled to be executed, we'll probably be taken to a special room."

Jenny looked around her and whispered, "Have you ever witnessed an execution?"

"No."

"Me either."

Mick glanced at her and smiled. She was thoroughly enjoying herself. "Listen," he whispered back, "some things you need to know."

"What?"

"If there's a prison riot, stay calm. Whatever you do, don't let them take you as a hostage."

Jenny didn't blink. "Okay." A pause was followed by, "Maybe I should stay out here."

"I'm just kidding. There's not going to be a prison riot."

"Very funny."

A guard appeared and indicated he would show them back. They followed him through a series of heavy metal doors. Down a long, white corridor, their footsteps echoed off the stark walls. They were taken to a room overly lit with fluorescent lights.

Mick and Jenny sat on one side of the table. Jenny scooted her chair next to Mick's and stared at the door.

"You okay?" Mick asked.

She nodded.

But she didn't look okay. Mick was suddenly sorry he brought her. "You can wait outside if you want. I won't give you a hard time."

Jenny forced a smile. "Are you kidding me? This is . . . is . . . great."

"Nothing's going to happen. I shouldn't have made that prison riot comment. That usually only happens when there's a full moon."

That made her laugh and she relaxed a bit. "He's going to be sitting so close to us. I could reach out and touch him! So, what are you going to say to him? Are you going to ask him questions like an interrogation?"

"Jenny, this isn't going to be dramatic; I promise you. I just want to hear what he has to say. He's reaching out, claiming he's innocent. The man's about to die. Why not hear what he has to say?"

"What if he starts screaming like a crazy man?"

"What kind of impression you must have about a day in my life!"

She shrugged. "It's more exciting than mine."

The door to the room swung open, and even Mick had to admit his heart was pounding a little heavier than usual.

The guard brought Sammy Earle in. He looked totally different from the last time Mick had seen him. Before, Earle had been a slick, nearly handsome attorney, with a white-toothed smile that he flashed at all the appropriate times. Now he was nearly all white, with heavy bags under his eyes, his mouth drawn downward. His shoulders were hunched as the guard laid his hand on his back and led him to the chair opposite Mick and Jenny.

Earle glanced at both of them, smoothed his thin hair down on the back of his head, and suddenly seemed to try to remember who he used to be. He stood a little taller and gave a courteous nod. "Hello."

The guard moved to a chair in the corner of the room. Earle sat down, his hands shackled, but he seemed oblivious. He offered a confident smile.

"Mr. Earle," Mick began, "we received a letter from you about your claim that you are innocent."

"I sent out a lot of letters. Can you tell me who you are?"

"You sent a letter to my brother, Aaron Kline, who was one of the officers who worked the case. He is deceased, so his widow, Jenny, brought it to me."

"Sorry to hear that."

"Thank you," Jenny said.

Earle studied Mick. "You look familiar."

"I'm Mick Kline, the man who almost took the fall for kidnapping your ex-girlfriend."

Earle's face lit with both surprise and disgust. He shook his head and grumbled, "That woman. That woman!"

The guard, who'd slumped in his chair, sat up a little straighter and focused his attention on Earle.

"I'm sorry," Earle mumbled. "But I loathe that woman. Taylor Franks. She is the reason for all of this mess."

"You claim to have been set up for the murder of Fiscall. You think it's Taylor Franks?"

"She has an alibi. She's not smart enough to pull something like that off anyway. But if she hadn't faked her own kidnapping to get back at me, I sure wouldn't be in this situation now."

"Because you wouldn't have gone to the DA's house to see what kind of information he supposedly had on you?"

"That's right." Earle sighed and stared at his bound hands. "It's been ten years, but I still spend my nights staring at the ceiling, wondering . . . wondering."

"Wondering what?"

"Who set me up," Earle said. "I don't expect you to believe me. I know it sounds far-fetched. As an attorney, if a guy came to me claiming what I'm claiming, I'd probably pass the case up. Especially with all the evidence mounted against me. Whoever did this was a pro. They knew exactly what they were doing."

"Who do you think would do this?"

"I have a lot of enemies. More than I can name. More than I can remember. But somebody remembered me."

"You think it's someone you represented? or someone who lost against you?"

"Could be either. Could be one of many ex-girlfriends. Could be a judge I made look foolish. Could be a fraternity buddy." Earle puckered his lips to stop the stream of other names that seemed eager to come out. He glanced at Jenny, then at Mick, then at the table. "I wouldn't call myself a decent person. The poor chaplain here is about to have a heart attack that I don't want to see him before I die. I guess nobody's told the guy no before."

Mick and Jenny glanced at each other.

Mick said, "You're not concerned about life after death, then."

"I wasn't that great at life, so I figure death will be much more of the same, whatever is on the other side." He shuffled his feet. "So why are you here again?"

"We just wanted to hear what you have to say," Mick said.

"I can't say much, other than I know I didn't kill that man. That's all I can say. I don't have anything to disprove the facts they prosecuted me with. I sent out those letters hoping someone who knew something would step forward. But then again, who would save a guy like me, right?" He chuckled and shook his head. "It's true what they say: what goes around comes around."

"You think someone may know the truth and is not saying anything?"

"Someone out there knows what really happened. Maybe it's just one person. But there is a killer out there. Somebody got away with murder." Earle ran a thumb along the metal of his handcuff. "The truth won't come along in time to save me. And that's the irony of it all, I guess."

"Why's that?"

"I was never much concerned with truth. I was only concerned with winning. I made the truth. But it turns out you can't really do that. Sure, you can fake it for a while, fool a few people, but truth is much more of a fighter than I really thought. The truth is that I probably deserve what I'm getting. So maybe that's truth's revenge. To hide itself from me when I need it the most."

Mick found himself speechless. Earle was a strange mixture of confidence and despair. He smiled graciously at the two of them, probably the same smile he'd used on many juries. His teeth were a dull light yellow, and the whites of his eyes were a crooked mess of red veins. Prison had made him someone else, but the old man hung on.

Mick knew that from experience, because he still fought his demons, though not as often as he used to. Mick looked away; he knew quite frankly that he could be sitting where Earle sat now. By the grace of God, he'd heard the truth and he'd listened. But only by the grace of God.

"I'm going to look into this," Mick said suddenly, causing everyone to glance up, even the guard who'd lost interest a while back. Mick glanced at Jenny, then back at Earle. "I can't promise anything."

Earle grinned like a small child. "I'm grateful you would try."

"Your execution is how many days away?"

"Don't bother with the date. It doesn't matter. I have a feeling I'm being sentenced to death for something other than what I went to court for."

"So you do believe in God. That He's punishing you."

Earle motioned to the guard. "I believe that somewhere out there is something better than I could ever hope to be. You look like a good man, Mr. Kline. Your eyes show your heart. I'm thankful you're going to search for the truth. But don't do it to try to spare my life. I'm afraid you will be trying in vain."

———

After lunch at a sandwich shop, Mick asked Jenny if she could swing him by the hospital so he could check on Agent Lancaster. As they walked into the lobby, Mick noticed the gift shop.

"Hold on," Mick said and walked in.

Jenny followed. "I've got gum if you want some. They charge double here."

"I'm getting some flowers."

"Flowers?" Jenny asked.

"Yeah. Flowers. Flowers are nice, aren't they?"

"Well . . . yeah, sure. Flowers." Jenny smiled, but Mick knew the raised eyebrow meant that she was withholding a lot of questions.

"We're working the case together. It's just a nice thing to do. She was pretty shaken up."

Jenny nodded, suppressing a smile.

"What?"

"Nothing. Flowers are good. Red roses are particularly thoughtful."

"Funny." Mick went to the counter and picked out a simple bouquet—with no roses.

Jenny waited for him outside the gift shop. Mick didn't bother explaining anymore. There was nothing wrong with flowers.

In the elevator, Jenny said, "She's hot, isn't she?"

"What are you talking about?"

"You think she's pretty." A mischievous grin spread across Jenny's face.

"It doesn't matter what I think. I'm just trying to be nice."

When they stepped out of the elevator, Jenny said, "Stop a minute." She turned him toward her and straightened his shirt. "Okay."

"Give me a break," Mick grumbled. "Since when is it taboo to bring a coworker flowers?"

"First of all, she's not a coworker. She works for a rival agency that most of the time you don't get along with. Secondly, you might want this." She handed him a piece of gum. "You did have an Italian sandwich for lunch."

Mick hesitated. If he took the gum, he'd look guilty. If he didn't take the gum, he ran the risk of his breath introducing him before he got there. The smirk on Jenny's face told him she knew she had him. He grabbed the gum awkwardly, since his good arm was holding the flowers, and his bad arm was in a cast and a sling.

"I'll wait here. Just remember—you're on pain medication."

Mick rolled his eyes and waved her off. He made his way around the corner, trying to stuff the gum in his mouth without dropping the flowers. He wiped his lips across his shoulder to assure there were no stray crumbs lingering from lunch. In the hallway outside Libby's room, he stopped and tried to gather himself. Oddly, there was a strange flutter in his stomach. Leftover adrenaline from his visit with Earle?

He reasoned with himself. It was, after all, appropriate to bring flowers to someone sick in the hospital, was it not?

Mick decided the more he reasoned, the more he was going to talk himself into a frenzy, so without further hesitation, he opened the door and waltzed into the room, as if the flowers were as appropriate as the unusually strong antiseptic smell that almost made him gag.

"Good afternoon," he said.

When he moved the flowers from in front of his face, he was staring at an empty bed. He looked at the bathroom, but the door was open, and the lights were out.

He heard footsteps behind him and turned around, expecting to find Libby. Instead he found a tall, thin man with translucent, pale skin and a smooth, hairless baby face. His hands rested in his pants pockets, and his head was tilted to the side in a nonchalant manner. His hair was combed perfectly into place, parted with precision.

"Hello there," he said, looking Mick up and down.

"I'm looking for Agent Lancaster," Mick said. "Has she been checked out?"

"Who are you?"

"Special Agent Mick Kline with the bureau."

The man eyed the flowers.

"Relative. Upstairs. Distant cousin. Having a baby. Babies. Twins. Boys. Charles and . . . Chuck." Mick cleared his throat. "I thought I'd stop by on my way and see how she was doing. Who are you?"

"Agent Toby Guber. I'm with the ATF."

Ah. The infamous moron. With the flowers in his good right hand, Mick couldn't shake his hand, so he nodded politely.

"They took her to surgery. She hemorrhaged about an hour ago."

"Hemorrhaged?"

"Brain hemorrhage. Her brain has been swelling, and they can't get it to stop."

"I saw Libby yesterday. She seemed fine. In fact, she said they were just keeping her here as a precaution."

The agent laughed through his nose. "Yeah. That's Lancaster for you. It's been serious from the beginning, and she knew it. Behind those cold eyes there's a woman who isn't as tough as she'd like everyone to believe." Guber shook his head. "So you're the agent who's got the dead body."

"That's me."

Guber scratched his nose and looked annoyed. "Well, I'd sure like to know what's going on there."

"Me too."

"Has Lancaster kept you up-to-date?"

Mick was amused. Guber wanted to know what he knew. Two could play at this game. "We were doing just that when we got called to the latest fire."

"I see."

"I guess this makes the fifth building burned, the third in two weeks. Was this one started on the inside first floor like the first three, or is the signature different, like the last one?"

Guber looked surprised. "Lancaster is not usually so generous with information."

"Must be my charm."

"Why don't you leave your card. We'll give you a call when we know something."

Mick set the flowers down and pulled a card out of his pocket. He stuck it into the empty card holder in the center of the bouquet.

Guber stared curiously.

"What're Chuck and Charles going to do with a bunch of flowers, right?" Mick smiled.

"Sure."

"Have you called Agent Lancaster's sister?" Mick asked.

"Um, we're trying to get a hold of her. She lives in DC."

"You should call her priest. Libby would want him here."

Guber sniffed away his surprise and nodded.

"Keep me updated," Mick said and walked to the door.

"It's going to be a while before we know how that fire was started."

Mick looked at him. "I meant on Libby."

"Oh. Right. I'll let her know you stopped by if she makes it through this."

chapter eleven

W ith his stomach queasy from pain medication, Mick stumbled up the stairs of his apartment, Jenny hanging onto his elbow cautiously. She unlocked the door for him and helped him to the couch.

"I feel horrible," Mick groaned as he crashed into the cushions.

"You did too much today," Jenny said, sitting on the coffee table and adjusting a pillow against his side. "You were supposed to rest, remember?"

"I guess I'm not eight years old anymore. You're eight and you break your arm—you just go on like nothing happened."

"How about some hot tea?"

"I'm okay. I just want to sleep."

"Make sure to eat something later tonight, though, okay? And call your mom. She'd kill me if she knew her baby boy broke his arm and nobody called her."

Mick nodded, already feeling groggy in his reclining position. "Thanks for praying with me."

"I hope the agent's okay. A brain hemorrhage is so serious. I'll keep praying." Jenny touched his knee. "I'll give you a call tomorrow. Which, may I remind you, is supposed to be another day of rest for you. You'll be back at work soon enough. Give yourself another day to recover."

"We don't need to call Mom. She's right here in front of me."

"Just remember how you're feeling right now when you decide to do something crazy tomorrow."

Mick patted her arm. "Thanks for taking care of me."

Before Jenny was out the door, Mick fell into a deep sleep, dreaming of fires and evil men lurking in the darkness with matches and gasoline. He saw Lamberson's body over and over, except his eyes were open and staring with horror at the last thing he saw before he died.

What was that last thing? Mick's subconscious worked out the obscure puzzle until morning, when he rolled over and moaned out his discouragement. His arm was throbbing again, but he was done with the pain medication. He managed to prop himself up into a halfway sitting position.

The phone rang. Mick tried to lurch forward to grab it, causing pain to jolt through his arm. He answered the phone with a grunt.

"Dude? You okay?"

"Reg . . . hi. I'm all right."

"You don't sound all right."

"I'm middle-aged. A broken bone is like a death sentence."

"I feel for you, man. I can't wait to come over and sign your cast, though."

"Maybe this will get the girls to pay attention to me."

Reggie was rolling with laughter. "You are something else. Well, I was calling with some information. They found matches and a lighter behind the paint factory. No gasoline, but another flammable substance, maybe cleaning fluid. And it was started from the outside, which is rare. The explosion was caused by the abandoned chemicals inside. Now we have two dead firefighters, which is going to bring in a whole lot more company."

Mick sighed. "Any information on the shelter companies connected with the other buildings?"

"We suspect they're there, but the paper trail is cold, and until we find the documents that prove it, our hands are tied."

"You've got the request into FinCEN, right?"

"Yeah, Mick. But you know how long that can take."

"Lamberson has to be connected somehow. He wasn't there by coincidence. We've got to figure out if he was killed because he was going to the grand jury or because of something else."

"It's a coin toss," Reggie said. "Dude, I'm glad you're home, by the way. Tom asked me to double-check, and I was afraid I was going to have to hunt you down."

"Tom thinks I'm going to do something crazy when I've been ordered to take time off?"

"You're being a good boy, right?"

"Pretty good. I tried to visit Agent Lancaster at the hospital. She had a brain hemorrhage yesterday afternoon. Have you heard anything?"

"No, nothing."

"Hopefully I can find out some more information."

"Let us know."

"Okay. I'll be in tomorrow."

"Hey, it's supposed to rain tomorrow so be sure and keep that new cast under a coat or something."

Mick smiled. He wasn't feeling so old anymore.

After a breakfast of Pop-Tarts and Diet Coke, Mick tried to get comfortable on the couch. It had been a long time since he'd watched weekday television. It was amusing for about fifteen minutes, and then he turned it off. He tried to pick up some clothes here and there, but with one arm he was even less motivated than usual.

He wandered around his apartment for half an hour,

then settled himself in front of the box Jenny had brought over. He'd told Sammy Earle he would look into the case, but he wasn't holding out a lot of hope of finding anything. Yet knowing that his brother had been interested in it beyond the conviction made him wonder if there was indeed something else to it.

Mick studied the court documents, which didn't tell him much more about the case than he already knew. He focused on some of Aaron's handwritten notes in a small notepad. He couldn't read a lot of his writing, but after an hour of going through everything, he noticed a name that kept coming up: Patrick Delano. He didn't recognize it in any of the court documents or remember hearing it in the media. But something about it seemed familiar. And there was no explanation of why the name was written among the other notes. Mick found it four times in various lists and documents, handwritten each time by Aaron.

Mick also found it interesting that Aaron had taken a particular interest in Shep Crawford, the homicide detective who had led the investigation into the kidnapping of Taylor Franks. It was ten years ago, but Mick could remember the detective as if it were yesterday. He was a strange bird, with eyes that made you want to look away. The detective had gotten sick the day before he was supposed to testify at Earle's trial, and another detective filled in, which wasn't unusual. The more important testimony came from forensics, anyway. Still, there was something about the detective that had interested Aaron, and therefore it now interested Mick.

After two hours of studying as much as he could, Mick needed a break. He decided he'd go get something to eat . . . and why not stop by the library and see what he could find out about a man named Patrick Delano?

Mick hadn't made it halfway to the library when he decided to drive to the hospital. He couldn't get Libby Lancaster off his mind. Nobody had called him about her condition, and he suspected they wouldn't. Patrick Delano could wait.

He assumed she was still alive. The death of an ATF agent would've made the news. But what kind of condition he might find her in was up in the air.

As the elevator doors opened, he stepped into the hallway and felt his body tingle with nervousness. When he arrived at her room, a man stood by the window. He was backlit so Mick couldn't tell who he was. It was definitely not Guber.

"Hello," Mick said.

The man turned and stepped forward out of the harsh light of the window. He was a priest. As he walked toward Mick, his ocean blue eyes—small, scrutinizing, but compassionate—met Mick's. He was probably in his seventies, with short white hair, barely holding its own on top. A grin balanced between two ruddy cheeks. Add an extra one hundred pounds to the thin man and he could've played Santa Claus. "I'm Father Samson."

"Mick Kline."

"You work with Libby?"

"Sort of. We were working on the arson case when she was hurt." Mick glanced at the empty bed. "Is she okay?"

The father nodded. "For now. She made it through another surgery last night. They're taking a CAT scan this morning." He looked at a book in his hand, then set it down next to the bed. "I brought her some word puzzles. She loves word puzzles."

"Have you seen her today?"

"Just briefly. She was still groggy. Told some guy he

was a goober and to get out of her face." The priest smiled. "That's my Libby. She doesn't hold back much."

"You've known her for a while?"

"Since she was a child. Doesn't surprise me she does dangerous work. I used to have to hunt her down in the church because she liked to climb the rafters."

Mick laughed. "She's a brave woman. She ran into a burning building to try to save the firefighters."

"I heard that. She's a fine lady."

"And a dedicated parishioner?"

"She never misses a Sunday if she can help it. She actually teaches the preschoolers."

Mick hid his surprise with a knowing smile. Now *that* surprised him. He couldn't really picture the woman bent down and talking gently to a bunch of four-year-olds. But then again, he hadn't seen her bolt into the burning building coming either. This woman was turning out to be quite an enigma.

The door to the room opened, and two male nurses rolled Libby in. When they transferred her to her hospital bed, she noticed her visitors.

"Father!" She smiled. Then she looked at Mick. He noted the smile didn't fade too much. "And Agent Kline."

"We've been having a nice chat about you," Father Samson said, walking to her bedside.

Mick stayed a few feet away, observing their relationship. Lancaster's hard demeanor melted as Father Samson touched the bandage around her head. "You've come through quite a night."

"Yeah. Apparently my brain's been swelling." She laughed as if it were no more important than an ingrown toenail. She faced Mick. "How long have you been here? Don't you have a dead guy to investigate?"

"I've got one more day of mandatory medical leave."
He moved his cast-ridden arm and shrugged.

"Ah."

Father Samson grinned. "Haven't you chased off
enough coworkers today, Libby?"

"Oh, Guber. That guy. He gets on my nerves."
Suddenly Libby spotted the flowers on the windowsill,
placed near the corner and nearly out of sight. Mick
suspected that Guber had something to do with the location. She frowned; she might have been observing a roach
crawling across the wood.

Mick swallowed and felt the urge to step in front of her
line of sight. Maybe the flowers should've gone upstairs to
Chuck and Charles.

"What's that?" she asked.

Mick pretended not to hear.

Father Samson glanced toward the window. "Flowers,"
he said and walked over to them.

Mick wanted to crawl under the bed. Instead he
announced, "They're from me." It was just instinct . . .
self-defense, really. That way he didn't have to endure the
surprised look on her face when she pulled his business card
from among the petals.

Libby's facial expression wasn't quite as easy to read as
the priest's obvious curiosity. Her gaze darted to the flowers
that Father Samson held. Then she slowly looked at Mick.
He thought he saw her suppress a smile. "How nice, Kline."

"Thanks." He shrugged. "Everyone deserves flowers,
right? Especially when you have to have brain surgery."

She stared at the blanket across her legs, then pulled it
up over her left shoulder.

An intense heat crawled up Mick's neck. "Well, I better
get going. Just wanted to check on you. Make sure you
made it through the surgery."

"I'm fine." Her gaze remained downcast.

Mick wasn't sure, but he sensed he'd said something wrong.

The priest didn't seem to notice. He was busy admiring the flowers.

"Take care, Kline," she said as he went to the door.

"You do the same. I wish you a speedy recovery."

"Yeah. And cows jump over the moon."

chapter twelve

Sergeant Patrick Delano tugged at the bottom of his uniform and dusted off his sleeves. He looked impeccable. He needed to look impeccable. Despite the insignia on his advocate's sleeve, Lt. Grady seemed to have little experience, but Patrick didn't mind. The facts could be presented by a donkey. The facts were the facts. They couldn't be disputed. At stake here was honor. And today—*finally!*—he would get his chance. Once they understood, he had no doubt whatsoever that freedom would be his again.

The bathroom door opened, and Lt. Grady said, "You ready?"

Patrick glanced one more time in the mirror. He met his own eyes. This was the moment of truth. *Truth.* He smiled, aware Lt. Grady was watching. There was nothing wrong with a confident smile. Lt. Grady was not wearing a smile but a sober frown.

"Sir, it will be okay," Patrick assured.

Lt. Grady stopped him just outside the bathroom. "Patrick," he said. It was odd that he used his first name. It made him uncomfortable. He'd been called Sergeant by so many for so long. Except one. Deborah. She always called him Patty. He glanced toward the courtroom doors. She would be here. He knew it. "You're going to come up against some tough questioning. You keep telling me you're prepared. It's not that I don't believe you. But I'm not sure . . ."

"What?"

"How you're going to handle this. You're a passionate man. I understand that. But sometimes that kind of passion doesn't . . . translate exactly right."

Patrick was several inches taller than Lt. Grady, though probably eight years younger. Still, Patrick knew a certain wisdom rested in his own eyes. It was the wisdom, the pride that came with combat. He was a *soldier*. Not a military man. A soldier. Lt. Grady did nothing more than study books to earn his rank.

"Passion, sir, is what got me here in the first place. Passion is the reason I was over there serving my country. And passion is what is going to set me free."

"I'm just not—"

"You put me on that stand," Patrick said. "My words will be like fire."

Lt. Grady bit his lip.

Patrick sensed unsettled fear in his eyes as he stared at him. Patrick had provoked a lot of fear in a lot of people.

"All right," the lieutenant finally said, in barely a whisper. "Let's go."

They walked side by side down the quiet hallway. October was proving to be colder than usual. It was only in the forties outside. As they walked into the courtroom, voices mingled and hushed. Not a seat was empty.

Patrick studied each row on one side of the courtroom. She was *here*. Yes, she was here. She had to be here. He looked for her long, dark hair, shinier than most women's. She almost always wore a headband. And pink lipstick. Pale pink. So beautiful.

He searched the other side. The Lasatter family sat in the front row, stern faced. Patrick knew they were grieving. Unfortunately, today they would know how pathetic their dead son was. It was a hard thing to tell, but war was as ugly as a rotten corpse.

"Come on," Lt. Grady urged, pushing his arm a bit. From the beginning of Patrick's trial Lt. Grady had looked uncomfortable in front of crowds. He wasn't a leader. He certainly wasn't a soldier. He did, however, know the law.

They reached the table. Grady's assistant, slob that he was, had papers strewn across the top.

"Sir," Patrick said, "let me help you with this." He shuffled the papers together and handed them over. "We don't want to look unorganized, right?"

Patrick looked over his shoulder. Deborah. She would be here; she promised. Maybe she was running late. The woman was the definition of love. She'd stood by her man, knowing that she was risking taking him back into her arms in a body bag. But he'd come back alive.

She'd wavered. The trial, Lasatter's death . . . had been hard on her. There was no doubt about that.

"You could be hanged?" she'd asked tearfully one night as he was explaining the court-martial.

Hanging was up for dispute. John Bennett had been hanged in 1961 for rape and attempted murder. Right before his death he said, "May God have mercy on *your* soul." Hanging was still in practice, but a lot of people thought it inhumane. He was not going to be hanged. Or executed. Or even imprisoned.

"I'm going to be fine. Once they hear my side of the story, they'll understand."

She'd nodded, but Patrick felt her uncertainty. As the weeks passed, Deborah had grown more and more distant. But she'd called two nights ago.

"You'll be there?"

"Yes."

"Promise me."

There was a long pause, but then she'd said, "I promise."

Of course, his side of the story had been plagued by his advocate's fears that no one would understand. He figured that was an advocate's job . . . to be afraid for you. But if push came to shove, the world would know the truth. He wasn't ashamed of it.

Court was in session. Colonel Marshall took the bench. He was a white-haired man who looked confident and wise. Patrick glanced over at Major Usher, his commanding officer. To his credit, he had been fair and nonjudgmental throughout the court-martial procedure. Major Usher acknowledged Patrick with a slight nod.

The jury was brought in. The men entered the courtroom now and sat down, all of them looking at Patrick. He offered a small, peaceful smile. They would have to agree. It would have to be unanimous. Capital cases had to be unanimous. This seemed to be the thing onto which Lt. Grady kept holding.

It seemed forever before he was able to take the stand. He watched Lt. Grady scribble notes. In front of him was his own pad of paper and a pen, presumably there in case he felt the need to look down. He did not. He stared forward and sat tall.

Finally he was called to the stand. Lt. Grady actually shivered as they stood up. Patrick walked confidently, held his head high. When he sat down, he scanned the crowd for Deborah. His calm heart beat faster. Surely she would not break a promise. That was not the woman she was. She was a soldier's wife. A *wife*.

Lt. Grady began the questions, just as they'd rehearsed.

The who, what, when, where, and why of it all. Patrick was careful not to sound rehearsed. Lt. Grady paused, turned to the jury for their attention, then dramatically asked the final question, "Is there a why, Sergeant Delano?"

Patrick replied simply, "If that question could be answered, then perhaps none of us would be over there in that war in the first place."

It wasn't the answer they'd talked about, but the shiny approval in Lt. Grady's eyes told him it was better. They smiled slightly at each other.

The prosecutor, Major Donald Howell, stood to begin his questioning. "Sergeant Delano, help us understand the situation you found yourself in that day in Vietnam. Describe the scene you saw before you."

"It was war, sir. The enemy had ambushed us. We'd been split up. I knew we had five men dead. I didn't know where the others were. We also knew the enemy was to our north. We could hear the gunfire. Every man was surviving on his own at that point. I knew the kids were scared. I was trying to track them down, one by one, and reorganize."

"You were in a wooded area?"

"That's right. It was the best place to hide and assess the situation. I didn't know where they were."

"What happened next? How did you find Private Lasatter and Private Earle?"

"It was coincidence, really. I heard movement. I snuck around some trees to see what the noise was. My weapon was loaded, of course. I came around a tree and saw Private Lasatter. He'd engaged his weapon. I didn't want to yell. I was afraid I would scare him. He looked so afraid. He was sweating and his eyes were wide. If I had called out his name, he would have instantly turned and fired at me."

"What was he doing?"

"I wasn't sure at first. I saw his attention on something,

but I couldn't tell what. I thought maybe he had the enemy in his sights. I saw movement about two clicks ahead. And then it just happened so fast."

"Please describe it."

Patrick shook his head. For the first time, he felt flustered. The scene was right before him, as if he were back there in the Mekong Delta. His nostrils filled with a bloody, putrid smell. "I just saw him raise his weapon. He was going to shoot Private Earle. He thought he was the enemy. I saw him engage the bushes, and from where I stood, I could tell it was an American soldier he was about to kill."

"So you shot Private Lasatter."

"I . . . I raised my weapon to shoot, and right as I did, my elbow hit the tree I was standing next to. I saw Private Lasatter fall to the ground. I had aimed for his knees, so I figured they just buckled and he fell. I saw Private Earle roll out from under the bushes. He was crying. He saw Private Lasatter. Then he saw me. And I . . ." Patrick felt his words coil.

"You what?"

". . . I saw the blood on Lasatter's chest."

"You knew you'd probably killed him?"

"I wasn't sure. I didn't know."

"Private Earle said you stood there for a long time. That you didn't come over to help."

"I was in shock."

"Sergeant, why don't you tell the court what you said to Private Earle?"

"I don't recall."

"According to Private Earle's testimony, when he beckoned you for help, you said, 'He was useless.'"

"No."

"You recall what you said?"

"I'm sure I said something like 'It's useless.'"

"But Private Earle testified that you said, 'He is useless.' He also said you looked angry."

"I can't say how I looked. It was a stressful time. I had five men dead—"

"Is it also true, Sergeant Delano, that you told Private Earle to 'learn his lesson about loyalty'? Private Earle testified he did not know what you meant by that."

"I don't recall saying that."

"So you recall everything else about that time except what you said directly after you shot and killed a fellow soldier?"

Patrick sat silently.

"Do you feel remorse?"

An annoying itch tickled his cheek, and Patrick clawed at it. He realized the courtroom had become very quiet. He looked at Lt. Grady, who was leaning forward across the table. Why was he staring at him? He looked at Major Howell, who stood there, glancing at the jury and then back at him.

"Sergeant?"

"What?"

"Do you feel remorse?"

Patrick felt a strange presence around him, a dark shadow that hovered behind him. "Victor Charlie. Victor Charlie. Charlie. Charlie."

"Sergeant? Victor Charlie?"

"Wouldn't you know that?" Patrick said, looking at Howell. "Wouldn't you know that's what we called the Vietcong? VC. Victor Charlie. Charlie. Wouldn't you know that?"

"I asked you if you felt remorse for killing Private Lasatter."

"He wasn't loyal."

Murmuring began.

Colonel Marshall pounded his gavel and quieted the room.

"He wasn't loyal?" Major Howell asked.

"Objection!" Lt. Grady yelled.

Patrick had never felt it this close before. It made him numb. He didn't understand it—two arms wrapping around him, squeezing him, making him feel nothing at all.

"Please direct Sergeant Delano to answer the question," Howell said.

"Sergeant," the colonel said, "are you okay?"

"I heard him one night. He was with another soldier. Private Jefferson. We'd set up camp."

"Objection!"

"Overruled."

"And they were whispering. Like Charlie. They were whispering."

"Objection. Sir, please. Sergeant Delano is obviously—"

"I was beckoned over there. I can't explain it, really. But I heard them."

"What did they say?" asked Howell.

"Objection!"

"Overruled."

"They said . . ." Patrick searched one more time for Deborah. He looked at all the eyes, trying to find her beautiful brown ones. Her smile.

"They said what?"

"There was going to be a mutiny. They were questioning my decisions. The stresses of the war were getting to them."

"What did you do?"

He never saw Deborah's eyes. But then he saw Private Earle's. He was sitting in the front row, slumped a little. Tears brimmed on his bottom lids.

"Why are you crying?" Patrick asked him.

"Objection!"

"I saved your life."

Major Howell started to say something, but Patrick interrupted. "Private Earle, are you listening to me? You sat up in this very chair that I'm sitting in, and you testified that I made a mistake. But did you thank me? Did you ever once realize that you'd be the man in the coffin if I had not saved your life? Instead, what do you do? You sit there and judge me. You tell the court that it was wrong what I did. You tell everyone that you cannot understand how it happened. You say that Matty Lasatter could not have mistaken you for the enemy, because he saw boots, not sandals. 'The enemy always wore sandals,' you said. Here I am on trial for murder because I tried to save your life, and you have turned against me. You decide to judge me. Yet here you are—living, breathing, crying for heaven's sake. Crying."

Patrick focused on the jury of three of his peers. "I saved this man's life. And he looks at me like I'm a monster. He takes the free pass, enjoys his life, but blames me. Did you hear what he said about me yesterday? the things he said?"

"Sergeant Delano," Lt. Grady said.

"No. It must be said. The man is unappreciative. He is greedy. He takes his life for granted." Patrick stared into Private Earle's startled eyes. "You will drown in the very blood that caused you to live."

"Sergeant Delano!" Colonel Marshall declared. "Stop this now!"

Patrick drew back. He looked at Major Howell, whose attention was on the jury. Lt. Grady was whispering to his assistant. Deborah was nowhere. She'd not even come.

Patrick thrust his chin forward and faced the jury. These soldiers would know. They would understand. If they'd seen any time at all in combat, they would understand.

Major Howell stepped forward. "Remember, Sergeant, you are under oath. Did you kill Matthew Lasatter because he was questioning your leadership?"

Patrick Delano offered the confident smile that he and Lt. Grady had exchanged moments before. "I may have pulled the trigger, but Matty Lasatter died because this earth didn't need him anymore."

chapter thirteen

1ook what just arrived," Reggie sang as he waltzed across the floor toward Mick's desk. He tossed the envelope to Mick.

"FinCEN." Mick ripped open the envelope. It had taken a week for this information from the Treasury Department's Financial Crimes Enforcement Network to arrive, which was actually fairly quick for that organization. But in the week that they'd been waiting, they'd hit dead end after dead end, especially with ATF's refusing to share information. Since Agent Lancaster had been out of commission, Guber had not been as liberal with the dissemination of information. So, as Tom had predicted, Reggie and Mick were going to have to track down their own leads.

"That's weird," Mick said as he scanned the documents.

"What? That I could look so svelte with an extra fifty pounds attached?"

"Yes. And the fact that all four of the torched properties have the same resident agent and address."

Reggie's eyebrows popped up. "Really." He came around and stood behind Mick, looking over his shoulder. "Financial Rock, Pratt Financial, Dugenstein and Associates, and Maple Tree Services."

"Yep. Those are the four companies that are listed as owning the properties."

"All with the same address." Reggie straightened up and smiled.

"Look who the treasurer of all these companies is."

Reggie bent down again and squinted. "Our one and only Joel Lamberson."

Mick swiveled around in his chair and faced Reggie. "We just got a gigantic piece of our puzzle."

"Yes, we did. Looks like we're going to be visiting our resident agent. Will he cooperate willingly, or shall we call the U.S. attorney and get a subpoena first?" Reggie was chuckling.

Mick grabbed a quarter off his desk. "Heads or tails?"

"Tails."

Mick flipped it, and it landed on his hand. He tossed it to the back side of his hand, revealing heads.

Reggie growled. "You always win."

"Sorry. But they like you better."

Reggie walked off toward an office with a door, this time without the waltz.

"You might want to mention we're probably going to need a couple more subpoenas this week."

Reggie waved him off and rounded the corner.

Mick continued to scan the documents. He had a date with 1754 West Bend, Apartment 15.

"Stand up straight," the elderly black man said as he measured Sammy Earle's legs and waist. He jotted down some notes. "All right. I'm done here."

Warden McAubrey patted the man on the back. "Thanks." Then he looked at Sammy and handed him a stack of mail. "This is from the past two days."

Sammy took it. He'd been receiving more hate mail as his execution neared. He'd stopped reading it.

"Eighteen days," he mumbled, sitting on the small chair that accompanied the desk near the corner of his cell. "Twenty days. I can't make much of a difference in twenty days when I'm locked up here."

"You could write some letters to people," the warden offered. "People you want to make amends with."

"Nobody wants to make amends with me." Sammy's parents had died when he was in his twenties. He had no other relatives who wanted to claim him. He'd been on his own for years and done nicely. But he knew that not even his law partners would come for a last visit. Nobody would.

"You don't have anyone listed on your witness sheet," McAubrey said, as if reading his mind.

"There won't be anyone."

"The chaplain would be here if you wanted him."

Sammy looked into McAubrey's calm face. "I told you I'm not religious."

"Whether or not you're religious is of no consequence, Mr. Earle. You're going to be facing God, with or without help."

Sammy's heart fluttered. He'd faced his own mortality many years ago in Vietnam. But it was different then. He had been fighting a war, an enemy, and he was sure of the cause, so he hadn't worried about the afterlife. If he'd died, it would've been for a noble cause, and God would've seen that.

But now, the evil enemy stared back at him through a dim mirror. "There are not enough days left for me to save my soul," Sammy murmured. "Maybe if I had more time, I could do good. But there's nothing I can do sitting in this cell. There's no one I can help. There's not a chance to make up for . . . who I've become."

The warden stepped closer to Sammy, his gaze intense for the first time. "If I were to live to be a hundred and fifty, there would not be enough days to make up for my sin either."

"That's hard to believe." Sammy sniffed.

"Is it so hard to believe we're all in a prison of sorts? Really? Before you had bars in front of your face, didn't you already feel trapped?"

"I never thought about my life much."

"It's not too late. God will forgive you."

Sammy threw the mail onto his small desk. "I'm more worried about whether or not I can forgive God . . . for allowing me to die for something I didn't do."

"Maybe God's more concerned with how dead you were inside before all this happened."

Sammy leaned against the cold cement wall and studied his small metal-framed bed . . . more like a cot. He had numbed his emotions so much with alcohol that he hadn't felt anything in years until he got to prison. And for the past ten years, he'd done everything he could not to think or feel, but it was nearly impossible. It was all beginning to crash down on him. His throat swelled with anger and sorrow, and he turned away, waving at the warden to leave him alone.

The cell door shut, and then footsteps walked away.

With an angry groan, Sammy swiped the mail off the desk, sending it sliding and flipping across the gray cement floor. "You don't have to tell me!" he whispered, balling up his fist and shaking it at the white mess at his feet. "I know I'm horrible! You don't have to send me letters telling me so!" Tears streamed down his face, and he smeared them across his face. He fell onto his bed and flopped an arm over his eyes.

He lay like that for a long while, letting the wave of false hope collapse and drain from him. A crowd of faces stared back in his mind, faces that he'd given little regard to over his lifetime. It was what his father had taught him before he died. It was how his father had dealt with him, as if he weren't worth the time to do much more than introduce at parties like a sideshow: *"This is my son, Samuel. Run along now. Don't be a bother."*

He'd spent years trying to prove otherwise. Years alone. His mother, though a kind woman, was weak to her husband's persuasive personality and spent her time catering to his needs. He liked beautiful women—and lots of them—but depended on his wife to be the one woman he didn't have to discard.

The strange formula that had caused Sammy to cower as a child was the same one that caused him to rise above others as an adult. The less attention he paid to those who wanted it, the hungrier the corporate world became for him. How easily he could spot weakness through a crowded room. Body language was oftentimes the key, though there was certainly the way people dressed or wore their hair.

In some ways, he became much more of a monster than his father had been. Though cold and distant, his father had never been cruel. But Sammy could be cruel. He could bring people to their knees. His favorite weapon was his tongue.

His father had met a terrible fate. He'd stepped in front of a train and killed himself. Sammy's was much worse. He did not have that last-minute choice not to step on the tracks. For some reason his father had decided not to take the second chance, and he stepped onto the tracks. What Sammy would give for that second chance . . . that choice not to die.

He rolled onto his side and stared at the dozen or so envelopes on the floor. He'd read probably a hundred over the ten years, all saying the same thing. Now, one in particular caught his attention from the sea of white. The ink was red. He grabbed it and ripped it open. Not many people used red ink. It was probably symbolic of their need to see his blood spilled.

A small white piece of paper was tucked inside. He took it out and opened it. Typed neatly in the center were the words:

I cannot save you. But there is one man who will.

Somebody knew he was innocent.

Mick opened the door to Mail Me, a slummy version of Mail Boxes Etc. But instead of a nice display of shipping envelopes, neatly stacked cardboard boxes alongside bubble wrap, and a high-tech copy machine, a wall of mismatched items greeted Mick to his left.

A small counter, stacked high with all kinds of boxes and envelopes, hid the source of a male voice on the phone. "Yeah, Carl, I got it the first time. I said I don't know. . . ."

The conversation went on as Mick studied the west wall. A collection of mailboxes, probably forty or so, looked to be the most orderly part of the store. Mick walked past the man, viewing a mostly bald head, as he approached the wall. Next to the mailboxes were corporate licenses, hung on display to satisfy the state licensing authority. If Mick were a betting man, he'd bet the owner of this shabby joint was acting as the resident agent, who normally knows nothing about the companies they represent. They just provide a place to hang the licenses. He'd seen resident agents represent as many as a hundred companies, sometimes even more, making money off the fee they charge to be the in-state representative.

"Carl, you could do me a favor and go kill yourself." And the conversation was over. The man stood and asked, "Can I help you?" His accent was clearly Northern. Mick guessed he was from Chicago. He wore a thin, cotton button-down three sizes too small and gaping at his belly button and his chest. Four heavy gold chains hung around his neck with a big nugget ring on one of his fat fingers.

"Mick Kline. FBI. What's your name?"

"Frank DioGuardia." He glanced over to the mailboxes, then at the badge Mick was showing him. "Look, I don't care what your badge says. I'm a businessman, and my business is to give my customers privacy. That's what they want—that's what I give them. I don't know what comes and goes in those boxes. None of my business. So unless you FBI guys got a subpoena—"

"We pride ourselves in being thorough," Mick said, handing it over with a smile. "Will this satisfy your requirements?"

DioGuardia sighed. "Yeah. What do you want to know?"

Mick handed him a piece of paper. "Do you recognize these names?"

"Sure. All four of these companies hang their corporate licenses here. I never see anybody picking up their mail, though. I'd say they've been around for a couple of years. I can check some paperwork on that and give you the exact date."

"What happens to the mail?"

"Every once in a while I get a call from a guy who tells me to forward it. The addresses change every four months or so. I don't ask any questions; I just do it. But he doesn't get that much mail. Maybe a handful, mostly from insurance companies, for all four businesses. Last month he called and had me send all four envelopes to the same address."

Mick was beginning to see exactly the kind of picture he thought he would. "Do you have the name of the guy who rents these boxes?"

"I got his card right here," DioGuardia said, reaching

below the counter and grabbing a box. Sorting through it, he found the card and handed it to Mick. *Joel Lamberson.* "Must've been who you're looking for by that smile on your face."

"Mind if I take this card?"

"No. They haven't paid their bill for this month anyway, and I'm in this strictly for the money."

He reached below the counter and pulled out another sheet of paper. "You can have this too. They're the addresses he'd have me send them to. The one at the bottom is the latest one."

"Thanks," Mick said.

"Yeah, just don't let this get around, you know?"

Mick shook his hand. "Try to stay off the evening news."

Mick groaned as he turned off the TV and stretched on his couch. It was only seven, but it felt much later. A slice of leftover light glowed around the edges of his window. He'd left work at five, which he hardly ever did, but admittedly he was tired, and his arm reminded him about its displeasure.

After a TV dinner, he decided to go through more of Aaron's box. He'd found out some interesting things about Patrick Delano after using the microfiche at the library. He remembered his name from ten years ago, when he was trying to find out more information about Sammy Earle in the kidnapping plot in which he'd been entangled. Delano's name had come up in a conversation about the Vietnam War, as a soldier who shot and killed another soldier, then escaped before he could be sentenced. But what he couldn't figure out was why Aaron had been interested in him in connection with Sammy Earle and the murder of the ADA.

An hour later, Mick turned his attention to the strange

letters he'd continued to receive. So far he had *S A T P O U T F O R U O*. He had tried to make sense of the letters but couldn't really put anything together. When he would finally assemble one word, like *four*, the rest of the letters wouldn't form a word. It was discouraging to say the least. Besides feeling violated that someone would be sending him some sort of code, it was particularly alarming to acknowledge his apparent limited vocabulary.

A shadow moved across his window and stretched across the floor of his apartment. Mick stood up. A knock soon followed. He went to the door, peered out the hole, and opened it.

"Agent Lancaster," Mick said, barely able to hold in his surprise. "What are you doing here?"

He noticed she had a cane in her left hand, and she was leaning on it with a lot of her weight. Her gaze was downcast, and she was stroking her hair across one side of her head.

"Are you okay?" Mick asked.

"I'm fine." She stood up a little taller and tried a smile. "I know it's probably weird that I'm here. Reggie was at the office and gave me your address."

"Please . . . come in." Mick could only imagine the self-satisfied smile on Reggie's face.

Mick opened the door wider for her and watched as she struggled to navigate her way in. After closing the door, he offered her a seat on the couch. She looked relieved to be able to sit.

"I'm surprised to see you up and around. I thought you might still be at the hospital."

"They released me two days ago."

"Well . . . you look good." Mick negotiated the words carefully. Her face was still bruised, and her limp seemed to add fifteen years to her age. But as Mick stared across the coffee table at her, all he could think was that this was one of the most beautiful women he'd ever seen. Her face was without makeup, and her hair hung against her shoulders with no certain style. But in her eyes, a strange, delicate balance of strength and humility shone through.

"You're staring."

"Oh . . . sorry . . ." Mick grinned away his embarrassment. "I didn't realize you injured your leg."

"I didn't. It's from the brain injury. The concussion. My motor skills are having a little trouble getting back on track. Doc says they can't tell me when it'll all get back to normal. It's just a hiccup in the recovery."

Mick was suddenly realizing how serious her injuries were, as if they weren't serious enough before. "Did you ride here?"

"Not allowed to drive or ride my bike for two more weeks. I took a cab."

"Can I get you something to drink?"

"Sure—" she smiled—"though I have to wonder what a bachelor like yourself might be able to offer me."

He hoped a wide grin might mask the fact that he was wondering the very same thing. He opened the fridge, and to his relief there was lemonade that Jenny had mixed for him. "Lemonade?"

"Really?"

He tried not to sound so surprised himself. "Yep."

"Sure. That sounds great."

Mick poured them both a glass and returned to the living room.

She was looking at the newspaper articles with the highlighted letters. She raised an eyebrow as he handed her the glass. "Official bureau business?"

"No."

"What is it, then?"

Mick bit his lip, a little embarrassed. "It's nothing,

really." She didn't appear satisfied with that answer. "I've been receiving these newspaper headlines over the past couple of weeks. Each headline has a letter highlighted. I'm not sure what they mean or who they're from. I figure it's supposed to spell something but . . ."

"But?"

"But it doesn't . . . as far as I can see."

Libby picked up the paper on which he'd written all the letters. "These are the letters?"

"Yeah."

"Do you mind if I try?"

Mick scratched his hairline. He wasn't sure if he wanted her to. What kind of message would she decode? Something about him? Or a case he was working on? Besides, surely he was capable. His mind worked on the various scenarios, but by the time he decided it wasn't a good idea, she was already at work. "Um . . ."

"This making you nervous, Kline?"

"Yeah."

She looked up.

"That's my good pen you're using."

She laughed. "I'll be careful."

"Thanks."

As she was writing down several word possibilities, she said, "How often do you receive these?"

"Every few days, sometimes several to an envelope."

"Postmarked from what city?"

"Dallas."

She wrote down a few more words, studied them for a moment, and then said, "These aren't from the Dallas paper."

"How do you know?"

"Different font, different writing style. See? Look, the person left some of the article below this headline. This writer doesn't work for the *Dallas Morning News*."

"How do you know that?"

"Read that paper cover to cover every single day."

Great. Beautiful, successful, and well-read. He wouldn't be surprised if he found out she was royalty too.

She went back to working and then said, "Did you receive one today?"

"I haven't checked my mail."

"Why don't you go do that. It may help me figure out one of these words if I get another letter. Who knows how many letters are to come, right?"

Mick nodded, a little stunned that he'd just turned complete control of one of the strangest mysteries of his life over to a near stranger, but headed downstairs to his mailbox anyway. He checked his mail regularly, though most bachelors he knew didn't.

"Hi, Mick."

Mick cringed and turned to find Alexia, the resident just below him, approaching. She'd asked him out three times over the last six months, refusing to believe that her skimpy, skintight outfits and drinking parties weren't attractive to him. With her beer bottle in hand, she juggled her keys and opened the box next to his.

Mick grabbed his mail and tried to make a polite exit.

"Who is she?" Alexis asked.

"Who?"

"The chick upstairs. I saw her at your door."

"Coworker."

"Hmm. Scandalous office affair, huh?" She glanced at his arm. "Oh! Are you okay? Your poor arm!"

"I'm fine. Really. No big deal. I've got to get back upstairs."

"I'm sure you do," she purred, sliding her bright pink nails through her bleached blonde hair.

He trotted upstairs quickly, hoping she wouldn't call after

him with some obscene remark. He'd never seen a woman work harder at partying and living on the edge. Her late-night parties had kept him up on more than one occasion. But he dared not go down and try to talk some sense into her, because "Your parties are too loud, so could you tone it down" translated in her world to "I'd like to come in and join the crazies."

Libby looked up as he walked back in. "Looks like you've got some other interesting information sitting over here." She nodded toward Aaron's box. "Don't worry. I didn't go through it. Just looked at the stuff sitting on top. Habit. Always detailing my surroundings. Sorry."

"That's not related to this. Just some stuff of my brother's I'm going through."

She smiled. "I solved your puzzle."

Mick walked to the couch. "You figured out what it said?"

"Yeah. Sounds like a personal problem to me." She flipped over the page and showed him what she'd printed out: *out of our past.*

Libby looked amused as she handed him the page. "Interesting."

"I don't know what it means," Mick said, setting his mail down on the coffee table.

He was studying the words, trying to understand what they meant, when Libby said, "Look at this." She held up an envelope. "Is this another one?"

Mick glanced at it. It was indeed.

"Mind if I open it?"

Why not? She'd already opened Pandora's box. Surely one more envelope wouldn't kill him. "Go ahead."

She took out the headline "Yearly Fall Festival Canceled." The second *Y* was highlighted.

"*Y*? Where does that fit? Is it the start of a new word?" Mick asked.

"Let me see the paper," Libby said, and Mick handed it over. She studied it for a moment, picked up the pen, and wrote something down. She handed it back to Mick.

The sheet now read: *out of your past.*

Mick felt a chill run down his spine. He sat in the chair across from Libby and reread the sentence.

"There's something else in the envelope." Libby handed a small square to Mick.

His mouth hung open. It was a newspaper picture of Sammy Earle when he was arrested ten years ago.

Libby glanced at the box near the coffee table. Mick noticed a picture of Sammy Earle was on the top of it. She had already put the two together. "Looks like they are related after all, eh?"

Mick was stunned into silence. What in the world was going on?

Libby said, "Tell you what. Let's get out of here."

"What?"

"I came by to thank you for the flowers and for your . . . kindness. Wanted to see if you'd let me buy you a cup of coffee at my favorite coffeehouse."

"What if I have a favorite coffeehouse?"

"You don't seem like a coffeehouse kind of guy. Besides, you understand I have to maintain most of the control in this situation."

Mick smiled and grabbed his keys. "At least I get to drive."

chapter fourteen

mick thought House of Blended Souls was a bit of an overstatement, seeing that the only people there were yuppie white folks, but the aroma caught his attention as soon as they walked up the porch steps.

Libby explained that this converted old house used to belong to a man who lost all his money in the coffee trade back in the twenties. "They say it's haunted," she said as she helped herself up the stairs using the railing.

"Well, that's certainly how I would want to spend all of my eternity. Hanging around the very thing that made me miserable on earth."

Libby smiled as she topped the last step, and for the first time Mick noticed the most charming gap between her two front teeth. It was small but added a lot of character to an already enchanting smile. Until now she hadn't grinned wide enough to see anything but a hint of white. He was making progress. If he kept up a good pace, he might get to hear a giggle.

Inside, a cozy atmosphere welcomed them, including a fireplace; leather chairs; small, intimate tables set in the corners; and soft, big-band music playing in the background.

"What kind of coffee do you take?" she asked.

"Usually the stale kind that sits in the pot all day. This is going to be a nice change."

"You'll be hooked. You might as well write it into your budget."

Mick gazed at the menu board. "I'm lost already. You might have to help me out."

"Do you like iced coffee?"

"Probably as much as I'd like warm soda."

"What about chocolate?"

"Sure. Love chocolate."

"Then how about a mocha?"

Mick glanced around and whispered, "Is that a chick drink?"

Libby laughed again. "I guess you never claimed to be cultured, did you?"

"I do take a certain pride in being able to down coffee as thick as molasses."

"Trust me," she said with a sweet smile, "you're going to love this." She stepped up to the counter and ordered their drinks, specifying detailed instructions about each one. Then she said, "Let's get that table in the corner."

Mick followed her over to the table by the window. Outside, the streetlights were flickering on.

"Do you come here a lot?"

"Sounds like a pickup line, Kline," she said with a chuckle. "Yeah, I come here a lot. Sometimes to unwind. Sometimes to work. Sometimes on the way to work. It's a cliché, I know. But it's relaxing. I like to come here in the afternoon. That's when all the writers converge with their fancy laptops and buzzing minds. They sort of check each other out from across the room, like they would love a peek at what the others are writing. It's fun to watch weird people."

"As if you don't have enough weirdos keeping you busy at work."

"Exactly."

A man with floppy, curly hair and an assortment of chains and hoops hanging from every piece of cartilage on his body served them their drinks and acknowledged Libby with a familiar smile.

"That's Pete," Libby said as he walked away. "He's working toward medical school."

"And we thought our young people weren't going anywhere."

"Just in their own way." She sipped her coffee. "Try it, c'mon. I can't wait to hear what you think. I even made sure they added whipped cream to yours."

"Here it goes." Mick took a drink. It was surprisingly good. He thought people just drank this stuff to be cool. "I like it."

"There are a billion combinations."

"I could get used to this kind of luxury." Mick settled into his chair and watched a group of teenagers mingle outside. "So what does Agent Libby Lancaster like to do in her free time?"

"Ha. What free time?"

"Overworked?"

"Yeah. Really overworked. I love my job. If I didn't, it would've killed me years ago. But when I do have free time, I like to read."

"Really?"

"I love novels. Any kind of novel I can get my hands on: pop fiction, classics, literary—you name it."

"I haven't picked up a novel in years. My brother, Aaron, was the reader in the family."

"Was?"

"He was murdered a year and a half ago."

"I'm sorry."

"I always wanted to love reading, though. I hear it's a nice escape."

"Amazing escape. I've always loved English. In school, I remember being so intrigued by the four points of conflict."

"You'll have to elaborate."

"You'll remember them. Man vs. man. Man vs. himself. Man vs. nature. Man vs. God."

"I guess I've never thought of conflict like that."

"It's nice to read about somebody else's conflict rather than my own." She laughed and fingered the rim of her cup. "Anyway, I love to go to the library and bookstores when I have time. What do you do for fun?"

"Chase storms."

Her eyes widened in surprise. "Chase storms?"

"Yeah. I used to chase women but I had to give that up."

"No kidding," she said with an amused smile. "Why is that?"

"Something to do with that man vs. God thing you were talking about."

She leaned forward on the table. "I'd love to hear that story."

"It'll take longer than one cup of mocha."

She glanced over at the coffee bar. "Well, then, I guess I'll just have to buy you another."

"I was hoping you'd say that."

"You're already hooked, aren't you?" She watched a couple walk away from a nearby table. "And look! The Scrabble board is free! I love Scrabble. You play, don't you?"

Mick swallowed a large gulp of coffee so he would have time to decide how to answer that question truthfully while covering up the fact that he was blushing.

Ira Leville watched Nicole from across the room, holding his warm scotch and measuring its effects against years of being married to a woman half his age. He'd never been an attractive man, but he'd been told by many women that he had enchanting eyes. They were sky blue, bloodshot most of the time, and buried against mounds of puffy skin, but smiling even when he was not.

And he was not.

Nicole was busy engaging one of the many guests at one of the many parties she planned throughout the year. She wore a tight, beaded, red dress and stood out from most of the crowd, which is how she liked it. She was currently flirting with one of his old business partners. It had been harmless flirting all these years. He really didn't think much of it. It was how she was . . . a free spirit.

But he could hardly stomach watching her now. He set down his drink and headed outside for some air. From the balcony of his estate that overlooked the sparkling city lights of Dallas, Ira looked calm. But as the evening breeze tickled his perpetually sweaty forehead, he fought the urge to scream. He'd been fighting it for days now.

And cursing Joel Lamberson's name. He hated that man and would've been rejoicing over his death had it not been so inconvenient. Truthfully, inconvenient was an understatement. Ira growled under his breath at the thought of Joel and pulled his suit jacket over his large belly.

He did not like things going on behind his back, and now someone was going to pay dearly for it. He just didn't know who. But he had his suspects.

"Out here by your lonesome?" Nicole's steamy voice made him want to choke. Her hand glazed against his shoulder and down his arm as she came up beside him. "You never did like these things." She smiled at him.

He could never look at her; not that she ever noticed. She was too busy spending all his money and charming all his friends, which up until recently had been a delight for him.

But then Joel had mentioned her name. He'd ambushed

him at the office, claimed to have stolen the documentation, and said her name, like they were acquaintances. As far as Ira knew, they had never met. But there had been a mischievous glint in Joel's eyes. Ira still didn't understand it all. "I'll be in touch," Joel had warned.

"You okay, baby?" Nicole said, clinging to his arm like a child. Her face turned to a pout, because what she really meant was "Why aren't you paying full attention to me?" She was spoiled, but it was his fault. He'd created the monster. When they'd met ten years ago, she was in her late twenties, fresh-faced, and working as a waitress at his favorite restaurant. Now she globbed on the makeup, dyed her hair, and pretended to be important.

He studied her eyes for a moment, which were big, brown, and hiding something. He knew it. He just knew it. "Just have a lot on my mind."

"Big business stuff, huh?" she said with a tease in her voice. "Well, I'll leave you to be with your brilliant mind. You want a drink? Cocktails galore in there."

"No."

She walked back inside, and Ira leaned against the balcony railing. He'd been betrayed once, and now he suspected twice, and that was two more times than was tolerable for him. He fingered his gold rings, grinding his teeth and grunting like a wild animal. He turned and watched through the open French door as Nicole crisscrossed through the crowd, her red dress sparkling in the light.

"Not you, Nicole. Please don't let it be you."

Mick studied the Scrabble board and then his measly choice of letters. Finally he saw it. One of the words ended in *D*, so he slid in an *O* and a *G*.

Libby smiled. "Dog."

In this game so far, she'd spelled *blanched*, *guru*, *innkeeper*, and *satiety*. He didn't know what that word meant but said "good job" anyway. He'd never enjoyed being beat by a woman so much in his life.

She scrutinized the board. "I think that's why I love this game. It's tedious."

"Kind of like your job, right?"

"Yeah. When I first thought of joining the ATF, I had this notion that I'd be chasing down criminals with bombs and guns and all sorts of exciting things. It still is exciting— and definitely interesting—but most days are spent chasing paper trails. I'm sure much like your work."

"That's all I do . . . study numbers and chase paper-work."

She sighed and leaned back in her chair, grabbing her second mocha. "I'm out of the loop."

"What?"

"They're cutting me off the case. Citing my injuries, of course."

"Libby, you *are* injured."

"Yeah." She stared at the cane next to her chair. "Guber rushes things. He's not thorough. It's meticulous work. Most people don't understand how hard arson cases are to solve. It's not how the fire started. It's why."

"Sure."

"It can sometimes take years, especially if the insurance company doesn't report it as fraud, or if we can't find who the insurance company is. Some of these companies are disguised by more than one shelter company. Each with different resident agents. This looks to be one of those cases. Guber's going to miss details by rushing things."

"You've found a shelter company?"

She bit her lip and looked at him. "One. There may be more."

Mick stared at the board and then, without thinking through the implications, blurted out, "There are four shelter companies."

A serious determination set into her expression. "Four. How do you know that?"

"FinCEN. We got the documents today."

"Ah." Libby seemed a little disgruntled. "I should've known they'd give the bureau priority." Then she said, "I didn't bring you here to share information with me."

"I know." He smiled. "But you're off the case. What possible good could that information be to you, anyway?"

A big grin spread across her face. "Right. What good?"

"We were investigating Lamberson on embezzlement at the corporation he once worked for. He was going to be called in front of a grand jury."

"Do you think this is all connected?"

"I don't know. We've investigated the company, called Welleson Bryer, pretty heavily, and I think we would've uncovered some of these company names. But who knows? Like you said, it can run deep."

"So you think your guy may have been involved with something else in which you were unaware?"

Mick shrugged. "Could be."

"All right," she said, as if there were words inside her mouth hoping not to escape, "I'll let you in on something we discovered. The building that burned with Lamberson in it . . . we found acetone."

"Acetone? Why would there be acetone? You're telling me this is a drug case? I didn't see any evidence of a meth lab."

"And that, my friend, is the way a male mind works."

"Oh?"

"I'm looking at the same evidence and seeing something else altogether."

Mick folded his arms. "And what would that be?"

"A female suspect."

"Why?"

"Because I think the acetone isn't from a meth cooker. I think it's from nail-polish remover."

Mick rested his chin in his hand and propped his arm on his knee. "Lamberson had alcohol in his system."

"I know."

Libby took the last few Scrabble letters into her hand and set them down precisely onto the board. Looking up, she smiled.

The new word was *endear*.

chapter fifteen

C haplain Barber was not what Sammy had expected. Throughout his time in prison, Sammy had seen several pastors and priests walk the halls and do services. They all looked the same: pious, self-righteous, and passionless. He imagined they would open their Bibles at the services and drone on about the goodness of God, the life of forgiveness. It had occurred to Sammy once that none of these religious men looked as if they thought they needed to be forgiven. Yet they were all too eager to point out the flaws of caged men.

Now he sat across from a man who looked like every other prisoner here. A multicolored tattoo of a dragon spewing fire ran the length of his huge, muscular arm. The sleeves of his black, fitted T-shirt were cut off. His jeans had holes in them, and he wore motorcycle boots. His head was totally shaved, and the only hair on his face was a thick, bushy goatee.

"Roy Barber," the chaplain said, extending a hand that looked like a baseball glove.

Sammy had never seen such giant fingers. He felt his hand swallowed as they shook. "Sammy Earle."

"Nice to meet you." His voice was a bit gravelly, and Sammy wondered if this saint might still be hooked on nicotine. His eyes roamed down to his shirt pocket, and sure enough, the outline of a rectangular box gave Sammy the evidence he needed. "Sammy, the warden tells me that you weren't too eager to meet with me."

"The warden tells me you were very eager to meet with me."

"It's true," he said. "You've only got a few days left. I can't say I've met too many prisoners who aren't thinking about what's going to happen to them when they die."

"Whatever it is, it's not going to be good, so why think about it."

"You're an educated man, Sammy. Much more educated than me. Don't you believe it's at least worth looking into?"

Sammy studied the chaplain. "What's your background, anyway? I mean, don't priests have to have some sort of training? You look like you just stepped out of a dark alley."

"I used to be in prison. I killed a man."

"Hmmm. Just like me, right? You and I are the same?"

"I don't know. You tell me."

"I don't know you all that well, so I couldn't say."

"You seem like you have a lot of bitterness."

"You and I are not the same. I never killed anyone."

"So the man with the worst sin has found God, and the man who still believes in his innocence will die God's enemy," the chaplain said.

Sammy sat back in his chair and stared at the paradox in front of him. "If I'm God's enemy, then so be it."

"You seem like a man who likes control, Sammy."

"I lost control of my life a long time ago." He studied the chaplain again. "I have to say I'm surprised by you. I haven't been much of a churchgoer, but you don't really seem like the kind of man who would wear a robe and carry a Bible around."

"Robes are overrated, but I do always carry my Bible."

He reached into the front pocket of his T-shirt and pulled one out.

"I should've known."

"Known what?"

"I thought that was a pack of cigarettes. For a moment there I thought we might be a little bit the same. I used to smoke. Gave it up for liquor."

The chaplain smiled and reached into his back pocket. He pulled out a half-empty pack of Marlboros. "Want one?"

Sammy couldn't help but laugh. "No, but if you have a flask hidden away somewhere, I'd be more than happy to share."

"Had to give that one up. It was a vice."

"And smoking?"

"A pleasure." He smiled.

Sammy shook his head. "I would've never thought a man like you and a man like me would have much in common. I used to be an attorney. Did you know that?"

"No."

"Represented a lot of rich people. I was, in fact, very rich. Lived in a big house and had nice furniture. Dated beautiful women. To tell you the truth, I was rather cheap. Looking back on it now, I would've spent more of my money. After all, you can lose it so quickly and never enjoy it. I did buy nice suits, but I had to match up with what my clients wore."

"Sounds like you spent it plenty well."

"Not on people, though." Sammy stared at his fingers, slim and dainty compared to the chaplain's. "I should've bought people things. Christmas presents. Dinner out."

"Do you spend a lot of time thinking about these kinds of things?"

"What?"

"Regrets?"

Sammy tilted his head and cocked an eyebrow. "Sure. Why not? I've landed in jail for killing a man that I didn't. Most of all I wish I hadn't gone to Stephen Fiscall's house that night. I wish I wasn't a man in need of such control that I felt like I had to go there and find out what that note was all about. That's what I wish. So much of my life would be different had I not felt the need for control."

"And now you have no control."

"I have some."

"Like whether or not you're going to let God have the last word over your life."

Heat flushed Sammy's cheeks and he looked away. Implying he still needed control. Maybe he did. That was the natural-born instinct of all human beings, wasn't it? It's what caused them to survive, to thrive.

The door swung open, and a guard said, "Sammy, you have a phone call."

A phone call? Sammy stood. "Who is it?"

"I can't remember the name. He is on the call sheet you provided the prison." The call sheet was a list of people allowed to call him. He remembered making it when he first came and had found it hard to come up with even five names besides his attorney. He was supposed to update the list every year, but he hadn't changed a thing. The guard gestured with his left hand. "Come with me, and I'll take you to a room with a phone."

"Thank you for your time," Sammy said to the chaplain.

"Maybe you'll let me return. I don't think we're done with this conversation."

"If a death sentence isn't a wake-up call for someone, then I'm not sure what is. The fact of the matter is that I don't care anymore. I don't feel many emotions, I don't have any hope, and I lost the will to live a long time ago."

The chaplain stood as Sammy walked past him. "I guess walking to that execution chair is going to be a piece of cake then."

Sammy didn't turn around but followed the guard down the hall. "You don't remember the name at all?" Sammy asked as they walked.

"I think they said something about Clark, maybe?"

"Doyle? Doyle Clarkson?"

"That's it."

Sammy nearly stumbled at the name. He hadn't heard from his trial lawyer in years. He occasionally followed Doyle's cases in the newspaper. Doyle hadn't aged a month, at least by his pictures, and in fact looked like he'd lost some weight over the years. He probably started working out. Doyle was always into fads.

The guard guided Sammy to a small, windowless room with a table and a corded phone. "Line two."

Sammy sat and hesitated as the guard stepped into the hall. He wasn't a big fan of Doyle's, and he figured Doyle was just calling to give his condolences or whatever you give when a former client is going to be executed. He figured Doyle would recite some speech about nobility and courage and have some excuse about why he couldn't make the "big day." He really didn't want to hear it.

But Sammy hadn't talked to anyone from his previous world in so long; it might be nice to hear a voice from the outside, even if it was going to be condescending.

He stroked the receiver and watched the blinking red light. Then he snatched it up. "Hello?"

"Hello, Sammy."

Sammy frowned. Doyle sounded strange. Was he sick? His voice was lower and softer . . . older. Sammy waited for Doyle to continue, but there was only silence on the other end of the line.

Finally Sammy spoke. "Look, Doyle, I'm not sure why you're calling. There's really nothing to say. Quite frankly, you stunk up my case in a royal way, and now I'm paying for it. It's what I get for hiring a high-priced, high-powered attorney. I should've given a kid right out of law school a shot. He would've worked himself to death for me. You thought your formulas and fabrications would work, and they didn't. No matter. I'm tired of this old life. I was tired of it before. You should know something, Doyle, just for the record . . . you're not going to find happiness at the end of your self-made rainbow. Yeah, maybe there's a pot of gold there at the end, but it only buys more gold. There's nothing tangible about it. Just so you know. Maybe if there's one last thing on this earth I can do, it's to tell somebody not to waste time, because it can disappear in a second anyway. I should know. And you know what? I'm ready to die. I am. Why not, right? Who cares? Who cares if I die? I made enough enemies in my life . . . I was guaranteed some sort of unhappy ending, so maybe I can't blame you completely, Doyle. Maybe not. Maybe you can walk away from all this with less of a burden."

Sammy almost chuckled, wishing he could see Doyle's face after his outburst. He found himself much more able to express his true feelings these days. Maybe he should tell Doyle what an idiot he looks like when he waves.

Another band of silence caused Sammy to sigh. "You're irritating me, Doyle. Have I stunned you into silence? Why are you calling?"

More silence.

But Sammy felt him there on the other end. He could almost hear breathing.

And then he said, "You've been doing a lot of ruminating, haven't you, Sammy?"

Sammy blinked as a cold chill tickled his back. "Excuse me? Who is this?"

More silence.

Sammy knew this wasn't Doyle. "What is this? Some kind of sick joke?"

"Are you angry, Sammy?"

"I'm not sure," Sammy said, drawing in a breath. He'd been caught off guard, but he settled himself. "Should I be?"

"You sounded pretty angry."

"Everyone's angry about something. I live with hundreds of angry men."

"But few are angry because of injustice."

"Who is this?" Sammy asked again. "Do you know something about my case?"

"A thing or two," said the amused voice. "I also know about being angry at injustice, Sammy. I know what it's like to be accused of doing something that you didn't."

All breath was sucked out of Sammy's lungs. He almost dropped the phone.

"Have you ever seen a caged animal, Sammy? An animal who doesn't want to be there? Have you ever seen that? Have you ever seen its eyes?"

Sammy leaned against the table, as if a casual, uncaring demeanor might come through over the phone. But his insides were trembling. "Can't say that I have."

"Oh yes you have, Sammy. Sure you have. You've seen my eyes."

Sammy swiped the back of his hand over his mouth. He felt like he was going to throw up. He knew the voice. He knew it. "Patrick." The single word, barely a whisper rolling off his tongue, caused tears to form in Sammy's eyes. "Patrick Delano." He straightened and wiped at his eyes. He made sure his voice did not quiver. "Why are you calling me?"

"Why not?"

"I thought you were probably dead."

"You know better than that."

"I should've guessed it." Sammy jutted his jaw forward. "I haven't thought of you in years."

"I've thought of you often."

"What are you trying to say here, Patrick? I'm not sure why you're calling, and I really don't care."

"You do know why I'm calling, and you do care."

Sammy stared at his trembling fingers. "It was you." He heard a faint laugh on the other end. "You did this," Sammy said, clutching the phone cord. The guard glanced in. Sammy turned his back.

"I won't take up any more of your time, Sammy. I know you don't have much of it left."

"Wait! Tell me if you did this! Tell me!"

"You said it. And your words have always had a lot of power, haven't they?"

The phone went dead.

"Patrick. Patrick! *Patrick*!"

Sammy dropped the phone into its receiver. He let out a little yelp, like a beaten dog. Could it be true? After all these years? He cupped his hands over his mouth and stared at the ceiling, his legs wobbling like they might on the day he would walk to his own execution.

chapter sixteen

his paper trail is a mess." Reggie sighed and groaned. "I don't think we're going to have a clue unless the insurance companies come forward with worries of fraud. And I'm assuming they're insured separately, so why would they?"

"I think we need to pay a visit to Joel Lamberson's wife," Mick said.

"Oh?" Reggie smiled. "We have the police report on it. Said her husband was going to the store—"

"Yeah, I know. But beta-ketopropane was found at the crime scene."

"Acetone? Are you telling me this is a meth case? You have got to be kidding me!"

"And that is how the male mind works, my friend. What if the acetone was from, say, nail-polish remover?"

Reggie's expression registered surprise. "Interesting theory. Strangely—and maybe you haven't noticed—but you are a male. Where'd you get that information?"

"The ATF."

"No, I mean *that* information. Fingernail-polish stuff."

Mick looked around and lowered his voice. "Okay, but this leaks to *nobody*. Got it?"

Reggie nodded eagerly.

"Agent Lancaster let it slip."

"She's off the case, isn't she? Due to her injuries?"

"Yeah."

"So, um . . . when did you see Agent Lancaster?"

"Don't act so surprised. You sent her my way."

Reggie's face lit up. "No! No way! You had a date?"

"What? Sssssshhh! What?"

Reggie chuckled. "Are you telling me that you and Medusa are getting friendly?"

"Keep your voice down."

"You *are*!"

"It's not like that."

"Like what?"

"Like what you're insinuating."

"That you're hot for Medusa?"

"First of all, Medusa is really too strong. She's more of a . . ."

Reggie sat there with his mouth hanging open.

Mick tried to find the right word. ". . . an Athena! Yeah. Athena."

Reggie crossed his arms. "Athena. I haven't read up on my Greek mythology lately."

"I'm just trying to find someone comparable in the Greek mythology structure. If you'd mentioned someone from the Bible, I would have come up with a comparison in the Bible."

"I don't know anybody from the Bible."

"The point is that Medusa is an exaggeration. That's all. End of discussion."

"How long did she stay?"

"We went for coffee." Mick cringed. That didn't sound good.

"Coffee! Like a date!"

"It wasn't a date. She just wanted to thank me—that's all."

Reggie whispered, "Dude, don't fool yourself. Women

don't drive all the way across town to 'thank' someone for visiting them in the hospital."

"She actually took a taxi."

"Whoa."

"Whatever the case, she told me about the acetone and that the warehouse fire had an even different signature than the others."

An assistant walked up and handed Reggie a fax. Reggie read it and handed it to Mick. "Looks like the warehouse is owned by a separate company. But who knows. It may be attached to the shelter companies in some way too."

"Or a deterrent."

Reggie rolled his eyes. "This is going to be another long case."

"Let's go see Lamberson's wife today." Mick stood and put on his jacket.

"Good excuse to get out of the office for a while."

Another assistant approached Mick. "You have a call. I didn't want to send it through before giving you a heads-up."

"Is it a woman?" Reggie grinned.

The assistant said, "The guy sounded really uptight. Wouldn't give me his name. Wanted to speak to you only."

Reggie said, "I'll pull the car around."

Mick nodded and told the assistant to send the call through. He answered it and barely had time to say hello.

"I know who it is," said the tottering voice. "I know for sure now. I know."

"Who is this?"

"Me . . . Sammy . . . Earle." He sounded like a frightened child.

"Sammy Earle? What—?"

"It was Patrick Delano."

"Slow down. Please. I'm not following you."

"*Patrick did this!!*"

"Did what?"

"Put me here. He's the one who put me here."

"Sammy—"

"I don't know how he did it, but he did."

Mick took a breath, trying to comprehend. Sammy was talking about the Patrick Delano that Aaron had been researching. The soldier who disappeared, who was court-martialed for the death of Earle's best friend in Vietnam.

"He's alive," Sammy uttered, whispering it as if it had some power over him.

"Why do you think it was Patrick Delano?"

"He told me himself. He called me."

"He called you?"

"Here at the prison, claiming he was my former attorney, Doyle Clarkson. That's how he got past the call sheet."

"What did he say? Did he say he killed Stephen Fiscall?"

"It's him. You must believe me. It's him."

"Tell me what he said, Sammy."

There was a long pause and then he said, "He asked me if I'd stared into the eyes of a caged animal."

"Did he actually say he was Patrick?"

"I recognized his voice. I swear it was him. And when I asked him if he did this to me, he . . . laughed."

"Did he give any indication of where he might be?"

"No." Sammy sounded as if he wanted to weep. "You're my only hope. I don't know if there really is any hope. He's hidden for this long."

"Why would he call you now?"

"He wanted me to know. And he wanted me to have time to think about it . . . days to think about it . . . before I died. As if being executed for a crime I didn't commit wasn't enough, he wanted to make sure I knew that he did this to me."

"Are you sure this isn't a sick prank?"

"I know his voice. I will never forget his voice as long as I live."

Mick sat down in his chair and tried to figure out what to do next.

"If only one person knows I didn't kill Fiscall, maybe that's enough for me." Sammy paused. "I don't think you'll be able to find him."

"Why not?"

"He's too good. He was an amazing soldier, mostly because he barely had a conscience, and he had this keen sense about people and things, like a sixth sense or something. He was able to control people in the strangest ways."

"I'll see what I can do."

Sammy was silent.

Mick knew Sammy needed more than that. "But I need to know something first, and you must be honest with me, Sammy."

"What?"

"Are you sending me notes in the mail?"

"What kind of notes?"

"If you're sending them, you would know."

"I'm not sending you anything. I swear it."

Later, in the car, Reggie glanced at Mick three times from the driver's seat before he finally said, "You okay, dude?"

"Yeah, I'm fine." He'd not slept well last night, his thoughts shifting between the mysterious headline messages and Libby Lancaster's beautiful smile. The little sleep he did get had been plagued with memories from long ago, memories he'd suppressed with much success over the years.

They were some of the worst days of his life when he had, much like Sammy Earle, been falsely accused of a kidnapping. But unlike Sammy Earle, Mick had been able to prove his innocence. It all seemed surreal.

"All right, here we go," Reggie said, pulling into the Lambersons' large circle drive. It was this humongous house that had been one of the first clues that Lamberson might have been embezzling funds. Four large, white pillars held up the porch overhang, and an oversized, bloodred door with an iron knocker stood out from beneath the shadow of the three-story home.

"Okay, you ready?"

"Yep."

Reggie had the honor of using the large knocker, and he banged it with the glee of a child. "If I had one of these things on my house, I swear it would knock down the entire door." He chuckled.

The door opened slowly. A small woman stood in the doorway, nearly swallowed up by its size. They had seen Mrs. Lamberson many times before but had never spoken with her. Dark, heavy circles rimmed her eyes, and she didn't offer a smile. "Yes?"

"I'm Special Agent Mick Kline with the FBI, and this is Special Agent Reggie Moore."

Her gaze shifted between both of them. "Yes?"

"We need to speak with you, please," Mick said gently.

She hesitated. "I've already spoken with several law-enforcement agencies. I think even the FBI."

"Yes, ma'am. But we have some unfinished business."

She combed her fingers through her hair, which was pulled into a bun at the nape of her neck. She looked older than Joel, but maybe his surprising death had fixed age onto her face. "Sure, come in."

She offered them seats in a small sitting area to the right of the entryway. All the furniture was stark white, and the only color provided in the room was from a large painting on the wall and the bronze lamps that sat on the white tables.

"Tea?"

"No, thank you," they both said.

She took a seat across from them, still messing with her hair and touching her face as if she felt naked.

Mick said, "Sorry to come by unannounced, ma'am, but—"

"Please call me Anita."

"We're sorry about your husband's death."

"I think I'm still in shock." Her eyes glistened. "The girls are not taking it well at all." She looked toward a large, spiral staircase and followed it up and out of sight. "Joella has hardly eaten since her dad died. Annie is just a basket case." She turned her attention back to them. "What can I do for you?"

"Anita, let me be up front with you. We were investigating your husband in an embezzlement case."

She didn't look surprised.

"But now we think that it might reach far deeper than our original case."

"He was fired from that job. He never told me exactly why."

"But you had your suspicions?"

Her nostrils flared slightly. "Joel was a very driven man. He hated to lose. He hated to be on the bottom."

"How did he take the firing?"

"Surprisingly well. In only a few short weeks, he began doing the consulting work."

"Consulting work for whom?"

"I don't really know. He didn't talk about work much. He didn't like to bring it home." She held a finger below her eye. "He was a good father. I know that. His girls adored him."

"Yes, ma'am."

"I know you probably think of him as a horrible person. Who knows what he did? But he was a good father."

"Was he a good husband?"

"Look at this place," she said, almost smiling. "He gave me everything I could imagine and some things I couldn't."

"Can you tell us anything about the night Joel died?" Reggie asked.

"I already told the police everything I know. He went to the grocery store to pick up a few things. He liked to go at night when it's not crowded. And he loved to look at magazines, those car magazines you see the kids buy. He was a kid at heart, always wanting new toys. I just assumed he was there looking at magazines. I got worried when three hours had passed."

"Do you have any idea why he was at that office building?"

"No. His car was found a few blocks away. Maybe it was a carjacking and they took him there and killed him." She started crying. "None of it makes sense. This is an awful world. A cruel and unfair world."

Mick said, "There is a lot of mystery surrounding your husband's death, and, like you, we want to know exactly why Joel died. But we're going to need your help."

"I don't know anything," she said. "I promise I don't. Joel . . . Joel sometimes thought of me as dumb. Not in a bad way. But he never thought I could understand all his business deals. And the fact of the matter is that I don't really understand accounting. I used to work in a beauty salon. Numbers don't make a lot of sense to me."

"Numbers make a lot of sense to me," Mick said, "and there are things that aren't adding up in this case. Anita, would you mind if we took a look at some of your husband's business files? I'm assuming he has an office here?"

She hedged. "I . . ."

"Anita," Mick said, standing as she did, "your husband is dead. Someone killed him, and we think it was over a business deal. The problem is, nobody understands what kind of business your husband was doing."

"I don't know anything."

"Do you know of any other office your husband had?"

"No."

"May we, then?"

Anita drummed her temples, sighed, and walked across the hall to a spacious office with French doors.

Reggie went straight to the computer. Mick opened some file cabinets and searched for anything that looked suspicious. But after fifteen minutes, he found nothing more than personal documents.

Reggie said, "There's nothing on here."

Anita stood in the doorway and watched silently. When they were finished, she said, "What are you looking for?"

"Just trying to find out why your husband was at that building," Reggie said.

She stared at the open file cabinet Mick was standing by. "Documents."

"Excuse me?"

"A couple of days after Joel died, his old boss Ira came by."

"Ira Leville? The CEO of Joel's former company?" Mick asked.

"That's right. They had kept in contact since he was fired. Ira looked so stunned. The whole time he was here, he couldn't believe Joel was dead."

"He came by to give his condolences?"

"Yes. And he said that Joel had been working on some business for him, and he wondered if he could see if the documents were here."

"Did he say what kind of documents?"

"No. I didn't think much about it. I didn't know he and Ira were still working together."

"Did Ira find what he was looking for?"

Anita shook her head. "He asked if Joel might keep documents elsewhere, besides his office, and I said not that I knew of."

"He never mentioned what those documents were?"

"No."

"Did he appear upset they weren't here?"

"He appeared upset. I think Joel's death really hit him hard."

One of the Lambersons' teenage girls appeared at the top of the stairs, staring down at the conversation. Anita looked Mick in the eyes. "If that's all . . ."

Mick understood her to be saying she didn't want her girls to know anything. "Sure. Thank you for your time."

She led them to the front door, and Mick and Reggie walked out onto the porch.

"What do you bet those documents are exactly what we need to link Lamberson to those shelter companies?"

"And maybe Ira Leville as well," Mick said. "Is it possible these two have been working together since Joel was fired?"

Reggie laughed. "I'd be shocked."

Mick gestured at the house as they got into the car. "That poor woman doesn't have a clue, does she?"

"I think she's starting to catch on."

"Maybe it's best if she doesn't know all the details. Looks like she really loved her husband. Believed he was a good man."

"Yeah, well, I guess we all have our dark sides. Some more than others."

"And some are better at hiding them too."

In the late afternoon, Mick took off early and drove to the Irving Police Department. He was not looking forward to the visit. It had been years since he'd seen Detective Shep Crawford, the man who had formed a malicious manhunt against him but had also been a strange ally. Mick had never quite understood Crawford's motivation for wanting to protect him, but in the end, Crawford's instincts had been right. Mick was innocent, and Sammy Earle was the monster.

Crawford had been described by more than a few of his colleagues as one of the most capable and savvy homicide detectives to ever work in Texas. Inside his eyes was a strange sense of genius but also an unbalanced, passionate urgency . . . urgency for what was never determined.

He'd won fame for solving unsolvable mysteries, but he never reveled in it, never wrote a book, never sought out the attention. He simply worked.

Mick found the homicide department on the second floor. After he showed his badge, a woman led him back to a cluster of cubicles.

A young detective greeted them. He looked fresh-faced and wide-eyed. Mick wondered if that's what he'd looked like when he'd gone to the academy.

Mick shook his hand. "Mick Kline. I was wondering if Detective Crawford is here."

From behind them a voice said, "What do you want Crawford for?"

Mick turned around and recognized the speaker. He had red hair, freckles, and was wearing a fancy silk shirt. He couldn't remember his name, though.

"Randy Prescott," the detective said. "You're . . ."

"Mick Kline."

"Mick Kline!" He let out a laugh. "My goodness. Last time I saw you, you were in handcuffs in the back of a police car."

"Yeah."

"How things have changed. I heard you'd joined the bureau." Prescott glanced at the other detective. "Look, why don't you come into my office, Mick."

Mick stepped up next to him, and they walked down a hallway.

"You've got an office now, eh?" Mick smiled.

"Yeah. I've been moving up in the ranks." He laughed. "Lead detective now. They've done some remodeling, so we have a lot more offices than we used to."

"Congratulations."

Prescott shut the door and opened the blinds to his office, letting in the warm, late-afternoon sun. He leaned against the windowsill and stuck his hands in his pockets. "So what brings you by?"

"I wanted to talk with Detective Crawford. He's not here?"

"Nah. He's semiretired now. He comes in every once in a while, just to shake the new guys up. He's a legend, and they fear and revere him. He makes fun of their clothes and tells them they stink up the place, and it makes their day."

"I guess you know that all too well."

"He's made me the detective I am today. The guy is amazing. After I got over the shock of his personality, I guess you could say, I decided the man had something to teach me."

"So how often does he come in?"

"Whenever he wants. Whenever there's an interesting case, he'll poke his nose around in it. Sometimes he gets involved; sometimes he doesn't. He likes to spend a lot of time at his beach house."

"Beach house?"

"Yeah. Down in Port Mansfield. Built it himself. It's kind of nice, actually. He brought pictures in. Is really proud of it. He has a boat and everything."

"I never really pictured Crawford retiring. He doesn't seem the type."

"It took a few people by surprise."

"When did he retire?"

"Last year. We wanted to throw him a big party, but he refused. He said his work was done, and he wanted to enjoy the last days of his life. He seemed happy. For the first time since I've known him, he seemed happy."

"Interesting."

"I've grown to respect the man. A few months back, one of those big newsmagazines inquired about doing a piece on him. But he declined. He never wanted the attention. He never did it to be respected. He always had this amazing sense of justice that seemed to drive him beyond himself, you know?"

"He was definitely a paradox. I can say that for him."

"Why do you want to see him?"

"You know Sammy Earle is about to die for the murder of Stephen Fiscall."

Prescott nodded. "I've been reading a few things in the paper. I'm ready for that rat to get what he deserves. It's like Crawford always said, 'Justice will prevail.'"

"Are you aware that Earle still claims he is innocent? that he was set up?"

A half smile slid across Prescott's freckled face. "I've heard his claims. He's been saying that since he was arrested. Doesn't surprise me. The guy always was a snake. Can't own up to the fact that he thought Fiscall had some dirt on him, so he killed him. Earle always needed complete control. When things went out of his control, he freaked out." He stood erect and took a couple steps toward Mick. "Is that why you're here? To talk about that case with Crawford?"

Mick shrugged. "Just wanted his take on it, that's all.

Earle is close to being executed. Just thought all loose ends should be tied up."

"There are no loose ends. If I'm not mistaken, what Sammy Earle did was pretty much your ticket to freedom."

Mick stiffened. "I would've been exonerated regard-less."

"Of course," Prescott said with an uneasy smile.

"Look, it's nothing big. I just wanted to talk with Crawford, see if he has any reason to believe it wasn't Earle."

"He doesn't."

"I noticed he didn't testify at the trial."

"That's not uncommon. They only needed one detective to give the details."

"And like you said, Crawford doesn't like the lime-light."

"Right." Prescott went to the other side of his desk. "You want to leave your card? I'll give it to him next time he comes in."

"Does he still live in that old, refurbished firehouse?"

Prescott nodded.

"I think I'll drop by."

"He's not one for surprises."

Mick smiled as he walked out the door. "It'll keep him young."

ick headed home. He wasn't sure he was ready to see the infamous detective. Not after the day he'd had battling a stubborn trail of misleading paperwork. If he knew Shep Crawford at all, he needed to have some sort of game plan, a few tricks up his sleeve in order to get anything meaningful out of the man.

Truthfully, a very large part of Mick thought Sammy Earle was grasping at straws. Maybe he made up the phone call from Patrick Delano. Maybe it was a last-ditch effort to save his own life.

But it wasn't so much Sammy Earle who had convinced him to do some checking. It was Aaron. It was as if his brother were speaking from the grave, trying to tell Mick there was more that he hadn't found out. Mick knew one thing: at some point Aaron had had his doubts too.

And someone else out there was trying to send Mick a message, as convoluted as it was. Someone went to an awful lot of trouble to highlight letters and make it some sort of complicated mind game. But who?

To make matters worse, Mick felt something very strange inside. For the first time in months, he thought he was feeling . . . what? Throughout the day, his mind kept drifting to Libby . . . her delightful smile, her eager work ethic, her sense of humor. And who would've thought he'd want the ATF in his life more than it already was?

At his mailbox, Mick was relieved to find only bills. Maybe the mysterious messages had ended. He trotted upstairs and unlocked his door. From the darkness of his apartment, he could see his red message light blinking. His heart jumped in anticipation. Without even turning on the lights or shutting the door, he walked over to his machine. He pushed the button, hoping to hear Libby's voice.

"Mick . . . hi . . . it's Faith."

Mick nearly dropped the mail.

"Listen, I was wondering if you were . . . if you were busy tonight. I just wanted to . . . um . . . just to see you. Our time ended so abruptly last time, and anyway . . ."

Mick squeezed his eyes shut. She left her phone number. Asked to see him. What was this about? Faith was one of the most gorgeous women he'd ever met, and he'd fallen a little too hard for her after Aaron died. But she hadn't been ready then. She'd had a lot of healing to do after her husband's murder.

". . . so if you get this, call me. I . . . hope to see you soon."

"Whoa." Mick walked to his door, closed it, turned on the light, and leaned against the wood. "This is seriously not happening." He chewed through two fingernails, trying to figure out what to do.

He decided to do what any God-fearing special agent with too many women on his hands would do.

He called Reggie.

"Well, you've never had this problem before." Reggie had laughed.

"Yeah, yeah, so tell me what to do."

Mick remembered Reggie's words now as he sat across the table from Faith at the same restaurant they'd chosen before. She looked as beautiful as ever. Her hair draped across her shoulders, luminescent against the candlelight. Mick's heart was pitter-pattering like rain. Though they'd been making fun chitchat since they'd arrived, there was a certain flush to Faith's cheeks that said she knew he knew there was more to come.

"Go for it," Reggie had said.

"Go for it?"

"Why not. Options are never a bad thing."

"I'm not sure these are options. They may be distractions."

And what was particularly distracting was Faith's smile. It had a sweetness to it that caused him to go temporarily insane.

Like agreeing to meet for dinner. Just hours before, he'd been infatuated with the one woman on earth who could get him to play Scrabble. Now the woman he'd helped back from a life of misery, a woman he saw himself able to take care of for the rest of their lives, was back.

She scratched her forehead as the waiter brought out a bread basket, and as the conversation lulled, Mick watched her wiggle in her chair. She was dying inside, and he knew how that felt. His heart was helplessly nagging at him to end her discomfort.

"I've been thinking about you a lot," he said suddenly. Did he just say that out loud? Was that his idea of rescuing her?

She looked up with surprise. "You have?"

I would've if I'd known you were thinking about me. Maybe you haven't been thinking about me, and I'm completely reading all this wrong, and I've just made a complete fool of myself. Somebody shoot me.

"Pass the butter?" he squeaked.

"Was that a question?"

Mick tried to recover. "Only if you object to me buttering my bread."

She laughed and passed it. She watched with interest as he buttered his bread, and then she said, "That's why I called."

"Really?" It came across heavy with relief, but he didn't care.

"Mick, I think we had something special, you know? I mean, back then I guess I didn't realize it. I was still recovering from a lot of grief. But time has passed. It's been over three years since Paul died, and . . ."

Mick tried his best not to speak.

She looked in his eyes, cast her gaze back down to her bread, and continued. ". . . and maybe it's too late. I didn't expect you to wait around for me."

Mick picked apart his bread, trying to discover what was in his heart. He hated being caught off guard.

"I'm sorry. I'm making you uncomfortable," she said.

"No, it's not that."

"You're so quiet."

Reggie's words hung in the back of his mind: *"Whatever you do, don't tell her about Libby."*

"There is someone else."

Her calm eyes swam with dejection. "It doesn't surprise me." She smiled. "You're a wonderful man."

"It's not serious. In fact, I don't know that I can even call it a relationship. We haven't even been on an official date."

"Maybe that's why you're here with me. Maybe you still have feelings for me."

Mick couldn't help the surprised expression that came with the shock of her forthrightness.

She laughed. "Close your mouth, Mick."

"Sorry."

"It's just that I can't help but think that what we had wasn't a fluke. There was a real bond there. You helped me out of such a dark place in my life, pointed me to the light. You gave me my faith back, my hope that life can be good again. And it is good. But there's still something missing in my life."

"I can't ever fill Paul's place in your heart."

"I know. I'm not asking you to. Maybe I'm asking that you make a new place." She grinned, and that grin was going to undo him.

Thankfully the waiter arrived with their meals. As they both silently bowed to bless their food, Mick didn't even bother to mention food in his desperate prayer to the Almighty for some help in managing his suddenly complicated love life. He was still squeezing his eyes shut, bouncing from one-word prayers to thoughts about his next move, when he realized Faith had begun eating and was looking curiously at him.

Clearing his throat, he took a big bite of his lasagna to buy himself a little more time. As he was chewing it to liquid, Faith finally said, "Listen, Mick, let me just put it this way. I made you wait—now it's my turn to wait."

"What do you mean?"

"I mean that I don't need a decision from you right now." She reached across the table and placed her hand on his. "It's unfair for me to come here and expect you to jump right into my plans for the future, right?"

Is that a trick question?

She smiled and let go of his tingling hand. "I want you to know that I think you're one of the greatest guys I've ever met. I've told you before how much you remind me of Paul. The way he never wavered in his faith, the way he stood strong in the convictions many people abandoned a long time ago. You're like that. You know what you believe, and you stick with it."

Except in this case, of course.

"Well . . . I, um . . . I . . ."

"It's okay." Faith laughed. "I can see you've never had this sort of predicament, have you?"

Mick smiled candidly. "I'm completely flattered that you would come here tonight and tell me these things."

"They're all true."

"What do you say we enjoy our evening together?"

"I'd say that sounds like a perfect plan."

It was 8 a.m., and Reggie had pulled up a large whiteboard and was armed with four colors of dry-erase markers. He'd even drawn a chart.

"You certainly have a lot more in common with Libby," Reggie said, putting a bright blue check mark by the word *interests* and then rolling up his sleeves.

"But I have more history with Faith." Mick sighed.

Reggie put a bright red mark by *past.* "In a moment of honesty, who do you find more attractive?" Mick hesitated and then shrugged. "Come on—don't deny that's important, even for a stout Christian man like yourself."

"They're both beautiful, but in different ways. Faith has that Grace Kelly way about her, you know? Kind of eloquent and gentle-natured. Libby is more down-to-earth, independent. Kind of tough in a real feminine sort of way."

"In other words, complete opposites." Reggie scribbled something in green.

Mick sipped his coffee and stared at the board.

Reggie asked, "What are you thinking, man?"

"I'm trying not to turn this into a mathematical formula."

"Let's talk negatives."

"That sounds like a math term."

"You can start worrying when I put the pi sign up. For now, tell me what the downside would be if you were in a relationship with Faith."

"I guess I fear that I would be stepping into Paul's shoes, shoes that I would never be able to fill."

"Good. Now what about Libby?"

"Well, that's easy. Could there really be a successful union between the FBI and the ATF?"

Reggie chuckled. "True enough."

"So far all we've talked about is work."

"Well, if there's chemistry when you talk about work, maybe that's a good sign."

"Good point." Mick leaned back and rocked in his chair, studying the whiteboard.

"Now, there's one more factor I have to throw in here, and you're not going to like it."

"What's that?"

At the very top of the board Reggie wrote the word *Jenny*.

"What?"

"You can't deny there are still feelings there."

"Yes I can! I mean, not deny, but I can . . . no . . . it's . . ."

"Dude, calm down," Reggie said, stifling a grin. "You're looking a little flustered—"

"Boys, we need to talk."

Mick and Reggie turned to find their supervisor, Tom, walking toward their desks. Reggie tried to block the whiteboard with his body.

"I need to know where we are in this Lamberson case. The phone's ringing off the hook, and the fax machine is nearly out of ink with all the junk ATF is sending us in an attempt to look 'helpful.' And can somebody tell me who this Guber guy is? He sounds like a mouse on the other end of the phone, and I have no idea who he is."

"He took over the case from Agent Lancaster, who still hasn't been able to return to work."

"Can somebody get him off my back?"

"Yes, sir," Mick said.

"We're waiting on a search warrant for Ira Leville's home."

"Isn't he the CEO of the company Lamberson used to work for?"

"Yeah. Lamberson's wife said he came looking for some documents after his death."

Reggie added, "And that they'd stayed in contact."

Tom appeared amused. "That sounds like an interesting angle. Go talk to Leville first, without the warrant. If he's got those documents, they're well hidden. I'd like to see him a little off balance, then watch him to see what move he makes. Any of the insurance companies come forward yet?"

"Not yet. I think we've probably got some international insurance companies involved here."

Tom glanced at the whiteboard, then looked at Mick and Reggie. "You boys keep up the good work. You're both doing a fantastic job." He patted Mick on the back and walked off.

Reggie sighed and fell into his chair. "We're lucky Tom still thinks he doesn't need glasses."

chapter eighteen

ira Leville had sent Nicole out the door three hours ago
with a credit card, plus an appointment at the spa. It
took all he had to smile at her with any sort of favor.
Deceit simmered on the surface of her eyes, and now he
saw it. He had been blind before, but inside the shiny glim-
mer of her charm was a dull, manipulative woman who
deserved nothing from him.

But until he could prove something, he was going to
have to pretend their relationship was real, just as she had
done for months.

In his heart of hearts, Ira knew she was capable of
deceit but had hoped that with enough attention and love,
she would remain faithful to him. Perhaps what was more
shocking than Nicole's apparent betrayal was Joel's. Ira
had practically rescued the man from financial despair,
but as he was well aware, if there is enough greed in a
man's heart, it can cause him to do the most wretched
things.

His own greed had remained in check for years. It was
the only way he could do business. He thought he and
Joel had similar ideals, but as it turned out, he'd grossly
misjudged the man he'd put so much trust in. He'd misjudged him in the wrong areas.

Ira had gone through every drawer in the house, every

cabinet, but there was nothing to be found. His beautiful Nicole, a siren in his midst, had gone to great lengths to hide the documents.

His hand swept over an eight-by-ten photograph of them on their wedding day. To think she was capable of murder on top of such deceit sent chills down his spine. He'd been unable to sleep in the same bed with her recently. Complaining about his back, he'd gone to one of the guest bedrooms, which had a firmer mattress. But he hadn't slept well for days now. His mind could not stop playing out the various scenarios that would somehow make him victorious in this situation.

First he needed those documents.

"Sir," said his butler from the doorway of his office, "there are gentlemen here to see you."

"Who?"

"They say they're from the FBI."

Ira turned to the window to hide the strain in his face. With the debacle that this had turned into, was he all that surprised? His heart shivered. With full knowledge, Ira Leville could've convinced any person of anything he wanted. But he did not know all there was to know, and the stakes had just soared to immeasurable heights.

Ira drew in a deep breath. "I'll be there in a moment."

He adjusted his tie and put on his jacket. He made sure he was wearing a watch. He smoothed out his hair and stuffed his pockets into their proper places.

He walked through the corridors of his home, his footsteps clicking against the expensive, foreign tile, and found the two men in the entryway, admiring one of his many pieces of art.

"Gentlemen, Ira Leville," he said, extending a hand. "I was told you're with the FBI?"

"That's right," said one man with a cast on his arm.

"I'm Mick Kline. This is Reggie Moore. We're special agents with the FBI."

"What can I do for you?"

"If you have a moment, we'd like to speak with you about the death of Joel Lamberson."

Ira did not avert his eyes but instead nodded. "Of course." He glanced steadily at his watch. "I have an appointment, but I can spare a few minutes."

He guided them into his large office and offered them both a leather wingback chair. "I've been watching the news, trying to find out anything else about his death."

"Why is that?" said Agent Kline.

"He worked for me. Was fired by the board of directors about a year ago. But I always liked Joel." He tried not to choke on his own words.

"For suspicions of embezzlement, right?"

"That's right."

"Did you stay in contact with Joel after he was fired?"

"A little. I felt bad for him; he had a family to raise."

"How often did you talk with him?"

"Maybe a handful of times. I'm not sure."

"Were you doing any business with Mr. Lamberson outside your company?"

"No."

"You're sure about that?"

"Yes. Why?"

"We're just trying to solve a crime, sir," Agent Moore interjected. "There are a lot of things that are not adding up about Joel Lamberson's death, including why all these buildings around town are being burned down."

"Joel was a keen businessman. I fully expect that he was wrapped up in some sort of business dealings."

"Just not with you."

"No."

"Did you visit Anita Lamberson after Joel died?" Agent Kline asked.

"Yes."

"What was your purpose for going?"

"To offer Anita our condolences. My wife went with me."

The two agents glanced at each other. "Your wife was with you?"

"Yes. We weren't able to make the funeral, but I wanted to tell Anita how sorry I was for Joel's death."

The front door opened, and Ira could hear Nicole walk in, chattering on her cell phone, shopping bags most likely hooked around each elbow. The agents turned toward her as she entered the office.

Ira stood and walked briskly toward her.

She met his eyes, looked at the two agents, and said, "Let me call you back." She closed her phone and smiled as she set down her bags. "Hi, darling."

"Nicole, come this way." He guided her by the small of her back, pressing his hand into her skin forcefully. "This is Agent Kline and Agent Moore. They're with the FBI."

"Oh," she said, offering a stiff hand. "Nicole Leville."

Both men stood and shook her hand.

"They're here about Joel's death."

She shook her head. "So sad." A small pout formed on her lips. He'd bought into her expressions all these years; why wouldn't they? Perhaps she was truly sad at her lover's death, though she had never given any indication of it. The evening he had died, she was supposedly out at her favorite club. When she had come through the door at 1 a.m., intoxicated and giddy, she had pulled up a barstool in the kitchen and begun eating ice cream.

Agent Kline said, "We were just talking to your husband about your visit to give condolences to Anita Lamberson and their children."

"She was very upset."

"Yes, I'm sure."

"Ira has had a tough time getting over Joel's death too. When they worked together, they were very close." She stood by Ira and put her small arm around his large waist.

"So you didn't attend the funeral?"

"No. We were in the Caribbean at the time, unfortunately."

"What did Anita say to you when you offered condolences?"

Nicole looked up at Ira casually, as if wondering which one of them would answer. Ira gave her a smile indicating she could answer. Why not?

"She just kept talking about what a great father and husband he was."

"Did she have any idea about who might've killed him?"

"She didn't really want to talk about that. We asked her if the police had found anything, but she said she wanted to concentrate on the good memories."

"While you were there, did either of you ask for any documents?"

Ira felt every muscle in his body stiffen. These agents knew *something*. What they knew exactly, he wasn't sure.

Nicole said, "What documents?"

"Anita mentioned you'd come over looking for documents."

"No," Ira said. "We weren't there for any business. Nicole brought a casserole, I think. And we were there for only about fifteen minutes."

"Just to clarify," Agent Kline said, "you had no business dealings with Joel Lamberson after he left your company."

"That's correct." Ira looked at his watch. He took a card from his breast pocket. "I have to go, but here is my

card. Please call me if I can be of any further assistance to
you."

Nicole showed the agents to the door, flipping her hair
off her shoulders and thanking them for coming by. When
she shut the door, she leaned against it and grinned at him.
"I found the most amazing sweater! I have to go try it on for
you."

"I'm late for work."

"Oh, c'mon! Don't be such a workaholic." She grabbed
her bags and trotted up the stairs.

Ira felt that familiar rage creep into the chambers of his
heart. It was the same rage he'd felt the night Joel had
ambushed him at the office. How could Nicole act as if she
didn't have a care in the world?

He'd underestimated her in the most astonishing way. If
he was going to live to see the light of day much longer, he
was going to have to find out where she'd hidden those
documents before the FBI did.

Reggie asked, "You want to grab some lunch?"

Mick stared out the car window.

"You're far away, dude. You thinking about Mr. and
Mrs. Rich Pants?"

Mick smiled. "You think Nicole was there . . . at Anita's?"

"I'm not sure. I don't see why she wouldn't be. Makes
sense she would go with her husband."

"But don't you think Anita would've mentioned her?"

"Yeah, maybe. But Anita looks like a shaken-up, unstable woman. Details like that aren't important to her."

"What'd you think of Ira Leville?"

"Seems to be hiding something."

"That's what I got too. We may need that search
warrant after all."

"That's going to be a tough one to get. There's no evidence linking these two men."

"Except Anita, who witnessed Ira going through her husband's office in search of documents."

"True. So what about lunch? I'm starving."

"Can't go to lunch today. I've got an errand to run."

———

The old, refurbished firehouse, rumored to be from the forties, stood quaintly unobtrusive on a corner in Irving. It looked homey, with flowers and a mailbox out front and an overly large garage in the back. There had been some changes, like the addition of a front door and a porch, which made it look more like a house and less like a fire station. But it still had that firehouse feel to it.

Mick pulled his truck to the curb. He hadn't seen Detective Shep Crawford for years, and that was fine with him. Even though Mick had also chosen a life of law enforcement, he never could get over the detective's ambiguity. In one sense, this man had saved his life. Had Mick not been in Crawford's custody at the time Stephen Fiscall was murdered, he might have been their first suspect. But it was the memory of the uncanny way Detective Crawford had stared into his eyes—with a quiet, unforced vengeance—that even now was causing a prickly sensation to cover his body.

There was the other side of Crawford—a strange, compassionate side—that had lent him to be Mick's ally, and at one point his only ally. Crawford had hinted that he believed in Mick's innocence, but it did nothing to explain his dogmatic tendencies.

Mick opened his truck door. Something about Detective Crawford had piqued his brother's interest, and Mick couldn't shake the feeling that Crawford might be the key

to finding some truth about Sammy Earle. Maybe he knew
more about the case against Earle than was ever reported at
court or in the newspapers.

Mick walked up the sidewalk and to the front porch,
small but tidy. He blew out a tense breath and knocked.

A few seconds later, the door opened. Crawford stood
there, his back hunched more than he remembered. He
peered out at Mick, with no recognition. The shadow of the
door kept those intense, piercing eyes hidden for the
moment. "You selling something?"

"No, Detective Crawford. You may not remember me,
but you chased me across half the state of Texas about ten
years ago."

The detective opened the door wider, revealing his
chronically fierce stare. While he looked Mick up and
down, Mick couldn't help but notice how much he had
aged. His hair was completely white now, a shaky hand
resting on the doorknob. He didn't look nearly as threatening as he remembered. "Who?"

"Mick Kline, sir."

His eyes flashed. He looked hard into Mick's face, not
a hint of a smile to be found. "Mick Kline."

"Yes, sir. Do you remember me?"

"How could I forget?" He stood a little taller, brushing
down the shirttail that hung over his cargo shorts. He was
wearing deck shoes. "What do you want?"

"Just a moment of your time, sir."

"Why?"

"It's a little complicated."

Crawford appeared distracted, pulling at a strand of
hair near his ear, his eyes distant, slightly cold. He studied
Mick one more time. "Come in."

Mick followed him inside. The firehouse had been
redone, with a spacious living area, an open kitchen, and

two hallways at opposite ends, leading out of sight. An iron stairwell circled up to a balcony. The decor was that of a man who looked like he'd fulfilled his ambitions of retiring near the ocean. Paintings of the ocean hung on otherwise bare walls, and a few wooden sailboats sat on tabletops.

He gestured that Mick should sit in one of the chairs in the living room. Mick noted plenty of books lying around in neat stacks.

Crawford was still eyeing Mick. He noticed the cast. "Are you staying out of trouble these days?"

"I am. I work for the FBI now."

This lit Crawford's shadowy expression. "The FBI." A smile-free chuckle caused pause. "That surprises me."

"What happened ten years ago changed my life. I decided to get my act together. I became a Christian, applied for the academy, and the rest is history."

"Just like your brother, Aaron. How is he?" The question was asked without the slightest bit of interest.

"He died."

Crawford didn't say anything, as if Mick were talking about his favorite houseplant.

"Look, I don't want to keep you any longer than necessary, but I wanted to ask you a few questions about the Sammy Earle case."

Crawford kept his eyes downcast. His thoughts seemed to linger a few sentences behind the conversation. He finally looked up. "What about it?"

"As you probably have read in the papers, Earle is about to be executed for Stephen Fiscall's murder."

"I don't read the paper. I don't keep up with the news."

Mick cleared his throat. "I see. Well, he's only got less than two weeks left before his execution."

He simply stared at Mick without restraint.

"Anyway, ever since Earle was charged with Fiscall's murder, he has claimed he is innocent."

Crawford snorted, the first sign of emotion. "These men who cannot fathom their own downfall," he said, shaking his head. And that was all.

Mick continued. "He claims he was set up."

Crawford said with a wry smile, "And you believe him. That's why you're here. You believe him."

"I think he's got some valid concerns." Mick was wavering on how much he should tell Detective Crawford about what he knew.

"So why are you here?"

"I'm just wondering if there was anything about the case that you can recall that might lend itself to Earle's claim of innocence. Any small detail that at the time didn't seem significant but now might be a clue to Earle's claim that he was set up."

A giant, condescending grin stretched across Crawford's face. He engaged Mick for the first time, leaning forward and propping his elbows on his knees. "Are you telling me this guy has actually convinced you that he didn't kill Stephen Fiscall?"

"I'm not convinced. But there are things that are worthy of exploring, especially if a man is going to die for something he didn't do."

"I believe in the justice system. You should too if you're going to do your job with any satisfaction."

"I believe in the justice system. But people are flawed. Sometimes mistakes are made."

"So it was a mistake that Earle's fingerprints were all over Fiscall's home? that there was motive in the note we found? that Fiscall's skull was crushed, and then he was shot to try to make it look like a suicide?"

"Like I said, Earle claims he was set up."

"Right." Crawford leaned back into his chair, crossed his legs, and observed Mick as if he were a filleted frog about to be dissected by an eager eighth-grade boy. "And you say you're with the bureau. What got you interested in this case in the first place, Kline? I mean, less than two weeks before a man's execution is a little late, isn't it?"

"I found some things of my brother's. A box of stuff about the trial. Before his death, he had been looking into Earle's innocence."

Crawford's smile faded deliberately. "So this was your brother's idea."

"It was my idea to pursue it."

"I see. Your brother always did have a great deal of influence on you, didn't he?"

"In the best ways imaginable."

"Religious fellow, wasn't he?"

"A Christian, yes. Now, back to the—"

"How did Aaron die?"

Mick felt himself growing frustrated. Crawford was avoiding the topic, which was striking a curious cord inside Mick's gut. "He was murdered."

"By whom?"

"Why does it matter?"

"Did they catch the person who did it?"

"Yes."

"Good. Then justice was served. I believe that no wretched man can live in freedom. Their souls decay until they are finally eaten up by their own disgusting bile."

"Detective Crawford, with all due respect, I'm not here to talk about Aaron. I really just want to know if you have any reason to believe that Sammy Earle did not kill Stephen Fiscall."

"I have no reason to think that Sammy Earle deserves

any sort of hope of getting out of the mess he put himself
into."

"Hope is a God-given right."

"Perhaps. But God has always been a little weak in His
efforts at justice, don't you think?"

"God isn't weak at all. His ways are higher than ours."

Crawford blinked slowly, as if tolerating Mick's explanation. "You Christians are always the same. Making
excuses for your God. The fact of the matter is that when
you can't explain why things happen, you chalk it up to
your God being mysterious yet somehow insatiably good.
How can you live like that? Really? It's an entire life philos-
ophy built on the idea of a God who can't control His
universe."

Mick clenched his jaw. "I didn't come here to debate
Christianity with you."

"Sure you did. Isn't that your real motive behind all
this, Mick? Your deep sense of right and wrong. Could you
live with yourself if, God forbid, you let an innocent man
die when you might've had the ability to save him? If Earle
is innocent, why not let God save him? Maybe we don't
need God after all. Isn't the need for justice an innate part
of our human nature?"

"The sense of justice is a part of human nature, because
we are made in the image of God."

Crawford stood suddenly, casually, looking down at
Mick. "You're a lot like your brother; you know that?"

"I take that as a compliment."

"I was sure you would." He walked to the kitchen and
took a bottle of water from his fridge. "There's nothing to
look for. Earle is making one last effort to save his own life.
Instead of repenting for his sins, he's decided to make up
some crazy story about being set up. I'm a little surprised
you're buying into it."

"There are others out there who believe he is innocent." Mick chose not to deliver the details of the letters he'd been receiving. The less Crawford knew the better.

This surprised Crawford, and as he screwed the lid off his water, his expression turned to amusement. "Interesting. So there's more than one sucker out there."

"Look," Mick said, standing and walking toward the front door, "I just thought you might be willing to offer up some ideas. You're supposed to be one of the most brilliant homicide detectives around. I thought you might find the idea compelling."

"I find it sickening. From the day Sammy Earle decided he thought he was a man, he became the worst sort of representative of the human race. He's a coward and a loser. Surely quite an embarrassment to God's lofty ideas of who man should be."

Mick opened the door. "Thank you for your time."

"One more thing," Crawford said, moving toward the door. "Did Earle happen to mention which of his many enemies he thought might have 'framed him' for murder?"

"He thinks it was a man named Patrick Delano."

"If memory serves me correctly, he was the man who killed Earle's best friend in Vietnam."

"That's right. He was convicted of murder, but he escaped and has never been seen since."

"Interesting theory. Really convenient, since this ghost of a man can't be found."

Mick made himself look Crawford directly in the eye. The man was full of self-righteous intimidation, and Mick was not one to be easily intimidated. Though Crawford's creepy ways did send a chill or two up his spine, he wasn't about to back down this easily. But in the moment they locked eyes, Mick felt an urgency to leave. The flutter deep inside his spirit surprised him as much as it scared him.

Crawford held his gaze a moment longer, then with a flick of his hand gestured for Mick to leave.

Mick walked briskly down the porch steps. He wanted to look back, but he didn't. Yet he was sure that from somewhere in the house Shep Crawford was watching him drive away.

chapter nineteen

It took Mick an extra two miles added to his usual five-mile run to settle himself down the next morning. He loved his Saturday morning runs, and the cool weather made it even better. He usually kept to three-mile runs during the week, but on Saturdays he loved to take the long route through his favorite park and blow off a week's worth of steam.

He couldn't get Crawford out of his brain. He'd dreamt about him last night, reliving that horrible night when, close to death, he'd had his showdown with Crawford. And lost.

Perhaps it was Crawford's blatant arrogance that had gotten under his skin yesterday. Or the way he knew that his disrespect for God would agitate Mick, which it did. Maybe that's what made Crawford so good at what he did. He knew what made people tick; he understood which buttons to push when.

That took one extra mile.

The second extra mile was devoted to thoughts of Sammy Earle. As strange and ominous as the anonymous notes were, it was probably the reason he was paying so much attention to the Earle case. It was a second source, and it was from someone who didn't want to be dragged into it. But who could it be? Someone who knew more than he or she should.

Once at home, Mick grabbed a Coke out of the fridge

and collapsed onto his couch. He clicked on the Weather Channel and kicked off his running shoes.

"Tropical storm Eve is making its way through the Caribbean, and all indications are that it will do nothing but strengthen as it heads toward the United States. Projection right now is still a guess, but it looks to be headed toward the Louisiana and Mississippi coastlines, perhaps even as far west as Texas if it keeps turning as it has been. . . ."

Mick turned up the volume. ". . . landfall as early as next week."

Perfect! Tornadoes from hurricanes weren't usually as impressive or powerful as other tornadoes, but it was still worth making plans to do some autumn storm chasing. Of course, a date might not be a bad alternative, though he was still trying to decide what exactly he should be doing about the dating predicament he found himself in. Back in the old days this would not have been a problem. But ten years of the straight and narrow had caused him to completely lose the deftness he might have once used for this kind of situation.

He knew one thing for sure: a shower was in order.

Thanks to Reggie's remark about Jenny, he was now spending his morning shower trying to decide if there was any truth to the statement that he still had feelings for Jenny. It had been many years since he'd fallen in love with her and she'd chosen his brother over him. Mick had to admit there had been some unresolved feelings that still lingered up until Aaron's death. He couldn't help but think he had let the perfect woman get away.

But as they shared their grief over Aaron's death, those feelings for Jenny had seemed to fade. He watched her life unravel without Aaron, and Mick wondered how he could have ever competed for her attention anyway. He'd willfully

sat on the sidelines and watched his brother enjoy a beautiful, uncomplicated marriage, all the while hoping that there
was, indeed, that same thing waiting for him in his future.

He was beginning to have his doubts.

And he was wondering if it was his grief over Aaron's
death that had masked his feelings for Jenny over the past
year. Maybe they were still there, well hidden but ready to
emerge at a moment's notice. He did care deeply for her,
but it seemed more sisterly now.

He shook the water out of his hair as he shook off the
thoughts. He got dressed and considered what he was going
to do for the rest of the day.

There were a lot of unanswered questions in his life
right now, and perhaps it was time to try to answer a few.

"Mick!" Jenny greeted him with a hug and a gigantic grin.
Her hair was twisted on top of her head, and she was
dressed in shorts and a T-shirt, without any makeup on,
which was how she looked best. "I'm just doing some cleaning. Come on in."

"Thanks." He walked in and smelled Pine-Sol. It was a
good smell. He always attributed that to the idea that somewhere nearby a woman was in complete control.

"What are you doing here?"

Mick smiled and found his way to the couch, where he
plopped down, let out a huge sigh, and shrugged.

"You don't know?" She laughed, joining him on the
couch.

"My life has suddenly become very complicated."

"How so?"

Again, he shrugged, mustering up the confidence and
words to try to explain all the thoughts that had pounded
him in the shower and then slid down the drain.

"You okay?" Jenny asked after a long pause.

"I went to see Shep Crawford."

"You did?" Her eyes widened. "Why?"

"To talk to him about Sammy Earle. The guy called me again, claiming his old Vietnam nemesis is alive and that he's the one who set him up for the murder of Fiscall."

Jenny shook her head. "Wow. So what did Crawford say?"

"Nothing that helped. But while I was there I felt this dread wash over me. I felt I was in danger."

"Really?"

"Yeah. It was kind of weird. We were having a conversation. Not a typical conversation, by any stretch of the imagination. The guy's weird and there's no denying that. But when I was leaving, I felt . . ." Mick couldn't find the right word to describe it.

"What do you think it means?"

"I'm not sure. I do know that Aaron had some interest in Crawford, but to what extent and why, I don't know. I can only imagine Aaron was thinking the same thing I was thinking."

"Which is?"

"That Crawford, being the lead detective in the case, might have picked up on some clues that he never mentioned. Maybe he was intent on getting Earle and didn't bother following up on something else."

"Doesn't sound like the Crawford we knew. The man was a perfectionist, if I remember correctly."

"You remember correctly. His home is still meticulously clean and organized."

"You went to his house?"

"Yeah."

"I remember Aaron talking about his house, but he didn't say much more than he thought it was an apt representation of Crawford." Jenny looked down. "In fact, Aaron didn't talk much about the man. But I always sensed he did a great deal of thinking about him."

"Tell me anything you remember about after Fiscall was murdered and I was let out of jail. When do you think Aaron started gathering some of this information?"

"I'm not sure. For a couple of weeks afterward, Aaron was in shock. I think he saw how close he had come to losing you, and it really shook him up. He followed the Sammy Earle case closely in the newspaper, and the next year I remember him following the court case. Maybe that's when he got interested. After Earle got convicted. But he never told me that he thought Earle didn't do it."

"Well—" Mick sighed—"Earle was my ticket to freedom that day. I would have been exonerated eventually, perhaps, especially if Taylor Franks would have shown up, but maybe Aaron didn't want to shake things up. Maybe he just wanted to prod around."

"Aaron never wanted me to worry about his work, so he didn't talk about it much. We had our lives outside of his work, and that's what he concentrated on."

"Do you ever remember him receiving any strange letters or phone calls?"

"I don't remember anything at all about it. I'm sorry."

"That's okay." Mick leaned back into the couch.

"You seem distracted and worried. You really think Earle may be innocent?"

"That, and I think I'm in love with two women."

"Really?"

"Yeah. I don't know what to do."

"Who?"

"Well, maybe I should keep that out of the conversation."

"Why?"

"Because I came over to make sure I'm not in love with three women."

Jenny's mouth dropped open a little, and she blinked as if she were trying to comprehend a complex mathematical equation.

Mick laughed at himself. He always did have a tendency to let reason fly out the window where Jenny was concerned. He'd made a fool of himself many times for her sake. There was no reason to stop now.

Jenny stared at her shoes in the exact same way she had years ago when he'd gone to the school where she worked to try to talk her out of marrying his brother. That same expression—compassion mixed with strain—now froze her features in place.

It was going to be painful, but he had to know—to get on with trying to figure out if there was a chance for love in his future at all.

She finally looked at him. He was surprised to find her smiling. With his arms still plopped on top of his head, he suddenly wondered if he'd put on deodorant. He let his arms drop to his sides. Maybe this would be a good time to add, *I'm just kidding*.

"We always had something special, Mick," she began.

He could almost finish her sentence: *something special as friends*.

But she stopped. Her mouth was open slightly, and her gaze was on his mouth, as if she was expecting him to say something next.

Strangely, he'd forgotten how to speak.

"Are you all right?"

"Yeah," Mick croaked. He cleared his throat. "What exactly are you saying?"

"What exactly are *you* saying?"

A sheet of dampness covered his skin, and he found

himself wiping his brow. He stood and walked to the other side of the small living room. He tried to find something to casually lean on, but there was only a fish tank. He eyed the fish, and they seemed to be eyeing him.

Great. An audience.

"I don't know. I just . . . I . . . I wanted . . ." He stopped himself after the third attempt to construct a sentence. He closed his eyes, and after mentally lashing himself for being so stupid, he gathered his thoughts, opened his eyes, and said, "I've always had feelings for you."

"I know." She smiled.

"And I really . . ."

Her beautiful eyes stared back at him with anticipation.

". . . really like these women."

The hint of pleasure on her face faded. "Then why are you here talking to me?"

"It was a stupid thing to say. I just thought . . ."

"What, Mick? I'm having a hard time following you here." Her tone was turning curt.

"For years I've had to remind myself you were Aaron's. I always respected that, Jenny. I never once infringed on your relationship."

"I know that."

"But Aaron's gone now."

They both swallowed . . . hard. It wasn't something they'd ever discussed before, and he wasn't sure the timing was right.

Tears formed in Jenny's eyes.

"I've upset you." Mick walked to the coffee table and swiped his keys. "I didn't mean to do that." He started to walk past her.

She touched his arm. "If you came here to make sure it's okay to move on, Mick, then yes, it's okay to move on."

Mick paused beside her. She smelled the same way she

always did, wore the same perfume she had since he'd known her. But her words had a double meaning. What was she trying to say? That he should move on and get over his feelings for her? Or that it was now okay for them to move on together, that Aaron would want them both to be happy? Her calm, graceful, teary eyes did nothing to help clarify her meaning.

"Go with your heart," she said gently, and without further ado, she tucked a few strands of hair behind her ears and grabbed her cleaning rag. "You want something to eat?"

"Uh, no, I gotta run," he said.

She smiled confidently at him, as if there had not been a horribly awkward conversation just moments before. Jenny's inner strength had been what had drawn him before. It was drawing him again. He knew instantly that Reggie was right. There were still unresolved feelings there. But he wasn't ready to admit they were anything more than that.

Mick tried to smile back. "I'll talk to you soon." He left, wondering if there was any bigger idiot in the world than he was.

———

It was four in the afternoon and two college football games later when Mick finally decided that perhaps flipping a coin was the best way to figure out who he should call for a date tonight. He'd been much better at this in high school.

He really liked and enjoyed being with both women, but most of what he knew about Libby came from their work experience, and most of what he knew about Faith came from helping her through the death of her husband. He needed to spend more time with each of them outside of what he'd known them for.

It was time for a new playing field. He turned off the TV.

Mick took out a quarter and assigned Libby heads and Faith tails. Surely fate would cooperate with his indecisiveness and help him out. Many football victories had been decided by such a flip.

The quarter twirled high in the air, glinting in the light, hit the floor, and rolled under the couch.

"Great." He knew he couldn't lift the couch with his arm in the cast, so with a groan, he maneuvered the couch aside with his good shoulder. But he couldn't see the coin.

"Forget it," he muttered, shoving the couch back in place. He reached in his pocket for another coin, but there was nothing. "This is terrific." He pulled the cushions up from the couch and found a shiny penny. He was losing credit already.

He flipped the coin in the air, more gently this time, and it landed on the coffee table. On tails.

"Faith. Faith, okay, Faith. Good." He went to his desk and found her number. Without any further hesitation, he dialed it. Her line was busy. Was this a sign? Maybe he should call Libby. Should he wait? His fingers drummed against the phone. And then, to his astonishment, it rang.

He snatched it up. "Hello?"

"Mick, it's Libby."

"Libby . . ."

"Yeah, Libby. You sound shocked."

"No, not at all. I was . . . I was just getting ready to call you." Oh, he wanted to barf. He said it with his eyes squeezed shut. So far, he was not making a good impression on behalf of dateless, God-fearing bachelors worldwide.

"No kidding. What timing. Why were you going to call me?"

"I, um . . ." Now he was truly nauseous. Libby was a much tougher sell. Sure, they had chemistry, but that was a far cry from an actual date, where he had to actually say the word. "Date."

"What?"

He fell into the chair by his desk. His knees were actually shaking. This was a pathetic display if he ever saw one. It felt just like junior high.

"Hello? Kline, you there?"

"Sorry. I'm just, uh, wondering if . . ."

"I think we're on the same page."

"Really?"

"Yeah. You've been thinking about those letters you've been getting, haven't you?"

"The letters?"

"I can't get them off my mind. I mean, mysterious letters, spelling out something about your past. Admittedly, I'm intrigued. So I've been doing a little investigation. I know, I know; it's your mystery. But I couldn't help myself. Besides, they won't let me go back to work, so I've got tons of time on my hands."

Time on her hands. That's good. Mick crossed his legs in hopes that his body language might drop a few hints to his flash-frozen tongue. "So how about we get together tonight and talk about it?"

"Can't. I have mass."

Mass. Right. "Well, does it last all night?"

"Uh . . ."

Was she thinking out an answer or an excuse? Mick decided he'd made a fool of himself once today, so why not make it twice? "I would love to take you to dinner afterward."

A pause. He could hear her breathing.

"Kline," she finally said, "are you asking me out?"

"I am."

Another pause, which gave him time to quadruple knot his tennis shoes.

"Okay. Yeah. Why not?"

Why not? It was strike two, and he wasn't even sure if he was in the game. "Great." He tried to sound charmingly enthused.

"I think you're going to find my research pretty interesting," she said.

"I'll look forward to it. How does eight sound?"

"Like enough time for me to pray for you." She laughed. "You don't know what you're getting yourself into."

That was the truest statement he'd heard all day.

chapter twenty

the small Italian bistro buzzed with Saturday night activity. Mick had made reservations, and a table for two near the window was waiting for them. He was glad he'd had four hours to prepare. It had taken him an hour to decide whether some gel in his hair would invite unnecessary banter, but he had to admit, it was Libby's feistiness that had attracted him in the first place.

Libby was dressed in a black lightweight sweater over a blouse, a short gray skirt, and matching tights. She looked stunning and extremely feminine. A small gold heart necklace dangled around her neck, and she rubbed it as if it were a good-luck charm.

He pulled her chair out, and that seemed to impress her. She watched him as he took his own seat. "You're quite a gentleman, Kline."

"You might want to wait until you see me eat." He laughed.

She laughed too. Good. She liked his stupid jokes, which made up about 86 percent of his personality.

She looked around the restaurant. "Charming little place. You bring all your dates here?"

He smiled. Nice try. "Only the ones who carry guns."

She laughed and then sighed. "I don't think that's going to be me much longer."

"Why?"

"I'm not recovering very quickly. My leg still isn't working right. I'm having some memory problems. I've even had a couple of seizures, though the meds seem to be helping. And my boss, though good at what he does, isn't known for his compassion." She shrugged. "So there you have it. I'm looking at desk work for the rest of my ATF career."

"I'm sorry. I guess I didn't realize your injuries were going to be debilitating."

"I didn't either. But life's full of surprises, right? Like when a bureau agent asks you out. That's surprising." She grinned away the sadness that had washed over her face. She glanced down at the menu. "What's good here?"

"The company."

"You're something else, Kline."

Cheesy compliments made up the other 14 percent of his personality. But he'd made her smile. And he liked to see her smile. She looked like she needed to do more of that, especially if her ATF career, at least as she knew it, was indeed ending.

After reading menu, she told him to order for her, which he took great pride in doing. Before long, they'd settled into an easygoing conversation. It seemed like only minutes, and dinner was finished. Mick ordered dessert, just to lengthen the evening.

As they waited for dessert, Libby pulled a folder out of her bag. Inside she'd jotted down some notes on a yellow piece of paper. "I figured out what newspaper those headlines came from."

"You'd mentioned you didn't think these came from the *Dallas Morning News*. I just figured since they were sent from Dallas, it was from that paper."

"It was the font and some other structural things about the layout of the headings that tipped me off. What can

I say? I was a journalism major before I decided to become a firefighter."

"Why did you become a firefighter? It's tough to break into that profession, isn't it?"

"Being a woman, you mean?"

"Yeah."

"It was. But I had nothing to lose. At that point in my life, I'd lost all direction and all interest in life. I found something I had a passion for, and that's what drove me."

"Why'd you leave?"

She hesitated, then smiled gently as the waiter placed the dessert between them and handed them each a spoon. She took a bite. "This is good."

"You're not going to tell me?"

"Tell you what?"

"Why you left firefighting?"

Her eyes closed in a long blink. When she opened them, she studied the dessert, but her eyes were distant with clouded memories.

"It's okay. You don't have to tell me."

"I really love working for the ATF," she said. "Maybe a desk job won't be so bad. It's what makes you tick, right?"

He grinned. "That, and a little storm chasing on the side."

"Can I go sometime?"

Mick could feel a smile stretch across his face. "I would love it."

"I would've never thought that about you, Kline. That you had an adventurous side."

"I'm kind of a paradox."

"I used to love to go skydiving, but I think that part of my life is over. Maybe some storm chasing would do me some good."

"Mark your weekends in April, May, and June."

"I've never had a man take up every weekend in my spring."

Mick laughed. She was charming his socks off. "So, tell me what you found out about these headlines."

"All of these headlines came from the same newspaper. In fact, they came from the same day. I got on the Internet, typed the headlines in, and after about two hours, I had them matched to one particular newspaper."

"Which one is that?"

"The *Wichita Eagle*. Is that significant?"

"Yeah. Could be real significant. I know someone who used to live in Wichita. Not sure if she's still there. What are you doing tomorrow?"

It took almost six hours to drive to Wichita, but the time flew with Libby by his side. Mick had picked her up after church, and they'd driven straight north on I-35.

He'd spent time at the office after their date last night, trying to figure out if Taylor Franks had returned to Wichita after her arrest for faking a kidnapping. She'd served only a few months of her sentence, and during that time, they'd stayed in touch some. But after she left jail, he hadn't talked to her at all.

Taylor Franks had been the beautiful, intriguing woman who had caused his life to be nearly catastrophic. But it was in that catastrophe that he'd finally found a sense of direction in his life . . . something that didn't require a football in his hand or a woman on his arm. He had turned his life around and entered the FBI Adademy.

It was what his brother had been trying to tell him for years—that he was created in God's image, that his life held purpose, that he had been willingly throwing it all away for booze and parties. Mick had been in his most desperate hour when he'd found salvation. And not once since then had he departed from it. Maybe that's why he hadn't stayed in touch with Taylor. She was a reminder of how close he'd come to losing everything.

But admittedly, he was intrigued by the idea that she might be behind the letters. It didn't make much sense. The postmarks on the envelopes were from Dallas, but knowing the papers came from Wichita was his first promising clue in this mess.

On the way to Wichita, Libby kept most of the conversation focused on Mick. She quizzed him about everything from his football days to his accounting degree, from the bureau work to his dating life. If she was half as meticulous in her job as she was in her questions, Mick knew she was probably the best of the best. For some strange reason, he didn't mind opening his soul to this woman, even if she wasn't quite ready to reveal hers.

At four in the afternoon, they arrived at Taylor's last known address.

"What a dump," Libby said as they got out of Mick's truck.

"Let's see what we can find out."

Mick and Libby made their way to the second-floor apartment, and Mick knocked on the door. He heard a television and footsteps crossing the floor. He glanced at Libby just as the door opened.

An old woman stood there in a gown and slippers, smoking a cigarette and glaring at the bright light. "Yeah?"

"We're looking for Taylor Franks. Does she live here?"

"Who?"

"Taylor Franks."

"I live here, and my name is Gladys."

"Did you know the previous tenant?"

"No."

"How long have you lived here?"

"Seven years."

"Thanks for your time."

The door slammed and Mick sighed. "Let's go talk to the manager."

The manager's office smelled like a grave, and he looked like he'd just dug one. He apologized by explaining he was having sewage problems in building B. "Always fix the mess, though," he added with a wan expression. "Sometimes it just takes a while."

"We're not from the housing authority," Mick said. "We're here to inquire about a former tenant named Taylor Franks."

"Franks . . . doesn't ring a bell."

"Do you have records on all your former tenants?"

"We keep them for a while."

"How long?"

"I don't know. There's no formula. Whenever we run out of room, we dump the files."

A man who looked like the manager's brother hurried in and said, "It's backing up into B-5 now! Hurry up!"

"If you'll excuse me," the manager said, rushing out the door but leaving a horrible lingering smell.

Libby was swatting her hand in front of her face. "I have a sensitive nose," she explained in a muffled tone.

Mick laughed. "Must make investigating fires really interesting. Keep watch, will you?"

"You bet." She stepped outside the office, and Mick opened a large filing drawer. He didn't find Taylor's name in the *F*s. Behind the desk was a closet door. Mick glanced back at Libby, who gave him a thumbs-up. She appeared relieved to be in fresh air.

The closet door was unlocked, and Mick was surprised

to see how big it was once he found the light. It was full of old boxes stacked to the ceiling. When he paid closer attention, he realized that the boxes in the back of the closet had years marked on them. He located two from 1995, thinking that might be a good place to start.

He opened the first box and found the last part of the alphabet. The second box had *A–J*. He quickly searched the files and soon spotted a label reading *Franks, Taylor*. He snatched it and headed out the closet door.

Outside, Libby looked nearly bored until Mick walked up beside her. "You found something?"

"Let's go."

The neon sign glowing with only one letter capped the squalid window of the diner. Mud and dirt smudged the glass, where a handwritten paper sign announced it was double-mashed-potatoes night. Even inside the truck, the greasy smell of fried food invaded their air.

Mick glanced down at the sheet of paper he'd pulled from the folder. "Becker Milton's Place."

"We got the right address?" Libby asked.

"Looks like it. I don't see anything that says Becker Milton's Place, though."

"So she last worked at a diner."

"Seven years ago. This isn't going to get us anywhere."

"You never know. This part of Wichita isn't terribly big. They may know where she is, even if she's not working here."

He felt Libby watching him.

"You okay?" she asked.

A few wispy shadows crossed the window. "I can't imagine her working here. She was a classy lady."

Libby looked amused. "Classy, huh?"

"I didn't know her all that well, but she once worked at the airport as a gate agent."

"Beautiful too?"

"I was in my twenties. Anything with long legs and a skinny waist was beautiful."

"Now you prefer a bulging middle atop a couple of Vienna-sausage legs?"

Mick cocked an eyebrow at her. "I prefer a woman with depth."

"Well, let's see what life has done to one Taylor Franks." Libby opened the door and struggled out.

Mick followed, wondering how his attraction to a woman a decade ago seemed to affect a woman he was attracted to now. After all these years, he still didn't understand the female species.

Cane in hand, Libby was blazing a trail toward the front door.

Mick tried to keep up. As they approached the diner, he said, "I don't suppose you want to explain why you're mad?"

"I'm not mad."

"You seem mad."

"I'm focused."

"Focused?"

She opened the diner door. Though Christmas was still three months away, a cluster of bells hanging from the door handle like grapes on a vine alerted the customers of the intrusion. They all stared at the two newcomers. Mick noticed there wasn't a plate in sight that didn't have a mound of potatoes on it.

A young, curvy waitress with a double chin watched them walk toward her, where she was wiping a dirty rag over a clean, red counter. "Help you?"

"Is your manager here?" Mick asked.

"Manager?" She was smacking something, but it didn't look like gum.

"Or owner?" Libby added.

"You mean Beck?" She called through a small window, and a few minutes later a large, grumbling man holding a spatula ambled through the double doors. His apron was hanging nearly to his feet because it wasn't tied in the back.

"Yeah?" he snorted to the waitress. "Yeah?" he repeated, redirecting his inquiry to Mick and Libby.

"These two are lookin' for ya," the waitress said.

His fat lips mumbled something as he walked toward them. He noticed a fly on the counter nearby and looked like if it got too close, he might just use the spatula.

"I'm Special Agent Mick Kline. I'm looking for a woman named Taylor Franks."

As the man leaned forward, he almost seemed to emit fumes. A whiff of onion burgers, spaghetti sauce, and butter caused Mick to cough. He glanced at Libby, who looked like she was holding her breath.

Beck's bulging bug eyes, complete with a web of bright red veins around each pupil, narrowed in scrutiny. "Taylor hasn't worked here for some time."

"So you do know her."

"A real pain. A complete and total human disaster."

Mick couldn't hold in his surprise. "What do you mean by that?"

"What do I mean by that?" Beck pulled a rag from his waistband and wiped each pudgy finger as he spoke. "I mean, I lost business because of that broad. I gave her chance after chance. Every time she assured me she'd get her act together, and she would for a while. But then things started slipping, and the next thing I know she's not showing up."

"How long ago did she work here?"

"I fired her about a year ago. For good."

"You'd fired her before?"

He shrugged, running his rag underneath his fingernails and studying his hand as if he were contemplating a manicure. "She was a persuasive woman."

This caused Libby to let out a short laugh, as if she had personally witnessed Taylor's persuasiveness in some weird time warp.

Mick eyed her but continued. "Do you know where we can find her?"

Beck dropped the rag to the counter. "Will it make you two go away? I got regulars in here that don't like company, if you know what I mean."

"Sure. We'll get out of your hair if you tell me where I can find her."

"Like I said, I haven't seen her in a year, but the last time I checked, she was living in the projects, eight blocks west of here. You can't miss 'em. Just follow the smell."

Mick couldn't believe what he was hearing. The Taylor he knew had such strong ambitions and had been doing so well back then. What happened?

Mick and Libby turned for the door.

Beck added, "And if you don't find her there, I'd check on the corner of South Broadway and Harry."

"What's there?" Mick asked.

Beck snorted. "A lot of fun if you brought some cash."

A group of dark gray apartments, squeezed between older, larger, redbrick buildings, looked almost like a plume of smoke amidst domineering flames. A few people milled about outside. Mick and Libby drew immediate attention as they parked and got out.

An old man smoking two cigarettes and sitting outside his door on a bucket stood as they approached. "What do you want?" he demanded.

Mick held up his hand, then his badge. "We're looking for a woman named Taylor Franks."

"Don't know nobody like that. We ain't on a first-name basis here."

"Have you seen a woman, late thirties, with brown hair around here?"

"Leave me alone," he grumbled and took his bucket and cigarettes inside.

"Should we split up?" Libby asked.

"No." Mick wasn't about to leave a woman, no matter how tough, alone in these circumstances.

Libby smiled at him. "I can take care of myself."

"That's what I'm afraid of. I don't want to be outdone by a woman."

A gruff, obese woman approached them cautiously. "Who you lookin' for?"

"Taylor Franks," Libby said.

Mick liked how she sensed this woman might be more apt to talk to a female.

The woman's eyebrows looked like a mustache across her forehead, and she raised them with interest. "That's what I thought you said." She smiled. "You with the police?"

"Why don't you tell us what you know?" Mick asked.

"I know that this woman's a nuisance."

"Are you sure you're talkin' about Taylor Franks?"

"I know who you're talkin' about. She lives right below me and makes my life miserable. She's a fruitcake if I ever saw one."

Mick tried to size up the woman, but she seemed intent on what she was saying.

"I could use some peace and quiet," she said. "I may be one of the only people around here that takes care of their home, but I do. I want this to be a place my children can come visit."

Libby said, "You say she lives right below you, ma'am?"

"The name's Rue. I'd be more than happy to lead the way."

A narrow window next to the door glowed orange through the threadbare white curtain that hung lopsidedly against the glass. After peering through it, Libby shook her head. "I can't see anything."

"We could try knocking," Mick said with a smile. He turned to Rue, who stood there with a pleasurable look on her face. "If we need any more assistance, we know where to find you."

Libby knocked, but there was no answer. "Now what?"

"Maybe we should kick the door in."

"I don't think that's such a good idea."

"How else are we supposed to get in? I didn't drive all the way here to turn around again."

"You know how much trouble you can get in for breaking and entering, right?"

Back and forth they argued until suddenly Mick realized the door was wide open.

Rue stood there grinning. "A little known secret . . . the keys work on all the locks. I thought I heard someone scream, so I opened the door to make sure she was okay."

Mick and Libby exchanged glances.

A heavy, stale odor drifted out. "I'm going to need some aromatherapy before this day's out," Libby grumbled.

Mick stepped into the doorway. He could feel Rue hovering behind them.

"Taylor?" Mick called out. The apartment was tiny, about the size of two hotel rooms. The orange light was the glow from a bedside lamp with an orange shade. The bed was a ratty mattress on the floor, with a sheet thrown over the top and a ripped quilt on top of that. It looked like a boy's college dorm room, minus the trashy posters, school pendants, and high-tech computer equipment. The walls were bare, the floor a sea of Chinese take-out containers and pizza boxes.

Rue spat. "What a way to live. She could use a maid."

Libby guided Rue outside, and Mick could hear her explaining why Rue needed to let them do what they needed to do . . . alone.

Mick walked toward the bed and scanned the room, trying to find something that would identify this as Taylor's. Nothing here even remotely resembled the Taylor Franks he knew. What he remembered of her apartment years ago was that it was clean, homey, and fragrant.

Of course, that was where his nightmare had begun.

Mick waded through the trash-strewn floor and turned to the doorway, where Libby was making her way back in. "This can't be her place," he said.

"Why?"

"I think Rue just wants this neighbor out of her hair."

"Could be. She was pretty adamant about how miserable it's making her life. But this isn't the Ritz-Carlton, either."

Mick laughed and said, "Well, we better get out of here before we find ourselves in trouble with someone other than Rue."

Then they heard a moan.

Libby stepped forward, putting her finger to her lips.

They heard it again.

Mick held up his hand as Libby started toward the darkened bathroom. "Stay here," he whispered.

Libby shot him a look but complied.

He approached the bathroom, trying not to make much noise. The moan grew louder. As soon as he stepped in front of the bathroom door, he could see two bare feet on the floor.

He motioned for Libby. Flipping on the light, he saw a woman, her head against the side of the toilet, her body lying motionless on the tile floor, her mouth gaping.

"Help me get her to the bed." Mick stood in the grimy bathtub and pulled the woman's shoulder up. His cast made it difficult to maneuver her.

Libby leaned her cane against the wall, then helped swing the woman's arm around Mick's neck. "You got her?"

"Yeah," Mick said, carefully dragging the woman to the bed, where he laid her down, sweeping her dark hair from her face.

"Is it her?"

"No," Mick said. The woman's cheeks were puffy, her eyes rimmed with red, encircled with dark purple. She was trying to open her eyes, falling in and out of consciousness. "Ma'am, are you okay?" He patted her cheek lightly. "What drug are you taking?"

The woman groaned, slapping away Mick's hand. She opened her eyes suddenly and turned her head, looking directly at Mick.

He froze.

"Mick?" Libby touched his shoulder.

"I can't believe it."

"What?"

"It's Taylor."

eat at your own risk," Libby said, walking through the door with two cartons of Chinese food. "I see why there're so many of these boxes here. That's all that's around. I've never wished so hard for a McDonald's."

Mick's stomach grumbled enough that he didn't really care. Libby tossed him some chopsticks, and he opened his box of meatless, veggie-less lo mein. He wasn't familiar with the restaurant or this town, so he didn't want to take any chances that the same knife that was used to chop raw meat was used to chop raw vegetables.

"Has she woken up?" Libby asked.

"In and out," Mick said, studying Taylor in the dim light of the room. They'd been here for three hours, and Taylor had done little more than groan. There was a flicker of recognition in her eyes when they'd first found her, but it faded into oblivion and she'd been nearly unconscious ever since.

Libby had told him it was white heroin. The norm used to be brown Mexican or black tar heroin. White heroin used to be called China White, a product of the Middle East. She said the amount of white heroin coming from the Middle East, and in particular Afghanistan, was starting to dominate the market again, most likely through France. Chopping off a head or two, she explained, had in the past kept the number of people down who were willing to take the risk. She'd heard a figure recently that heroin production was up 300 percent from prewar levels.

One of the casualties was prostrate on the other side of the room.

They'd examined Taylor's arms, glad to see she didn't have collapsed veins. If she was a user, she was either new or an occasional user. They found one syringe and one small plastic bag, plus cotton balls and a spoon with burn marks on the bottom.

Mick couldn't believe this was Taylor Franks. Ten years ago, she'd been a vibrant, beautiful woman with bright eyes and an enchanting smile. Life had really messed her up. Now her hair was long and stringy, her face swollen from what Mick could only guess was alcohol. She was wearing a short skirt and a skimpy top, so Mick had found a blanket and covered her up.

Across the room, Libby ate her Chinese food and observed silently.

After a few minutes, Mick asked, "You okay?"

"Sure. Just wondering what this crunchy thing is that I keep encountering in my fried rice."

Mick laughed.

"So, were you two pretty close?"

"No," Mick said. "We never got to know each other that well."

"You seem to care about her," Libby said, casting her gaze into her Chinese box.

Mick stood and walked over to where Libby sat, pulling up a heavy box and sitting down on it. "She's had a tough life. When I knew her she looked like she was getting her life together until Sammy Earle tried to destroy it. I'm just sad that it's come to this."

"I hope she can clue you into what those letters were

about." Libby stared across the room at Taylor. "She looks like she was an attractive woman at one time."

Mick shifted on the box. Something about this conversation was making him uncomfortable. He studied Libby. She looked hurt. "Hey," he said gently, "what's going on with you?"

She smiled and continued to eat.

"You look upset."

Libby set down her food and sighed, leaning on her knees and shaking her head, avoiding Mick's eyes. "Am I that transparent?"

Mick swallowed. He wasn't even sure what she was talking about, and he didn't have his woman decoder, Reggie, with him. His worst nightmare was when a woman asked a question, because as far as he could tell, there was hardly ever a right answer. Or if there was a right answer, it was said in the wrong tone.

Libby glanced sideways at him and smiled away a painful expression, seemingly unaware that he hadn't answered, which was a good thing. She bit her lip, as if there were something dying to come out, but it had to get through her clamped teeth first.

"You can tell me," Mick said. That sounded good. Women liked to talk about their problems, and since Mick was uncertain what problem he'd caused, he was willing to be enlightened.

She flicked her hand in the air, grabbed her food, and stuffed her mouth.

Mick smiled. Nice try. He'd used that trick before. "Tell me what's on your mind. Looks like we've got all night."

"Reminds me of some of those long stakeouts I used to do. I was usually the only woman around, so I'd be forced to listen to the guys talk about sports stats, how their wives were making their lives miserable, or women who weren't their wives. They'd talk about that stuff as if I weren't even sitting there. They wouldn't even ask for my opinion."

Mick grinned. "You don't seem like a woman who waits to be asked for it."

"You got that right." She winked. "And there were a few times I let them have it."

"So what's on your mind?"

She sighed and stood, limping to the front window without her cane. She peeked out the curtain into the still, somber night. "It's just insecurity, Kline. Pure and simple. Insecurity."

"About what?"

She turned and leaned against the door, her hands braced behind her. She looked him over, probably wondering if she could trust him.

Mick tried to look meek and sincere. He could feel a lopsided, clumsy grin emerge for no reason, so he self-consciously put a hand over his mouth, which probably made him look ridiculous.

"It's just been a long time since I felt pretty."

"Why?" Mick asked.

She rubbed her arm, the one that had been ravaged by fire. "I get self-conscious, you know? I wonder how anybody could see me as attractive. In a moment of honesty, can you really say that I'm attractive when you look at me?"

Mick had had enough experience with women to know this was definitely not one of those times when a pause was going to make a remark more substantial. So without hesitation, he said, "Libby, honestly, I don't even see or think about that burn scar. I mean, I noticed it one day when you took off your jacket, and I wondered how you got it, but that was it. Sure, burn scars are pretty distinct, but they're just like any other scar. It gives you character. I think you're beautiful. And whether or not you have a huge scar on your arm is inconsequential in my world."

He tried not to smile, but he did think he answered that very smoothly. And he meant it. Libby was one beautiful woman, and it shocked him to think she thought otherwise of herself.

Libby smiled a little and said, "I was talking about the gap between my teeth."

Mick slapped his hand over his mouth again before he muttered a muffled apology.

She started laughing to the point where she was holding her stomach.

Mick kept silent. He wasn't about to say anything else.

Finally Libby grinned at him. He couldn't imagine why. "Kline," she howled, "you are so gullible!"

She walked back over to her chair and sat next to him. A twinkle of delight shone in her eyes. "I couldn't resist. Of course I was talking about my scar. I have a horrible sense of humor and a terribly masculine laugh, which only adds to some of my insecurities."

Mick knew there was a reason he liked her so much.

"The scar runs down half my leg too. And now my other leg doesn't seem to work anymore. Who wants to date a woman with two bad legs?"

"How about a guy with one bad arm?"

A bashful flush glowed on her cheeks. "It's just hard for me to imagine that a scar like I have is no big deal."

"Then you haven't been spending enough time with yourself lately."

A warm, engaging smile spread across her lips. She patted his knee.

Another long, loose groan escaped from Taylor, but this time she rolled to her side and opened her eyes. "Where am I?"

Mick and Libby stooped to her bedside. Mick pushed her hair out of her sweaty face. After looking at Mick then at Libby, Taylor closed her eyes again.

"Taylor, it's Mick Kline. Do you remember me?"

Her eyes fluttered, but then she engaged him. Her mouth was open, and she stared at him in a vacant but open way, as if her mind were sorting through memories from long ago.

With a shaky hand, she grabbed his arm. "Mick?" She said his name again, and her head snapped toward him. She looked at Libby and began breathing hard. "Mick!"

"Calm down," Mick said, pushing her shoulders back into the pillow. "Don't move. You're going to be okay."

But she didn't calm down. She scrambled backward, hitting the small table with the lamp, causing both to crash to the floor. The lightbulb broke, and now the only light was the blue glow from a distant streetlight barely showing through the small window.

"Libby, see if you can find a light switch," Mick said, his eyes focusing in the dark as he watched Taylor's silhouette crawl toward the darkest corner of the room, whimpering and jabbering nonsensically.

Libby was making her way around the walls, trying to find a switch to the one light that hung in the middle of the room. "Found it!" she said, but when she flipped it, nothing happened. "Mick, be careful."

"Get away!" Taylor screamed, crouched in the corner.

"She's probably having hallucinations," Libby said, approaching from behind Mick. He could only see Libby's outline, as she was backlit from the window. "They can become pretty violent. See if you can talk her down."

"Taylor, it's Mick. I'm here to help you."

"Help me? How did you find me?" she asked between sobs.

Mick dropped to his knees so he would be on her level.

She'd shoved herself into the corner, with her anorexic-looking arms wrapped around her knobby knees. She was peering out at him between the chunky strands of hair that fell over her face.

"Why would you think I'm going to hurt you?" Mick asked.

"You shouldn't be here," she whispered, scanning the room as if there might be someone hiding in the shadows. "You have to leave."

"I can't leave you like this," Mick said, his voice hushed like hers. "You need help."

Taylor shook her head. "No. Go. You must go. Please. If you care at all about me, you must go and never speak about this again." Even in the dark room, Mick could see the terror in her eyes.

"Why are you afraid?" Mick asked. "What are you afraid of?"

"Just *go*."

Mick looked at Libby, who was standing behind him. "Is she hallucinating? Is she seeing something in the room?" he whispered.

Libby studied Taylor. "I don't know, but she's very scared. Whether it is real or imagined is hard to say at this point. Heroin is a crazy drug."

Mick tried to inch his way forward. Taylor was shivering. "Tell me why you're scared, Taylor."

Taylor didn't answer. She just watched Mick's every move, her body tucked into a protective ball, her eyes intense and wild.

Libby put a steady hand on Mick's shoulder, a sign she was ready to do whatever was needed if something unexpected happened.

"Taylor," Mick tried again, "I'm here because I think you've been sending me messages about Sammy Earle."

Taylor whimpered, and big tears fell from her swollen eyes. "Please, just go."

"I want to know why you sent me those letters, what you were trying to tell me."

"How did you find me?" she cried. "You weren't supposed to find me."

"My friend Libby here figured out that the headlines came from a Wichita paper, and I only know one person in Wichita."

"Mick, if you care at all about me, you have to go." Even though she was still whispering in a hoarse, unstable voice, it was the first time she sounded like the Taylor he once knew. "I can't tell you why, but you have to go."

"Tell me why you wanted me to look into Sammy Earle's conviction."

She shook her head. "Please go. You have to go. I'm going to die if you don't go."

"We're here, Taylor. Nobody can get you. You're safe."

A joyless laugh escaped her lips. "I'll never be safe again. And it doesn't matter where you are; he can still get me."

Mick was now only three feet away from her. He wanted to reach out and touch her, calm her, but she was still pent up into a tight, unwelcoming ball. It looked like she was about to draw blood from where her fingers were clawing into the skin of her knees. "Who? Sammy? Taylor, Sammy is locked away and probably going to die in a few days from lethal injection. Don't you remember?"

Taylor watched him silently, timidly, like a confused, caged animal. "I'm begging you to please go."

"I can't."

"You can. You can walk out of here and never come back. Please. If you don't . . ."

"You have to tell me what's going on."

"I can't speak of it. I can't think of it or I'll go crazy."

"What were you trying to tell me about Sammy?"

Her eyes glossed with a strange, distant compassion.

"You sent me these coded, mysterious messages telling me to look into my past, or some such, and there was a picture of Sammy Earle attached. Why?"

"He was a bad man."

"I know you were scared of him, but he's locked up now. He can't get you."

"He doesn't deserve to die."

Mick glanced at Libby, who could only shrug. He looked back at Taylor. "He killed a man."

"You have to go now."

"Taylor," Mick said, "I'm not leaving until I find out why you sent me those messages and what you were trying to get me to do."

Her nostrils flared with aggravation, but Mick could see he was breaking down her resolve. If he could just get her to open up about the letters, maybe he could figure the rest out. Of course, she was strung out on heroin, so getting to the bottom of this was going to be a significant challenge.

Mick inched closer to her. When he was within two feet of her, he said, "Taylor, tell me what's going on. You know you can trust me."

She appeared to be fading again, her eyes taking slow blinks, but she focused on Mick, wiped her nose, and clenched her jaw in determination. "I can't tell you everything. If I do, I'm going to die."

"Tell me what you can, then."

"You need to look into Sammy's trial." Her eyes gazed steadily into his, as if he might be able to pull more information from them.

"What about Sammy's trial? He was convicted of murder."

"Things aren't as they seem."

"That's what Sammy says."

Taylor wiped at a tear streaming down her face. "Sammy doesn't understand. He doesn't know."

"But you know."

In the light that barely lit the room, Mick could tell Taylor was turning pale. He slowly reached out and took her hand, which was cold and bony.

"That's all I can tell you. Please, you must figure it out. You have to. Sammy shouldn't die."

"Why do you care about Sammy? He tried to destroy you."

"He doesn't deserve to die. And that's exactly what is going to happen if you don't stop it."

"But how do I stop it? He was convicted of murder. There was a ton of evidence, including a motive."

Taylor moved a shaky hand to her hair, brushing it away from her face, as she continued to lock eyes with Mick. "Just promise me that you'll be careful. Please, you must be so careful."

"Careful about what? Taylor, Sammy is locked up. He can't get you or me."

"I'm not talking about Sammy."

"Then who?"

"I can't speak his name. He is so evil."

Mick dropped her hand because he saw her mouth a word. It made him catch his breath.

And then Taylor lunged forward and vomited.

chapter twenty-two

armed with two large coffees and a plug-in air freshener, Mick and Libby made their way back to Dallas.

"I can hardly smell it; I promise," Libby had said as he washed out the bottom of his undershirt.

Taylor had managed a direct hit on his shirt and part of his jeans, leaving him with only his boxers unscathed. So he'd removed his shirt, tried to rinse out the small amount that was on his undershirt, and managed to wipe most of it from his jeans, all the while trying to keep from gagging and starting the entire process over from scratch.

This was not the way to woo a woman. One, he'd introduced her to a woman he'd been romantically involved with, and although that was years ago, he realized one should never underestimate the fact that time means nothing to a woman. Secondly, he smelled like rotten Chinese food, and no amount of charm was going to do away with that smell.

He noticed Libby was keeping her coffee close to her nose.

Mick was distracted. Taylor had spoken a name . . . not with words but with her lips. And that single name continued to send strange chills down his spine in unpredictable waves. Libby hadn't seen it, and Mick hadn't told her. It was too much to explain at this point. And he wasn't sure he believed it, anyway. It came from the lips of a woman on heroin.

Aaron had been interested in the same person, which is what had led Mick to Shep Crawford's house. Yet Mick had assumed Aaron was interested in Crawford because he thought Crawford might've known more than he had revealed.

Taylor had thrown in an entirely new angle—albeit lacking a lot of detail and sense—that Mick hadn't even fathomed. Why would he?

How would Taylor know Shep Crawford? She might've known his name, but why would she be scared of the homicide detective who had put her abusive ex-boyfriend away? It made no sense, and it was making his head hurt.

"You're quiet," Libby said, sniffing her coffee.

"Sorry. A lot on my mind. Thanks for taking this trip with me. I'm sorry we're going to be getting back to Texas so late."

"Time well spent."

"I'm glad you think so."

"Listen," Libby said, "I . . . back there . . . what I said about insecurities . . ."

"What about it?"

"I usually don't talk about stuff like that. So can we just pretend we didn't talk about it?"

"Absolutely not. Besides, it was kind of nice seeing a softer side of you."

"I don't really have a soft side."

"Come on, Libby. There was nothing wrong with what you said back there. You were being honest. Dare I say vulnerable?"

"Dare you not."

"You still haven't said how you came to battle a fire and lived to tell about it. Maybe we can trade war stories."

"You have war stories? What happened? A string of long division jump out of a payroll record and slap you around?"

Mick glanced at her. "Funny."

"Sorry." She smiled. "See what I mean? I'm not soft."

"Yeah, well, you can keep the insults coming all day. I know what I know."

She slumped in her seat and stared out the window. "It's a grotesque scar, but if I were a guy, it'd be a sign of my manliness. I can't make this scar work in my favor, no matter how hard I try."

"Libby, there's more to a person than what's on the outside."

"Right. That's what you tell ugly kids when they go to school, but at the end of the day, they don't have a prom date, and life stinks."

"Maybe. But more times than not those kids grow up to be the kind of people who change the world and make a difference."

She breathed in more coffee. "I'm not changing the world, Kline. I may stop a criminal or two, but I'm not changing the world."

"What's it going to take for you to call me Mick?"

She looked at him and laughed. "Kline doesn't sit well with you?"

"Makes me sound like I design clothes."

She paused before saying, "I guess I'm having trouble understanding exactly what our relationship is. We started working on a case together. And now I'm helping you chase ex-girlfriends down. *Kline* seems safe."

"Well, when you decide you want to be unsafe—maybe take a risk—call me Mick."

She raised an eyebrow, and they drove on in silence.

"Where have you been?" Reggie stood at his desk as Mick wearily made his way to his own desk, an hour late. "Dude, you look horrible."

"Not enough sleep," Mick said in a scratchy voice that begged for a cup of coffee. He held up a finger to Reggie's pending question and made it over to the coffeemaker, where he poured two cups and carried them back to his desk.

"The last I heard from you, you were wondering which of the many women in your life you should ask out . . . and now look at you."

"Not many. Two, Reg. Just two."

"Three." Mick was about to retort, but Reggie added, "And I don't know if your present condition says you had a good weekend or a bad weekend."

"Long story," Mick growled.

"Well, you can tell me on the way to Leville's place. We got the warrant." Reggie grabbed his coat and gun.

"Reg," Mick said, catching his arm as he swept past.

"What?"

"Can you do this with Stephenson?"

Reggie stared at him. "Are you kidding me?"

"No."

"You're not coming? And you want me to go with Stephenson? You know I can't stand Stephenson."

"Some things have come up."

Reggie sighed. "You are the single biggest diet wrecker I have in my life."

"It's important."

"Which in your world usually translates to 'I'm doing something I shouldn't be.'"

"Reg, I have to go investigate something."

"Let me guess. You can't tell me what it is," Reggie grumbled and looked around before saying, "You owe me big time. I mean it. *Big. Time.* Football tickets. Basketball tickets. A vacation in San Antonio. All of those will work."

Mick slapped him on the arm. "I know I owe you."

Reggie let out one more disapproving sigh, shook his head, and marched toward Agent Stephenson's desk.

Mick glanced back at Tom's office, which was empty. He snagged his two coffees and headed down the stairwell.

Mick was the oldest person in the cybercafe by about fifteen years and was noticeably missing multiple piercings, a display of his navel, unkempt hair, and extra-small clothing. He tried to fit in, so he figured the first thing to do was order some coffee, and thanks to Libby, he knew how.

He moved to the other side of the counter where they yelled your name and left your coffee waiting for you. A couple of boys looking confident despite their blond afros studied Mick before going about their business.

"Nick!" A hippie-looking kid shoved a coffee to the edge of the counter.

Nobody claimed it.

"Excuse me; did you mean Mick?"

The kid's face remained expressionless. "Says Nick here."

"I ordered a mocha."

"Good for you."

The espresso machine's frothy noise cut off any further attempt at solving the mystery of who the coffee belonged to.

Mick took it and found an empty computer in the corner, across from another one that was occupied by a skinny kid playing a game that caused him to yell at unexpected moments.

Mick wanted Internet access, but not on a computer that would be linked to him. He was about to dive into unknown waters, and he wasn't sure how dark or dangerous they were going to be. He blew hot air into his hands and launched Internet Explorer. He was not a pro at surfing the Net, but he had managed to figure out how to get to ESPN's Web site and check football scores, and Jenny had taught him how to Google.

Mick cringed at the thought of her name. Reggie was insinuating things that weren't true, and it was about to drive him crazy. He was over Jenny; he was sure of it. And his stupid little remark to her a few days ago, well, that didn't help things. He refused to believe that after all this time Jenny was still the only one he was capable of loving. It didn't even seem possible.

Mick typed in *Shepman Crawford*.

Hundreds of options showed up, mostly tied to quotes or criminal investigations. Mick waded through them, not even sure what he was trying to find.

He skipped a few pages and looked at the less popular selections. He pulled up a picture of Crawford at a Veterans Day parade. Crawford looked stoic and purposeful, staring at the parade with a defined pride, seemingly resisting the urge to salute something. He was pictured with two other people, none of whom looked aware their picture was being taken.

Did Crawford serve in a war? Vietnam?

Mick typed in *Shepman Crawford Vietnam*. At first he didn't find anything, but toward the bottom of the third page, a sentence caught his eye: *Shepman Crawford's service record in Vietnam showed exemplary . . .*

Mick noticed it was from a Florida newspaper, and he clicked on the Web site. It was an article published last year about a small memorial set up in part to honor the soldiers who had died in Vietnam from that Florida county— twenty-five in all. Mick scanned the article and found where a man named Shepman Crawford was mentioned: *"It was a hard decision, but we decided to include Shepman Crawford in the names of the memorial even though he is still listed as MIA."*

Mick sat back and studied the screen.

The kid on the other side of the table was watching him and said, "If you're stuck, I can help you. I can win any computer game."

"Thanks," Mick said. "I'll let you know."

The kid shrugged and went back to his game.

Mick's head was spinning. He continued to read the article, where the journalist described the stone memorial and the small controversy about Crawford's name being added.

He no longer has family alive, but about twenty years ago, they had a funeral for him, which gave them some closure in their lives. "We simply have to assume that this young man lost his life over there. We need to remember his sacrifice too," said Paul Cunningham, the man who began the crusade to build this memorial.

Mick blew out a heavy sigh. This was unbelievable. Could this be the same Shep Crawford who is alive and walking around? And why did everything about the Sammy Earle case keep leading back to Vietnam?

Cyber Kid popped his head up again. "I swear, man, I can help you."

"I'm not playing a game," Mick said. "I'm using the Internet."

"Look, I taught my eighty-seven-year-old grandfather how to use the Internet, so you're not going to be a problem."

"How do you know I'm having problems?"

The kid laughed, shook his head, and went back to his coffee and game.

Cyber Kid's real name was Travis, and he had a knack for talking and typing at the same time. He was smacking his gum furiously, which Mick supposed at one point smelled like bubble gum but now smelled like rubber coffee. Still, Travis had taken him further in the last thirty minutes than Mick could've gotten in five hours of trying on his own. His supervisor, Tom, still couldn't believe how incompetent Mick was with computers, but Mick explained that it was his incompetency that helped employ the computer researchers who made up half the third floor at the bureau.

"It's all about the search engine," Travis had explained while typing away and flying through pages so fast Mick could only see colors and jumbled letters pass by.

Mick now had enough information about Shep Crawford to be very worried. According to Vietnam records that Travis had somehow accessed—Mick was not going to ask how—Shep Crawford had disappeared in Ia Drang during a four-day battle against the North Vietnamese that left two hundred U.S. soldiers dead. According to the document, Crawford's disappearance had been controversial, as he had supposedly been seen by other soldiers the fourth night of the battle. By the next morning, though, he was missing. Some had thought he might have been kidnapped. Nobody knew for sure. It was in November, just a month after Crawford had arrived in Vietnam at the age of twenty-one.

"Wait," Mick said as Travis landed on a fuzzy picture of group of soldiers crowded around what looked like a burned home in a village.

"There," said Travis. "There's his name."

Mick squinted and, sure enough, there was Crawford's name, along with the names of the four other soldiers. But the picture was so fuzzy, he could barely even make out his face. "Can you find any more pictures like this with Crawford?"

"I can break into the national headquarters for Internet Security, so I'm betting this isn't going to be a problem, though this guy doesn't seem too popular. I can't find much on him." His fingers flew across the keyboard as he chomped his gum. "Here's another one, but it looks pretty fuzzy too."

Mick bent down and peered at the screen, where another group of five soldiers stood with their arms locked around one another.

Travis pointed to Crawford's name at the bottom.

As Travis was about to continue, something else caught Mick's eye. "Stop." He knelt beside Travis and read the name three names down the row from Crawford's. "Delano."

"What?" Travis asked.

"Does that say Delano?"

Travis nodded. "Yeah. Crawford, Jones, Tuttle, Delano, Sueza."

Mick stood up and paced a few feet back, grabbing his head and trying to understand. Patrick Delano and Shep Crawford knew each other? What was Crawford? Some AWOL soldier?

"You okay?" the kid drawled in a Texan surfboarder accent. "To relieve stress, I play this game where you get to shoot gang members."

Mick shot him a look that returned his attention to the keyboard. "See what else you can find with Delano and Crawford. I'm going to get another coffee. You want something?"

"Yeah. Double macchiato, soy milk, with a double shot of Irish cream and a sprinkling of cinnamon."

"You're a little young for alcohol, aren't you?"

The kid's lips trembled with an emerging laugh. "It's a flavored syrup."

"I was making a joke." Mick tried to sound as convincing as possible.

He went to the counter, ordered another mocha, and told the guy, "And Travis's usual." He hoped that would work.

He didn't really want another mocha; he was jittery enough. But he needed to walk away for a second, get his thoughts together. He had a very big piece of the puzzle, but he didn't know exactly which puzzle it went to. If Shep Crawford was indeed AWOL all these years, it might explain some of his more eccentric behaviors. But why would he become a homicide detective? And how would his service record not be detected in background checks?

Mick carried the coffees back to the computer and handed Travis's his.

"Thanks, dude. All I could find was a bunch of information on a trial where this Delano fellow was accused of killing some guy named Lassater in Vietnam."

Mick nodded. "What about some information about Patrick Delano's escape from prison?"

"Escape from prison. Whoa. You know some fascinating people." A few keystrokes and two mouse clicks later, Travis found an article about it in a Virginia newspaper.

Mick quickly read through it. He jotted down the name *Billy Wedestal*. He was the prison guard on duty the night Patrick Delano disappeared and was questioned by authorities, but he couldn't explain the disappearance other than when he went to check on Delano in his holding cell, he was gone.

Travis checked his watch. "I gotta go. I've got class."

"Thanks for your help."

"Sure. No problem. I'm here every day at this time if you ever need more help. Just remember, Google is highly overrated."

"Gotcha."

Travis grabbed his backpack and said, "Listen, dude, I can show you how to download a ton of music without paying for it, and there's no way the FBI can track you down."

"No kidding."

chapter twenty-three

r eggie actually said "humph" as he carried a box that he'd tagged to the evidence vault. When he passed back by Mick's desk, he flung his nose in the air and set his eyes forward.

Mick trailed him. "Reg, I'm sorry. I really am."

Reg turned on his heel. "What time is it?"

Mick scratched his nose. "It's . . . um . . . 5 p.m."

"And what time did you leave this morning?"

"Um . . ."

"Nine."

"Yeah."

A pizza delivery boy entered the FBI offices with a stack of four large pizzas.

Reggie excused himself, paid for the pizzas—which was custom for all case agents to do—and hollered at the other agents that dinner was served. Mick opened a box.

Reggie slapped his hand. "Uh-uh."

"Reg, c'mon," Mick moaned. "I know you're mad at me. But I swear, I wouldn't have put you in this position unless it was completely necessary."

"This pizza is for the agents who were out at that stupid Leville mansion listening to those stupid rich people gripe about how stupid the FBI is. So unless you were called stupid today, you're not getting a piece of pizza."

Mick qualified, actually, but he wanted Reg's trust back

more than he wanted a piece of pizza. Mick lowered his voice. "Can we just talk for a second?"

Reg raised an eyebrow and looked around. "Brother, if this is how you treat the women in your life, no wonder you're single."

Mick tried not to sigh, especially since Reggie was acting exactly like a woman right now. "If I tell you what's going on, will you forgive me?"

Reggie folded his arms. "Maybe."

Mick could see curiosity sparkle in his dark eyes. He pulled Reggie into a quiet corner of the office. "Okay, this is going to sound insane, so bear with me."

"What's insane is that you let me work that entire search with Stephenson, but go on."

"Did Tom ask about me?"

"Lucky for you, his wife is having surgery today."

"Remind me to send a card."

"Remind me not to clobber you when this is all over with. Now, what have you gotten yourself into?"

Mick paused, trying to figure out the best way to present this kind of craziness. "A guy named Sammy Earle is about to die for the murder of a DA ten years ago. This is the same guy who was tied to my case when I was accused of kidnapping that woman."

"Wasn't Earle the boyfriend of the woman you were accused of kidnapping?"

"That's right. Well, a few weeks ago I started receiving these mysterious notes in the mail, with letters highlighted out of newspaper headlines. They were intended to spell a coded message. The message was *out of your past*, and included with the last letter was a picture of Sammy Earle."

Reggie seemed to forget his grudge. His arms dropped to his side, and he listened intently.

"Jenny told me that Aaron had investigated the case

further after Earle was arrested, and she brought over a box of stuff he'd collected, including the case files and newspaper articles. He seemed to be interested in Shep Crawford."

"Who is that?"

"He was the homicide detective who eventually caught and arrested me."

"Okay . . ." Reggie leaned in, wanting more.

"So I go visit Earle in prison. All these years he has maintained that he is innocent, that he was set up. Of course, nobody believed him because of all the evidence that seemed to prove otherwise. Anyway, Earle claims the man who set him up is Patrick Delano. Delano is a soldier that Earle served with in Vietnam, who was court-martialed for killing a fellow American soldier, who was Sammy Earle's best friend. Earle testified against Delano at his trial. Delano was convicted of murder, but he disappeared before they put him in prison."

"Go on."

"I couldn't figure out who was sending me these strange messages. Turns out that the headlines were cut from the *Wichita Eagle* newspaper."

Reggie looked impressed. "How'd you figure that out?"

"Uh . . . long story. Anyway, I knew of only one person who lived in Wichita. And that was Taylor Franks."

"Who is . . . ?"

"The woman I was accused of kidnapping. Sammy Earle's ex-girlfriend."

Reggie looked blank.

"Stay with me. So I go to Wichita over the weekend to find out why she sent me the mysterious messages."

"Are you trying to tell me that it was Taylor Franks, Sammy Earle's ex-girlfriend, who was sending you notes trying to get you to look into Earle's case?"

"I guess that was her intention. What she didn't intend

was for me to find her. The envelopes were postmarked *Dallas*, so she had someone send them for her. But when I showed up at her apartment in Wichita, she was strung out on heroin. She's apparently now a prostitute."

"Did she admit to sending the notes?"

"Pretty much. She was scared to death that I found her. And she seemed to be scared of someone in particular. I kept reassuring her that Sammy Earle was behind bars."

"So who was she scared of?"

Mick caught his breath. This one was hard to say . . . to believe. "Shep Crawford."

"Shep Crawford? Wasn't he the—?"

"Homicide detective."

"How does she know him?"

"I have no idea. Taylor wasn't involved in the case that I know of, unless Crawford interviewed her, but all the stuff Aaron had, including case files, doesn't show him interviewing her. It was mostly the prosecution that did that."

Reggie shook his head. "That's very weird."

"It gets weirder."

"I can't imagine how."

"Can I have a piece of pizza yet?"

"No."

"I wanted to do some research on Shep Crawford so I went to a cybercafe."

"You're kidding."

"I'm not. I got on the Internet—"

"*You* got on the Internet?"

"I swear it. I got on the Internet and found out that a man named Shepman Crawford served in Vietnam. He disappeared in Vietnam in 1966 and is still listed as MIA."

"Are you kidding me?"

"Nope. And check this out: Shep Crawford knew Patrick Delano. They served together in Vietnam."

Reggie was now slack-jawed. "Wow. That is unbelievable."

"So that's what I've been doing all day. Trying to figure some stuff out. I'm almost certain that it's the same Shep Crawford."

"Now what?"

"Pizza?"

"Not yet."

"I'm going back to Wichita. I left Taylor at a Catholic halfway house, whose people promised not to turn her in. I need to find out how Taylor knows Crawford and why she's so scared of him."

"What about this Delano guy?"

"Earle claims Delano called him to taunt him about setting him up. He said he recognized his voice, that there was no mistaking it. Delano has managed to hide all these years. I doubt he's going to be easy to find."

"You'll have to go visit Crawford, confront him on this."

"I already visited Crawford. And I don't mind telling you, that man completely creeps me out."

Reggie looked like he was thoroughly creeped out too. "Well," he finally said after a few moments of silence, "I'll tell you what the most unbelievable part of the story is: that you researched on the Internet."

"Can I have some pizza now?"

Reggie nodded, gesturing toward the pizza boxes.

Mick hadn't realized how hungry he was until he was walking toward the food. His stomach rumbled and even felt a little nauseous. He flipped open a pizza box. All the pizza was gone. He went to the next box, and it was empty too. The third and fourth were the same.

Reggie suppressed a smile. "What can I say? These guys have been working since nine."

Mick groaned and returned to his desk, hoping to find a box of crackers tucked away in a drawer. He found only a package of half-eaten Life Savers. He went to Reggie's desk, sure he would find a PowerBar or cauliflower or something else from nature. There was nothing. He rattled in his pocket for some change. Sixty-five cents would buy him a small package of Cheetos at least.

"Hungry?" he heard a woman ask.

Mick spun around to find Libby standing behind him, leaning on her cane and grinning. She held up a sack. "I've got some bagels. A gesture of trust from your friendly ATF agency."

"Hi. Yes, I'm starving. What are you doing here?"

"You don't think I'd let a search warrant for Ira Leville's house go unsupervised, do you? I know you're the lead agency on it, because that's the only way the bureau will play nice, but I'm here to make sure nothing slips through the cracks."

"Does that mean you're back to work?"

She handed him the sack. "On a part-time, highly supervised basis. If I blink wrong, I'm back on medical leave."

"Well, then, you better stop winking at me so much."

"Wishful thinking, Kline. So—" she smiled—"why don't you show me that evidence vault?"

―――――

Mick volunteered to finish up the search-warrant return for the judge and also the chain-of-custody report. Reggie looked beat, and his wife had called five times wondering when he would be home. Mick, on the other hand, had only a dark apartment and SportsCenter waiting for him, plus he'd left Reg alone all day. It was the least he could do. Thank goodness for Libby's bagel.

236

She'd left thirty minutes ago, and they'd done their fair share of flirting, but Mick sensed that a lot of her walls were strategically placed so there was no chance for anything deeper. She'd bared her soul once, and apparently in Libby Lancaster's world, that was one too many times. Mick wasn't sure how he could convince her that her scar wasn't going to bother him.

Then there was Faith Kemper, a lovely woman who had no bodily scars but was certainly scarred in her soul. Was she really over Paul's death? ready to move on? Or was Mick being set up again, only to be disappointed by a tenderhearted woman who had been emotionally wrecked?

And Reggie wasn't going to let him forget Jenny. But he wanted to. Badly. Jenny was the woman he'd lost, and for once in his life, he was ready to let her go. He *needed* to let her go.

It was after eleven when Mick finished the paperwork and got home. He was lucky. Some searches could last twenty-four hours. The fact of the matter was that nothing found in Leville's home was of any interest to them. Libby had left disgruntled. Mick wasn't happy either. Somehow Leville tied into this, but he'd apparently covered his tracks well. And he was now alerted to the fact that he was a prime suspect.

Mick threw his keys down and collapsed onto his couch, punching on ESPN and watching the highlights. His mind couldn't stop going over scenario after scenario, trying to figure out how in the world he was going to connect all the dots in the mystery surrounding Sammy Earle, a man who was about to die for a crime he quite possibly didn't commit. How would Mick find Patrick Delano? How would he confront a man like Shep Crawford about his military record? His stomach quivered at the thought.

He reached into his pocket and pulled out a small piece

of paper with a single phone number on it. It was a California area code, and it was only 9:30 p.m. on the West Coast. Mick had easily found this man's phone number and address on the computer at work.

The question was, would he talk to Mick about an incident that had happened nearly four decades ago? Mick dialed the number.

After three rings, a tired-sounding man answered the phone. "Hello?"

"Is this Billy Wedestal?"

There was a long pause. "I haven't been called Billy in years."

"What are you called now?"

"First of all, who is this?"

Mick drew in a deep breath. "My name is Mick Kline. I'm with the FBI in Dallas."

"Dallas." The man slurred his *s*'s; Mick thought he might be a little intoxicated.

"Yes. I was wondering, Mr. Wedestal, if you would mind talking to me about a case I'm working on. You're in no trouble at all. I just need to ask you a few questions."

"I'm not in any trouble?"

"No, sir. But I think you may be able to help me catch a very dangerous man."

There was another pause, then, "Don't call me Billy. I always hated that name anyway. Call me Bill."

"All right. Well, Bill, this involves something that happened in 1969."

He laughed. "I can't remember last week. I don't think I'm going to be much help."

"You'll probably remember this. It concerns the disappearance of Sergeant Patrick Delano."

Bill stumbled his words, finally saying, "I don't want to talk about that."

"Sir, please, you're in no trouble. I just need to know some things."

"I said I'm not talking about that!" Mick could hear the alcohol's effects in his voice.

"Bill, please. There is a man about to die for a crime that he probably didn't commit, and I have to get to the bottom of it."

"I don't see how I can help."

"I need to know more about Delano. He could possibly be behind a murder."

"Delano hasn't been seen since he disappeared."

"On your watch, sir."

"I know that! I know it."

"Can you please talk about it? tell me what happened?"

"There's nothing to tell. He disappeared during my guard duty. Like a ghost. He just disappeared."

"Sir, I don't believe in ghosts. Something happened, and he somehow escaped. If I knew how, it could possibly help me find him."

"You're not going to find him. No one will ever find him."

"What makes you say that?"

"He's a master of disguise. He made everyone think he was this valiant soldier. But in the end, he turned out to be a psychopath."

"You think he was a psychopath?"

"He was a monster."

"Do you draw your conclusions from what he was on trial for?"

There was silence on the other end.

"Or is this from personal experience?"

"I told you I don't want to talk about this."

"Mr. Wedestal, don't you think it's time the truth came out?"

"They asked me all these questions too, back when I was twenty-five years old and didn't know anything about the world. Now I know that I'm working minimum wage at a factory. I lost my job, my dignity."

"You can get it back. Tell me the truth about what happened, and you could save an innocent man."

"Nobody's innocent."

"You're willing to let a man die?"

"It's not my concern. Besides, what I know wouldn't save anybody."

"What do you know, Bill?"

"Only things about myself." Mick could hear him guzzle something. Then he repeated, "Only things about myself."

"What things?"

"A man doesn't willingly reveal his weaknesses, does he?"

"If it might help another man, I would reveal mine."

Bill sighed. Mick could hear him drinking something again. "I'm a pathetic human being. I've been divorced three times. I don't even know my children. I just wait here in my house, watching the tube, wondering when I'm going to die."

"You have a chance to do something extraordinary now."

He heard Bill laugh. He was gulping again. This might be helpful in getting him to spill the beans—if he didn't pass out first.

"I was so young," Bill said. "I just couldn't . . . I thought it would . . ."

Mick clamped his mouth shut. Something told him to let the guy talk. Maybe he'd forget there was someone on the other end of the phone.

"There were things about Delano that you were drawn

to, you know? He had this thing about him, like he was the perfect American soldier and if you were good enough, you might be like him someday. You wanted to be like him. Even with him behind bars, I remember thinking that. I thought he was wrongly accused. He convinced me of that. We became . . ."

Mick stayed silent.

"And then—" Bill's voice grew strained—"he turned on me. He found out the one thing that would destroy everything for me. He found out my secret. I still don't know how he did it, but he did. And he blackmailed me."

Mick couldn't hold it in any longer. He was not destined to be a negotiator. "Blackmailed you to do what?"

"What do you think?" Bill roared over the phone.

"You helped him escape."

Silence. No guzzling. Hardly any breathing.

"To keep my secret quiet." His voice lowered to a whisper. "Sometimes in my dreams he comes back. I can see his face. He's going to kill me. Because I'm weak. That's why he's going to kill me."

"But he's never been in contact with you since."

"You'll never find him. You should just stop looking. The entire government tried to find this man, and he vanished, as if he never existed. There have been men like you. Men who think they're special enough. But you're not. Let it go. Patrick Delano will never be seen again until he wants to be seen."

chapter twenty-four

it was a little after 7 a.m. when Mick arrived at the office, his eyes stinging with the sands of embattled sleep. The coffee wasn't even going yet, which made the additional flight of stairs he was about to climb that much more daunting.

Out of breath, he walked the hallway toward Abigail's office. It had been a while since he'd seen her. He was looking forward to it.

Dr. Abigail Grenard had become a friend and ally when Mick was trying to find Aaron's killer. She was one of the few people who believed his theory and ended up being a key factor in catching Faith's husband's killer too.

Before that, even her name had sent chills down his spine because she was the in-house psychiatrist. Being sent to her was like being sent to the grave. Except the grave wasn't as humiliating.

Her door was closed and Mick sighed. She was probably not in yet. He was hoping he could catch her before her day began. He tapped lightly.

"Come in."

Mick opened the door. Her long red hair fell over her face as she bent over her desk with an open file. Glancing up, her mouth popped open with surprise. "Mick Kline!"

"Hi, Abigail."

She rose, hurried around her desk, and greeted him with a hug. "What brings you by?"

"Coffee." He smiled, looking over at the fresh pot she had brewing.

She went to get him a cup. "I hope it's more than that!"

"It is. But I don't speak well until—" she handed it to him—"there. Yes. Thank you."

She laughed. "Have a seat."

"There was a time I'd have rather sat on needles."

"Oh, the looks on your face were priceless, Mick. When Tom ordered you to be evaluated after your brother died, I knew I had a real piece of work on my hands."

"Kept your job interesting, eh?"

"I can't say that any of the other agents took me on that wild of a ride, no." She chuckled. "So what are you working on these days, dare I ask?"

"You probably shouldn't, and I should probably keep my mouth shut about it, but it is a tantalizing case."

She nodded toward his arm. "Heard about what happened. You okay?"

"Yeah. I heal a lot slower these days though."

"This 'tantalizing case' . . . am I to assume it's not official bureau business?"

He shrugged. "You never know."

"Oh, boy," she said, rolling her eyes. "What have you gotten yourself into now?"

"Nothing big. Just trying to keep a probably innocent man on death row from being executed next week because he was set up by a psychopathic Vietnam soldier who may have connections to a local homicide detective."

Abigail's eyes widened. "Sorry I asked. No, I'm not. Give me details. You know how I love to profile a good psychopath."

Mick leaned back into his chair, set his coffee down, and wished he could clasp his hands behind his head. The cast made it impossible. Instead, he crossed his legs. "That's not why I'm here."

"It's not?"

"But I do need your help."

"For what?"

"Your profiling expertise."

"Sure, Mick. Whatever I can do, you know that. Who needs to be analyzed?"

"Three people of the opposite sex."

At this moment Ira Leville thought he might know what his mother had been feeling years ago when she was declared insane. She'd lived out the rest of her life in a mental hospital, and the few times he visited her, she circled her room like a toy train on tracks.

His entire life he had made sure to keep his emotions in check. That was why this boiling anger that made his limbs shake throughout the day was such a surprise. He'd never known rage like this. But then again, he hadn't been betrayed like this either.

Nicole had been doing a very good job of acting. Those classes he paid for two years ago were apparently paying off. She'd sensed his displeasure but continued to ask what was wrong. It made him even angrier. She knew he wouldn't speak the words to condemn her. Right now, she held the power. Somewhere she'd hidden the documents. Ira suspected he would become her next victim in the not-so-distant future. She was smart enough to let time go by. Even a car accident would look suspicious now with the FBI sniffing around for clues.

He'd never regarded Nicole as a patient woman, and he

wondered if she would indeed be able to pull off what he suspected.

But he wasn't going to wait to find out.

Ira waited in a busy restaurant parking lot, crunching down on his cigar and switching through the talk radio stations to shut out the madness in his head.

His car door opened, and a man he'd never seen before slipped into the front passenger's seat. He wore dark sunglasses and had unusually tidy hair. The tie was a nice touch. He shut the door and never looked at Ira. "You have the money?"

"Half of it."

"When, where, and how?"

"This one is complicated."

He smiled. "Yes, love is always complicated, isn't it?"

"This is business. I need her alive until I find the documents and can leave town with them."

"You're under surveillance, are you not?"

"Small amount. They took everything from my house and didn't find anything, so I think they'll shift their attention in another direction."

"Where are the documents?"

"I don't know yet, but I will find them. And soon. When I do, this should happen quietly and quickly."

"I don't normally ring bells before I do it."

Ira poked the cigar back into his mouth and gave it a good chew. "I'll be in touch. The money is waiting for you at the location we discussed." He handed him a key.

The man adjusted his sunglasses. "Most men who want their wife killed have a specific way of wanting it done. They want to know if she'll suffer, or they want to make sure she does."

"I just want her dead. But not until I get what I need."

"How long is this going to take?"

"The timing has to be perfect. But it won't take long. Pretty soon, Nicole will wish she'd never spent a dime of my money or looked at another man." Ira paused. "Go. I'll contact you soon."

Abigail looked to be waiting for Mick to answer. She'd helped him sort through the three women in his life and given good insight into why one might be better for him than another, but like any good psychiatrist, she liked to ask more questions than give definitive answers.

"So," Mick finally said, "you're saying that instead of focusing on each of these women's strengths, maybe I should look at my own weaknesses and see which woman would balance me out?"

"It might be a good start. All of these women sound wonderful, Mick. I don't know that you could go wrong, but there is also a risk with each one and some baggage that comes along too, so you need to look from the inside out, in my opinion."

"You get paid for this?" Mick laughed.

"I'm much better with FBI agents and psychopaths. Women aren't my specialty."

Mick rubbed his face. "My weaknesses, huh? Okay, well, that's not going to be hard. I can make a long list of those. Or maybe I need a woman who needs to be saved. I don't know."

"At the end of the day, you're just going to have to follow your heart. Now I'm talking as a woman, not a psychiatrist. You can't solve this like one of your cases. It's a matter of the heart, not the head."

"I just don't know how it's possible to go from a completely dateless life to this."

"You'll figure it out. Nobody will be able to tell you

who the right woman is. It may be the most obvious. Or the least. Or it may be none of them."

Mick stared at the ceiling. "Surely with three I have at least a chance. I know my luck is bad, but it can't be that bad."

Abigail laughed. "Hello? Where are you? You just went to a faraway place."

Mick tore his gaze off the ceiling. "Sorry. A lot on my mind."

"You don't fade out like that when you're with other women, do you? Women hate that."

"I'm unusually unfocused." Though on one blind date Mick could remember, the woman had blabbed so much he'd retreated inside his head and actually solved a case he was working on. It was one of Reggie's favorite stories to tell at parties.

"Well, let me know how it all turns out for you."

"I will." Mick walked to the door and then turned around. "Hey. I've never asked you. Why aren't you married?"

"I'm still looking for a man who doesn't feel the need to save me."

Mick and Reggie spent the entire morning working the Lamberson case. Since Ira Leville's home had turned up nothing significant, it seemed they were back to square one. They weren't going to be able to crack this case until they found the documents linking Lamberson and Leville to the five burned buildings.

Mick was having a hard time concentrating anyway. Earle's execution was five days away, and he hardly had a thing that would prove Earle innocent.

After lunch Mick left quietly, avoiding questions about

where he was going, and headed straight to the cybercafe. He was eager to get more information, to see if he could link Delano and Crawford somehow. He entered, wondering if he had to actually order coffee to use the computers.

"Hey there!" He saw someone waving at him from over the top of a computer. It was Travis. Mick smiled and waved back. "Hey, come on over here, dude."

Mick walked over to him. "Hi, Travis. How are you?"

"You're not going to believe what I've found."

"Found?"

"Yeah. On those guys."

"What guys?"

"Alzheimer's lately? Don't you remember? I couldn't get this stuff off my mind. I've been working nonstop."

Mick hurried around to the other side of Travis's computer. "What I had you look up? You're still—?"

"Oh yeah. And I found a ton of stuff. It's pretty crazy. Look at this." Travis pointed to the screen. "Don't ask how I got this information, either."

Mick bent down and studied the screen while Travis explained. "Found something on one of the other guys—Jefferson. His file is much less classified than Crawford's, because Jefferson's body was found. But they're grouped under the same heading and have been investigated together."

"What are you saying?"

"They were both murdered in Vietnam."

"You're saying Shepman Crawford is dead?"

"Yep. It's a highly classified file. He's listed MIA, but you won't even find that in current records because of this murder. In fact, if you just read Crawford's file, it simply shows his service record. I guess this was a real controversial thing, and they wanted to keep it quiet. Especially since both men weren't killed by the enemy, if you know what I mean. Jefferson's body was found about a year after he disappeared. He was shot in the head. Crawford's body was never found, but he disappeared when there was no chance the enemy could've been involved."

"When did this happen?"

"Jefferson was killed six months before and Crawford twelve months before."

"Before what?"

"Before Matthew Lasatter was killed. Patrick Delano is listed as a suspect in both Jefferson's and Crawford's murders, but there was no proof."

"Where was Jefferson found?"

"Buried. About half a mile outside their camp. A dog dug him up."

Crawford dead? His body never found? None of this made sense. His suspicions about Crawford being an AWOL soldier were increasing. But how could he prove it?

"These files are not easily accessible, you said?" Mick asked Travis.

"These files technically don't even exist. According to some of the memos I pulled up, which wasn't all of them, the military was pretty freaked about this stuff. They were already dealing with bad pub on the war, and they didn't want it leaked that they might have some whacked-out serial killer on their hands too."

"So the military doesn't list Crawford as dead."

"Yeah. They probably have some of his service record listed as classified, like details from 1967 on. I'm just guessing, though. I can look it up if you want me to."

Mick checked his watch. "Shouldn't you be in school?"

"I'm homeschooled. Besides, I had to get away from my mom for a while. She's driving me crazy with this college thing. I swear she's got a hundred pamphlets from a hundred different colleges. I'm tired of talking about it.

I don't even know if I want to go to college. I already make, like, two thousand bucks a month designing Web pages."

Mick pulled out his bureau card and slid it across the table to Travis. His eyes widened. "Maybe you should think about going into the FBI. Just a thought."

Travis picked up the card. "Am I in trouble?"

Mick put on his authoritative voice. "No, young man, you're not. But whatever you do, I absolutely do not want you to look up anything concerning other soldiers who served with these men and their current residencies. Do you understand me?"

Travis grinned. "I wouldn't dream of it."

"Good. And don't even think about calling me only by pay phone once you don't get the information."

"I won't be in touch."

Mick nodded and walked out. He got in his truck and dialed the Irving Police Department. He needed to know everything Randy Prescott knew about Shep Crawford, if anything. This was going to take a lot of finesse, but he was up for a challenge.

"Irving Police Department."

"Detective Randy Prescott, please."

There was a pause.

"Hello? Detective Prescott, please."

"I'm . . . I'm sorry . . . I . . ."

Mick frowned. "What's wrong?" Maybe his fancy satellite cell phone wasn't connecting well.

Then he heard sniffling. "Don't you watch the news? It's all over the news."

"What is?"

"Detective Prescott was found murdered in his home this morning."

reggie's large hands were folded together, fingers entwined, and resting in front of his mouth, as if he were holding in a thousand words. He simply stared at Mick, not saying a word.

"Say something."

Reggie didn't move.

"What's on your mind?" Mick tried again.

Reggie's hands slid down into his lap, and his head began to shake. Words always followed the shaking of the head. "Can't you just stay out of other people's business? I mean, can't you just stay away from it?"

"I wouldn't be involved in this if my brother hadn't seemed to think something was off."

"Yeah. Something's off, all right. You're trying to tell me Irving's lead homicide detective may be an AWOL soldier who faked his own murder, who could possibly be involved in some way with this morning's murder of another homicide detective. What's off, Mick, is that head of yours. I can't believe you're sitting here telling me all of this with a straight face."

"I know it sounds crazy. But I've got a lot of information to back up this theory. A lot of classified information."

"Where did you get this information? The boogeyman?"

"Look, let's just say I stumbled onto it with the help of

someone who is much more competent with computers than I am."

Reggie was still laughing. "My favorite part of this story is how you went to the home of this murdered detective donning a hat and sunglasses to try to blend in with the crowd."

"He was there!" Mick said.

"Yes, Mick, that's because he's a retired homicide detective. How shocking that he might want to investigate how one of his colleagues was killed."

"The thing is . . . I went to visit Prescott last week, remember? I wanted to know how to find Crawford."

Reggie stopped laughing. "We talked about Crawford, and Prescott told you where he lived. That could have sent Crawford over the edge. Maybe he felt betrayed. The guy's nuts. And you went to talk to him. This doesn't sound good."

"I wasn't sure about anything at that point. My brother listed Crawford as a person of interest, so I went to find out why. Now I'm starting to see. Aaron suspected something about Crawford when that DA Fiscall was murdered. I'm only trying to put the pieces together. Earle is scheduled to die in five days. There's a small chance the man is innocent. He deserves at least one person looking into his claims."

"That's the problem with you, man. You think you've always got to save somebody. Maybe you should've been a lifeguard."

"Reg, tell me I'm crazy and that I should completely walk away from this thing because there is absolutely no chance anything about my theory could be true, and I'll do it."

"You're crazy and there's no chance that anything about your theory is true."

"Okay, that just means I need to do a little more

convincing." Mick leaned back in his chair. "Aaron told Jenny once that Crawford was known as the Blood Man."

"Convenient name for your would-be murderer. What gave him that nickname?"

"Back in the seventies, Crawford was convinced that blood would be the key identifier in crime scenes. And the rumor was that he marked everything he owned in his own blood so it could be identified as his."

"I've heard of artists mixing their own blood into their paint so it could be identified through DNA as an original art piece, but that story sounds a little far-fetched."

"Like I said, it was just a rumor. Maybe it's true, maybe not. All I know is this feeling I get in my gut. There's something off about this guy. Don't know what it is. He gives me the creeps."

"Mick, as your partner and more importantly your friend, I'm telling you this is not a good idea. Let the police handle the murder, and keep as far away from it as you can. You have this knack for getting yourself into unnecessary trouble. Isn't there a storm you can chase or something to satisfy your urge for danger?"

"There's a big hurricane headed toward the Gulf."

"Good. Great. Go chase yourself a hurricane."

"I can't get Earle off my mind. An innocent man could die."

"And you could give me a heart attack, but you don't ever seem to be concerned about that."

"Do you still have that old blood light?"

"It's an antique, and yes, I do." A pout emerged. "Why?"

"I may need to borrow it." Mick tried to smile. He thought Reggie's collection of out-of-date police equipment was a little odd, but it might come in handy now. So far Reggie had collected three hundred pieces and swore it would make him a millionaire when he retired.

"Oh no you don't. Absolutely not."

"I'll be careful with it."

"What in the world do you need that for?"

"I'm going to see if the rumors are true."

"You're not."

"I am."

"Have you lost your mind?" Reggie whispered. "You're going to break into his house?"

"I didn't say that."

"I'm not giving it to you."

"Okay. I'm still going. I need to find out anything I can about this guy. I've got to figure out if he knows where Patrick Delano is and if he's connected with Prescott's murder. Nobody at the police department suspects a thing. I'm the only one with information that could lead to the truth."

Reggie growled at the ceiling. "I know you. And I know you're going to do this no matter what."

"Pretty much."

"The only reason I don't want you to go to jail is because then they'd partner me with Stephenson, and I'd be guaranteed an early death."

"You don't trust me with your old equipment either."

"They're antiques, and you're right about that." He finally stopped looking at the ceiling. "I'm going with you. But you have to promise me one thing. If we don't find anything out of the ordinary at Crawford's house, you will let this go."

"I promise if we get caught, I'll tell them I put a gun to your head and made you come."

━━━━━

Daylight was fifteen minutes from fading as Mick and Reggie pulled up to Crawford's house in Irving. They'd just

watched a news report on Prescott's death before leaving
the office. Crawford had not spoken to the press, but they
could see him in the background working the scene. The
report was supposed to be live, and Mick prayed that it
was.

"Okay . . . this is not good," Reggie said as they both
noticed a dark van parked in the drive.

A man was coming around the side of the house and
spotted them immediately. He stopped abruptly.

Reggie was shifting into Drive, but Mick stopped him.
"This could be our ticket in."

Another man rounded the other side of the house.

"Or our fast road to the grave. These guys look like
they're up to no good."

"Then our badges may come in handy. Come on."
Mick opened the car door and headed straight for the man
standing by the van staring at them. He could hear Reggie
following closely behind.

"Can I help you with something?" the man said. His tone
matched his image—tattered jeans, an even older-looking
shirt, a bandanna around his head, and several obvious
tattoos.

Mick glanced into the van. Painting supplies. He looked
at the other man, who was wiping his hands off on a rag. A
paintbrush was sticking out of his pocket.

Reggie was standing close enough to him he could hear
him breathing.

"You guys finish it up today?" Mick asked.

The man glanced over to his friend, then back at Mick.
"We'll have more work in the morning. We're almost done,
though. Who wants to know?"

"Sergeant Crawford."

"Look, he wanted the job done today, and we worked as
hard as we could. I told him it wasn't likely we'd be able to

finish, but he insisted. Paying us nearly double. Made us start working on the house last night. We put up some lights and got to work. Worked most of the night and morning, then took a couple of hours for a break. Been working ever since."

Mick shook his head. "Crawford, he's something else."

"Who are you again?" the guy asked.

Mick held out his hand. "I'm Calvin, his interior designer." He looked at the house. "I can tell that he chose the color. A little darker than before."

"He said it was fine."

"He always thinks he knows best." Mick turned back to him. "You're closing up shop for the night?"

"My men are exhausted. We'll be back in the morning and be finished by noon. We haven't seen him all day anyway."

"He left early this morning?"

"Yes."

"Did he leave last night?"

"No. He met with us, told us what he wanted, and then went into his house and we didn't hear another peep from him. He told us under no circumstance was he to be disturbed."

Mick faced Reggie. "All right. Well, let's get started. Go get the light."

"The . . . ?" Reggie looked confused.

"The paint light? Hello? Do you think we can do the paint analysis without it?"

Reggie walked back to the car.

"We're analyzing the durability of his interior paint. He's thinking about redoing the inside as well. It's so high-tech these days—all you have to do is put a light on it and it'll tell you everything you need to know about the quality of paint."

"We only use high-quality paint. We've been in business for twenty years."

"I'm sure. This only does interior anyway." Mick felt his pockets. "Oh no."

"What?" the guy asked as Reggie came back with the light, looking particularly nervous with a strained smile on his face.

"I forgot the key." Mick asked Reggie, "Did you grab the key?"

Reggie shook his head, still smiling awkwardly.

"Great!" Mick barked. "Crawford's going to kill us! You know he wanted the analysis done by this evening!"

"I thought you got it," Reggie said softly, trying to add to the script the best way he knew how.

Mick ran his fingers through his hair and looked at the paint guy. "He give you guys a key?"

"No. He said to stay out of his house. Said if we needed to use the bathroom, do it in the trees."

"Crass old guy. I've been trying to teach him to mind his manners." Mick sighed loudly. "We don't have time to go back and get it."

The paint guy leaned in. "One of my guys was taking a smoke break and leaned up against the back door to the garage. The door fell open. He quickly shut it and that was it. We didn't go in. I swear it."

Mick patted his arm. "I believe you. Thanks for that. We would've been in deep you-know-what."

"Paint fumes," Reggie said.

Three other men had gathered around, loading stuff into the van, then climbed in. As the van backed away, Mick walked around the garage to the back of the house.

"Interior designers?" Reggie whispered.

"Hey, that was genius at work back there."

"Yeah. Good thing they didn't spot our guns, which interior designers aren't notorious for carrying."

"Hey, clients can get vicious."

"Yeah. This one in particular."

At the back of the house, there was a dark blue wooden door that led into the garage. Mick took his shirttail and turned the knob. It opened to a garage so tidy it made the military boot camp standards seem tame.

Mick started to enter, but Reggie grabbed him. "Why are we going in there? Crawford has an alibi! The painters said he was here all evening."

"Maybe the painters are here as an alibi. Maybe Crawford wanted to give the appearance he was here when he had in fact slipped out via one blue back door."

"And *walked* to the crime scene?"

"He could have parked his car nearby. There are no windows in the garage so nobody would know if there was a car here or not. He could've walked through the trees to the road over there. Easy."

"Good grief. Let's start looking for conspiracy-theorist jobs for you. Once we finish serving time, of course."

Mick moved to the door that led into the house. A screen door opened with a creak that echoed off the garage walls, and then Mick used his shirttail again to try the house door. It opened. He turned to Reggie, who was growing pale. "We'll be in and out in a jiff. Come on—bring that light and let's see if the rumors are true."

They hurried inside. Mick followed the beam of his flashlight around to see if an alarm was activated. There didn't seem to be any alarms. A lot of American flags, though. They entered the kitchen and living area, where Mick had been before. "We'll start in here, see if we pick up anything, then maybe move to the bedroom or upstairs." Their gazes followed the iron staircase that led to a balcony that had a fireman's pole running up the middle of it. This was definitely one of the most unique houses he'd ever seen.

They crouched in the darkness. Reggie was breathing hard.

"How exactly does this work?" Mick asked.

"We'll turn it on. It's a black light, so wherever there's blood, we should see darkness. The light is basically swallowed up by the blood. So be on the lookout for something dark."

"Okay. Turn it on."

Reggie flipped the switch.

Both men gasped.

chapter twenty-six

the warden took Sammy to a small room with a small table and a white phone sitting on top.

"Thank you," Sammy said as he sat down. He took out a piece of paper from his pocket. He couldn't believe how much his hands were shaking. He'd seen other lawyers' hands shake from time to time over the years, especially during closing arguments, but he'd always taken pride in his steadiness and smoothness.

Each finger trembled as he punched in the numbers. The last digit caused pause. What was he doing? How foolish. His finger dropped onto the six and the phone rang.

"Hello?"

Sammy couldn't get himself to speak.

"Hello? Who is this?"

"JoAnne, it's Sammy."

Silence.

What had he expected? Squealing delight? "I . . . just wanted to tell you something."

"I don't want to talk to you."

"You don't have to talk. Please, just listen." Sammy expected to hear the phone slam down in the receiver, but her steady breathing indicated she was still there. "JoAnne, I only have a few more days to live. They're going to execute me for a crime I didn't commit. But that's not why I'm calling. Someone pointed out to me that not many people get a chance to know exactly when they're going to die. I have that chance, and so I'm trying to make some things right."

He swallowed. He could still hear her breathing. "I just wanted to tell you that I'm sorry for . . ." The words caught in his throat. That he could remember, he'd never said *I'm sorry*. ". . . for how I treated you all those years when you were my secretary. It was shameful. You are such a good person, and I treated you so badly. I'm . . . I wanted to ask for your, um . . . for your forgiveness."

While Sammy waited for JoAnne to say something, he stared at the graffiti etched into the wood tabletop. All kinds of vile words and pictures. He'd never been one to be vile. There was a certain amount of dignity partnered with his insolence. It was what had made him so feared in the courtroom. And so hated.

"You're a pig, Mr. Earle. You always have been. Do you expect sympathy now? The only thing that's making you repent is the fact that you're going to be executed. How sincere is that? You've had years in jail to contact me. You do it now?"

"JoAnne, I'm truly sorry. I've had time to think and ponder my—"

"You are one of the most despicable people I have ever known. All those years working for you were some of the worst of my life. I just want to go on and never have to see you again. Good luck with the execution."

The line went dead.

Sammy glanced around at the guard, who wasn't paying much attention to anything except the sports radio broadcast that was floating down the corridor and past the small room.

He cleared the line and quietly dialed the second number on his sheet of paper. He was allowed all the phone calls he wanted.

He listened to the phone ring. Five times. He was about to hang up when he heard a woman say, "Hello?"

"Doyle Clarkson."

"I'm sorry. . . ." Her voice trailed off as she said something to someone in the distance. "He's just leaving the office."

"This is Sammy Earle." Once his name had carried a lot of weight as a lawyer. Now he was hoping it carried a lot by his upcoming execution.

"Hold on. . . ." Her voice trailed off again, muffled as if she held the receiver to her chest. A minute ticked by.

"Sammy, it's Doyle." He was on speakerphone.

"Doyle . . ." Sammy didn't know what he should say. He wasn't sure why he was calling. Maybe just to hear somebody's sympathy, even if rehearsed and insincere.

"I was going to call you," Doyle said. "I've been in the middle of this trial. It's a big one. You would love it. Lots of rich people lying about their indiscretions." He cleared his throat. "How . . . how are you doing?"

"I'm afraid."

Doyle was silent on the other end.

What could Doyle say to him? It was going to be painless? That was no consolation. Sammy didn't want to die, even if it was in his sleep. Over and over he'd imagined the drug going into his vein, his eyes rolling into the back of his head, and sleep coming over him like a gigantic, warm wave of ocean water. But it wasn't the sleep he'd strived for through alcohol and other means. It was the sleep of death, and he assumed he would fight it, try to stay awake for as long as possible, staring at stern, emotionless faces through a dirty Plexiglas window. "Are you going to come?"

He could hear Doyle suck in a breath. "Sammy, I wish I could. I'm going to be in San Diego. You know I would be there if I could."

Sammy closed his eyes. How many times had he used that line on a woman, a friend, a client? "Sure," he whispered.

"I don't know what to say, Sammy. This is horrible."

"I guess I was just calling to say good-bye."

In the background Sammy could hear the secretary announce that someone of importance was holding on line two.

"Okay, Sammy."

"Before you go . . . are you a religious man?"

"Religious? No, I can't say that I am."

"Maybe you could . . . if you could just pray for me."

"Of course."

Sammy hung up the phone. He looked at the palms of his hands. They were wet. He felt his face—it was wet. He was crying. He hadn't even realized it.

He stared at the phone, cradled in its receiver. He'd just spoken to the outside world for the last time.

"I can't believe this," Reggie whispered. He turned the light, scanning the walls, the bookshelves, the tables. Everywhere they could see small spots of blood. It was on every single thing in the room. "It's all marked in blood. Look over there. Each book has a blood mark on its spine."

"Even the furniture," Mick whispered back. "This is crazy." He gripped Reggie's shoulder and pointed toward the boots by the door. "Did you see that?"

Reggie pointed the light directly toward the front door, where a pair of old work boots sat. On the tip of the right one was a quarter-size dark spot. Two smaller marks were on either ankle.

Mick walked over to it and crouched. He carefully

picked up the boot, then moved it to the small window by the door, where the porch light was seeping in.

"What is it?" Reggie asked.

Mick pulled back the sole from the boot. "It's blood. There on the toe." He turned toward Reggie. "And it looks fresh." He set the boot back down exactly as he'd found it and returned to Reggie.

"What now?"

"We need to find out what's upstairs."

"He could be home any minute."

Mick brushed past Reggie and climbed the staircase to the balcony. Reggie followed behind him, carrying the light.

Mick stopped, holding out a hand for Reggie to do the same thing.

"What's wrong?"

"You're not going to believe this." Mick stepped forward cautiously. In front of him was a huge wall, and on that wall was something the likes of which he'd never seen.

"What is that supposed to be?"

They gazed at what looked like childish scribble all over the wall in black marker, with a little red bleeding through. The words were written on top of one another, creating a mad web of nonsense.

"I think we should get out of here." Reggie started backing down the staircase.

Mick couldn't stop staring at the wall. He'd never seen anything like it. He could pick out certain words: *Justice. Punishment. Freedom. Honor.* Some written over and over again. But other words weren't as distinguishable.

"Mick, let's get out of here. *Now.*"

From the balcony window, Mick could see car lights coming from a distance, rays bouncing off the dark street. It could be any car. He willed himself not to panic. But as swiftly as he could, he bounded down the stairs.

Reggie was already halfway out the back door. Mick stopped in the kitchen, noticing a picture of a lake house in his flashlight beam. Maybe Crawford's? He read the address across the top of the door—1148. Prescott had mentioned that Crawford had a beach house in Port Mansfield.

In the garage, Mick grabbed Reggie. "Turn the blood light on real quick. Let's just see."

Reggie took in a deep breath and nodded, flipping the switch. They looked around. On every tool, every table, every storage container was a small stain of blood. Reggie flipped the light off. "Come on. We're out of here."

They moved through the back door and started around the back corner of the house. Mick held out the arm with the cast, stopping Reggie's dart toward the car. "Wait," he whispered.

"What?"

Mick stared at the lights, still distant, reflecting off the pavement of the dark street. "That car should've passed by now. Those beams haven't moved."

"Come on," Reggie said. "We need to get out of here."

They hurried to the car and took off in the opposite direction of the lights.

Mick glanced back, trying to spot a car in the blackness of the night, but all he could see were distant shadows. He turned to Reggie. "You okay?"

Reggie stared forward.

"Say something. Are you okay?"

Reggie looked at him. "I felt a chill when we walked into that house, even before I turned on the light. I think the blood on that boot was Prescott's."

"Now what do we do?"

"I don't know. But we have to make sure it's the right

move. I think we're dealing with a very dangerous man."
Reggie whipped the car onto Bryers Street, heading away
from the office.

"Where are you going?" Mick asked.

"I need a six-pack."

"You don't drink."

"Of donuts."

Reggie went home, but Mick decided to stay at the office
for a while. He was trying to work the Lamberson case,
but his mind kept drifting back to what he had seen in
Crawford's house. It was beyond eerie. And the fact that
there was fresh blood made it worse.

But now the question was, what were they supposed to
do? They couldn't very well announce they'd broken into
his home, though technically the door had been unlocked.
Mick suspected that door was unlocked because it was the
very door Crawford had used to sneak out.

The news reports said that Prescott was probably killed
sometime between eight and ten last night. Crawford
would've had an alibi with the painters being there. He
could've snuck out, driven his car that was hidden down the
road, and come back after the painters were gone, parking his
car inside the garage. The next morning, he would've been
seen leaving the house in his car. Nobody would suspect a
thing.

But Crawford had made one mistake. He'd forgotten
to lock the garage door.

It was only a theory, but then again, they were dealing
with a madman. What kind of person would mark everything he owned in his own blood yet seemingly have such
an indifference to human beings?

The other missing puzzle piece was how Crawford was

linked to Patrick Delano, if at all. Did the men still know each other? Did Crawford know where Delano was hiding?

"I've been thinking."

Mick whirled around in his chair. Libby stood over him, smiling.

"Hi!" Mick hopped up. "What are you doing here?"

"Looking for you," she said, leaning on the cane she held in her right hand.

"Here I am. Come sit down in Reggie's chair."

"Thanks." She hobbled over and sat down. "There's been something that has continued to bother me about Lamberson's death."

"What?"

"I keep wondering why the fire was set one office away. Why not set the fire where you want to destroy all the evidence?"

"Try to make it look like an accident?"

"Possibly, except there was nothing there that would start a natural fire. Assuming our suspect has average intelligence—and that's assuming a lot—surely he would know that an arson investigator would be looking for how a fire was started. This fire was started on a desk using acetone. You don't see that around a lot unless you're talking meth labs. And like I said before, some fingernail-polish removers still contain acetone."

"Okay . . . so what are you getting at?"

"Women are more emotional, and a woman would have a harder time torching the body of someone she loved, even if she did kill him. She might be able to do it if the body wasn't nearby. It would help her become unattached."

"Who do you suspect?"

"A woman."

He laughed. "Okay, okay. You don't have to tell me,

though I would assume it's Nicole Leville." Mick engaged Libby's serious eyes. "I'm glad you came by."

She smiled. "You are?"

"I am." He checked his watch. "You up for a late dinner?"

She stared at her hands. "That's the other reason I came by."

"To ask me to dinner?" Mick grinned.

"No. I'm . . ." She glanced up at him and sucked in a mouthful of air, then blew it out with a steady push of her cheeks. "I'm going away for a while."

"You're going away? Where?"

"I just need some time to think."

"About what?"

She wiggled her cane. "This." She pointed to her leg. "That. I was at the top of my game, and it came crashing down in an instant. ATF's got Guber in charge, and I'm supposed to just 'take it easy and do what I can.' I don't think I can keep doing it. I'm used to being in charge. I hate taking orders, especially from Guber. I shared my theory about a woman being Lamberson's killer, and he laughed and attempted some stupid, half-witted joke about women and nail polish. He thinks there's a third person involved that we haven't identified yet. So he's out chasing rabbits. He's got our men scattered everywhere, when in fact, I think the killer is in our own backyard."

"Are you thinking of quitting the ATF?"

"The doctor told me yesterday that there's a good chance my leg will never work properly again. I could do desk work, but that's not me. I have to be out in the action. I'm miserable, and I don't think I could ever get used to it this way."

"What would you do?"

She shrugged. "Who knows? That's what I want to

figure out. Maybe teach at the academy. Maybe do private investigative work."

"Maybe I can help you figure some of this stuff out. Over dinner."

There was a glistening of emotion in her eyes. "Look, the other thing is that—" she rolled a pencil between her fingers—"it's just that I'm starting to have some . . ."

"Some what?"

"Some feelings for you."

"You are?"

"That's a hard thing for me to admit. I'm not the kind of woman who lets a man influence her life. But you have. I think about you a lot, and I just need to go figure this all out. Figure out what I want in life, what's important to me."

Mick couldn't hold back the rather large smile that had overtaken his face.

"You're laughing at me."

"I'm relieved. I thought I might be the only one feeling like this. I kept wondering if you were having as much fun as I was."

"Are you kidding me? We've given an entirely new definition to the term *shameless flirting*."

He laughed, then leaned forward on his desk. "Libby, one of the things I like about you is how many risks you take."

"Yeah, and look where it got me." She pounded her cane against the floor.

"Maybe that one didn't turn out so great, but maybe this one will. You took a risk by telling me how you feel about us."

She lowered her eyes. "I just need some time to sort things out. It's been a long time since I've been in a relationship, and the last one I was in didn't turn out all that great. There's not a lot of things I fear in life. I want to make sure this isn't one of the few."

"Take all the time you need." He stood up. "But before you start your sabbatical, maybe you need a good, nourishing meal."

She laughed. "You're relentless, Mick."

"Only about things that are important to me." He moved to help her out of her chair. "Are you free?"

"Well, never free, but always available."

Laughing, he walked her toward the door, and the only thing that was going through his head was the fact that she'd finally called him Mick.

mick surprised Libby by taking her not to a restaurant but to his favorite hot-dog vendor.

"I guess you're going to tell me they have the best hot dogs in town?"

"No. But they do properly refrigerate their condiments."

They sat on a park bench, and Mick told Libby his suspicions about Crawford and about breaking into Crawford's house.

Libby was in midchew and nearly choked on her food. She managed to swallow and then said, "Are you serious? You didn't really do that. Please tell me you didn't do that."

Mick squirted a pack of mustard on his hot dog. A faint smile was all the indication she needed.

"I can't believe it!" she whispered.

"Let me tell you what you won't believe. The blood, Libby. It was everywhere. Mostly small spots on every single thing in his house. Books. Tables. Televisions. Walls. Paintings. Knickknacks. We turned on that light and saw blood everywhere."

"That is unbelievable. Almost as unbelievable as you breaking into a homicide detective's house."

"We technically did not break in. The door was

unlocked. It's definitely trespassing, but that's it. We didn't take anything."

"Still. That was awfully gutsy. Especially if what you suspect about this guy is true."

"I found fresh blood on one of his boots. Between the sole and the shoe. I pulled back the leather and there it was—it had seeped into the welt."

"You think it was that murdered detective's?"

"I do."

"And you still think Crawford is somehow connected to that guy on death row?"

"There's a big missing link there, but yeah. I received some information this week that a man named Patrick Delano, who Sammy Earle thinks set him up, is connected to Shep Crawford. Crawford is listed as MIA, though suspected dead by the government. Murdered, actually. But that's not listed in his service record. It simply says Crawford served in Vietnam. The rest is classified, except to his family, who knew he was listed MIA."

"I probably shouldn't even ask this, but how did you find out about that if it's classified?"

Mick smiled and looked down. "You shouldn't ask. So, where are you thinking about going on this sabbatical of yours?"

"That was the worst attempt at a change of subject I've ever seen. But if you must know, I'm not sure yet myself. I think I'll just start driving somewhere, you know? See where I end up."

"Sounds like a life plan to me."

She laughed. "Maybe it is. Everything's pretty uncertain now anyway."

"When are you going to leave?"

"I'm not sure." Her cell phone rang. "Excuse me. Hello?"

Mick studied her as her attention focused on the phone conversation.

She snapped her phone closed. "Are you finished eating?"

"I can be."

"Good. How would you like to join me for a little eavesdropping?"

"Well, I've already trespassed tonight, so why not? Who would we be eavesdropping on?"

"Ira and Nicole Leville."

"You wiretapped their home?"

"Nope. We mounted a camera on top of a utility pole outside their house to monitor when they come and go."

"Okay. Which tells you what?"

"When they're inside Mr. Leville's Cadillac."

"Significant because . . . ?"

"Because we were issued a Title 3 for the use of telematics."

"Telematics? Are you talking about the thing a lot of those cars are equipped with where you can punch a button if you're in a car accident or need roadside assistance? Then an operator comes on in a nice, pleasant voice to assist you?"

Libby grinned. "That's the one. We instructed the company to open the channel and record the conversations inside the car. It basically works like a two-way radio. Apparently we got some good stuff. They're asking for me back at the office. Want to come?"

"Yeah. But I thought you'd been downgraded."

"It was my idea to use the Cadillac. Guber thought it was a stupid idea, and I told him if it didn't turn anything up, I'd stay out of his hair for the rest of the investigation."

"Sounds like you'll be burrowing near his scalp for a while."

"What's he doing here?" Guber asked as Mick and Libby stepped into a medium-sized room crowded with a ton of equipment at ATF headquarters.

"He should be here," Libby said. "Without the information Agent Kline gave us, we couldn't have established probable cause for the Title 3. Lamberson's his guy. He needs to know what happened to him."

Guber sighed heavily and shook his head but refocused his attention on the small man sitting in front of a large display of computers. "Let's see what we got, Ray."

Ray's fingers flew across the keyboard, and as he typed, he talked. "Pretty much the first fifteen minutes is nearly complete silence. I guess these two lovebirds were giving each other the cold shoulder. So I'm fast-forwarding through all of that. Now here's where things get interesting."

Everyone leaned in to listen.

"You've been acting weird lately, Ira. I don't know what your problem is, but I wish you'd just let it out. Do you want to have another heart attack?"

There was more silence.

"Fine. Whatever," Nicole continued. "Why are we even going to this stupid party? I'm not in the mood to smile and shake hands and pretend everything is okay."

"Do whatever you want at the party. I don't care." The strain in Ira's voice was apparent. "Just get out."

Ray added, "I think they've pulled up to the country club at this point. There was a lawyer party or something there."

"Aren't you going to let the valet park the car?" Nicole asked. Greeted by silence, she said, "You don't want to walk in with me. I get it. Maybe you'll get lucky and not have to talk to me all night." She could be heard getting out of the car and slamming the door.

Ira said to a distant voice, "I'll park it myself." Then his window rolled up, and out rolled a string of expletives directed at his wife. After he ran out of words that made the women in the room blush, Ira mumbled something that couldn't be understood.

"I didn't catch that. Let's hear it again."

Ray rewound the tape and turned up the volume, but it still couldn't be deciphered.

"Hold on. Let me bring some of the other noise down and see if I can isolate the voice." His fingers zipped across the keys, and then he replayed it. "This should work."

"I will not share my bed with a murderer."

"That's pretty much it. They leave the party, and Nicole makes a comment about what some lady is wearing, and that's the end of it," Ray said.

"So Ira thinks Nicole murdered Joel," Libby said.

"That's what it sounds like to me." Guber turned to Mick. "We may have just delivered your suspect to your front door."

"Good job, Agent Lancaster," Mick said. "Your instinct about using the telematics system paid off."

"Thank you, Agent Kline," she said. "So I guess we've got to focus on those documents. Any signs that any of these insurance companies are going to come forward with suspicion of insurance fraud?"

"We don't have any information on that," Mick said. "It seems to be the biggest hurdle. These perps knew what they were doing, and everything is buried really deep. Unless one of the carriers suspects foul play, I think we have to find other means."

Guber turned back to the computer. "Nicole Leville is one cold lady. Kills her lover and betrays her husband. Ira

Leville is one angry guy, and for good reason. He got double-crossed by his wife and his business partner."

"I think we're short on time. It sounds like Leville is out for revenge," said Libby.

"But he's going to try to find those documents first. I don't think he'll do anything to Nicole until he does," said Guber.

"Unless he uses her to get to the documents. He sounded pretty angry and desperate. I wouldn't rule out cruel and unusual punishment here if he can't locate the documents in a timely manner," Mick said.

"We're talking almost a million dollars' worth of insurance claims." Guber sighed. "All right. We're going to have to be watching both of these people. And be very careful. Either one of them could lead us to the documents. Nicole is sensing something is wrong, so I imagine she'll be moving the documents very soon, just to be cautious. We can count on your full support, Agent Kline, as well as your discretion?"

Mick nodded.

Guber slapped his hands together. "All right, folks. Then let's get busy."

Everyone cleared the room, and Libby walked Mick to the elevator. She was wearing a self-satisfied smile.

"It worked," Mick said.

"Yeah." Mick could see how much she loved her job. She gently patted him on the arm. "Thanks for dinner. I didn't get a chance to tell you that."

"Then I'll have to take you out again so you'll have another chance."

"We'll talk soon." She pecked him on the cheek and walked off.

The elevator dinged right on cue with his cheesy smile.

Mick's body ached with fatigue when he entered his apartment. It was just past eleven o'clock. He didn't bother switching on the light as he found the remote control on the couch and punched on SportsCenter. His stomach rumbled, but he was too tired to even nuke a Hungry-Man or two.

Halfway listening to the scores and watching the images from the highlights buzz by on the screen, Mick settled into the couch and tried to relax. His nonstop mind was keeping good pace with his nonstop heart, but it was time to regain control of both.

After a few minutes, he switched over to the Weather Channel to see what Hurricane Eve was up to. He'd been following her path, and last he'd heard, she'd turned sharply and was headed toward the Gulf of Mexico.

One of the meteorologists was standing in front of a green screen of live pictures from a windy, stormy Cuba, where Eve had just passed through the Caribbean Sea and over Pinar del Río, missing Havana but doing significant damage to the Isla de la Juventud on its way. It was now in the warm Gulf of Mexico waters, where the meteorologist explained it was pulling energy from the open waters. It was already a Category 4 but would probably be a Category 5 by landfall. And its target was Texas.

There was a great urge inside him to go down south, try to catch the storm and photograph it, but he had enough going on here to keep him plenty busy. He watched the winds and the storm surges. They cut from the meteorologist, safe and comfy in the harbor of the news station, to the unlucky reporter who'd been assigned to get a firsthand report. The reporter's clothes whipped violently against his body as he tried to maintain some sense of professionalism while struggling to keep the microphone near his mouth and a stubborn earpiece in his ear.

Mick laughed. These guys lived for moments like this. How stupid was it to stand on the north shores of Cuba with a hurricane passing through? But this guy was risking it, probably hoping to tumble across the street in some show of meteorological heroics, only to hop up unscathed, still holding that ever important microphone.

When they switched to other weather, Mick went to the kitchen and noticed his answering machine blinking. He punched the button, hoping it was Libby, fearing it might be Faith, for whom he still had strong feelings.

Instead he heard a surfer voice. "Dude . . . it's not Travis, and I'm not calling from a pay phone to not tell you that I didn't find out some important info. The soldier's name isn't Jay Hume, and he doesn't live in Dallas at 1155 Mercury Street. He doesn't own his own tire shop. He didn't serve with Crawford and Delano. And I won't keep looking unless I don't hear from you." There was an amused chuckle on the other end. "Bye."

Mick laughed and tore off the piece of paper he made notes on from his notepad.

Behind him came a frantic knock. He heard his name being called, muffled from the other side of the door. He rushed to the door and opened it.

Jenny stood there, her fair complexion pale. She rushed past him, pulled him in, and shut the door, locking the dead bolt.

"What's wrong?" Mick said, grabbing her shoulders to calm her down.

"He came to my house!" she whispered.

"Who?"

"Detective Crawford! Shep Crawford!"

Mick let go of her shoulders. His body went numb.

"About thirty minutes ago. He came unannounced, knocked on the front door like he was a friend or something."

"Did you let him in?"

"No. I stood at the door and talked to him. I was in my pajamas. It was bizarre." She walked to the couch and sat down.

"Tell me everything that happened."

Jenny's hands were shaking as she gestured through her story. "Well, he's standing there at the door, and I didn't know what to say. I didn't recognize him at first, and then he introduced himself and I felt my knees get weak. It was something in his eyes, you know? He was pleasant enough, but there was this . . . this thing in his eyes. I don't know how to describe it. It was just there."

"What did he want?"

"He wanted to speak with Aaron. He said he wanted to talk to him about the Sammy Earle case, that it wasn't a big deal, but he wanted to know what Aaron knew about it. His interest, he said, had been renewed."

"What'd you tell him?"

"I told him Aaron was dead." She blotted her eyes with the back of her hand.

"Then what did he say?"

"He said he was sorry to hear that. And he turned and left."

"That's it?"

"Almost. He turned back and said, 'If we're both lucky, Sammy Earle will end up dead too.'"

Mick closed his eyes, trying to get a grip on the anger that was beginning to erupt inside his chest.

"Are you okay?"

"You need to leave town."

"Why?"

"I can't tell you everything. You shouldn't know it anyway. But I want you to go stay with my mom and dad for a few days until I get this settled."

"That's a full day's drive—"

"You're going to fly. I want you on a plane first thing in the morning. You'll spend the night with Reggie and Marnie, and Reggie will escort you to your house to get a few things before you go."

"Mick, don't you think you're overreacting a little bit? I mean, I know the guy's a little weird and everything. I won't lie—his visit kind of shook me up. But you don't think I'm in any real danger, do you?"

"I think Crawford's trying to get at me, and he'll do it however he needs to."

"What makes you think that? Maybe he just came to get information, like he said."

"Because, Jenny, Crawford already knew that Aaron's dead."

om Bixby shook his head and laughed, but not out of happiness. It was that kind of expression where a smile hid an angry grimace and held back an attempted strangling.

"Tom, I know this sounds crazy," Mick said, "but I wouldn't be here if I didn't think this was legit. I told you about all those notes I was receiving. This is just one more piece to the puzzle."

Tom patted down the hair on top of his head. That joyless smile was still plastered across his face. "I leave to take care of my wife. It's a medical leave. What can happen, right? Kline, you're like a maverick. I never know what's going on with you. I mean, I just figured chasing those stupid storms of yours would satisfy this need to get in the middle of things you shouldn't, but I guess I was wrong." He sighed heavily. "What about the Lamberson deal? Please tell me we've made some progress."

"Yes, sir. We're working closely with ATF—"

"Ha. That's a good one."

"No, seriously, sir. We're cooperating with them; they're cooperating with us. We're closing in on a suspect, who we believe is Ira Leville's wife, Nicole. She has motive, and we think she probably has the documents too. That's what Leville believes anyway. We're monitoring their activity. There is a good chance these people are planning to kill each other. The ATF was issued a Title 3, and they recorded a lot of helpful information."

"I want the report on my desk as soon as possible." Tom sat down and needlessly shuffled papers. "So what do you want, Kline? Why are you in my office?"

"I want permission to contact the governor if necessary."

"As a bureau agent?"

"Yes, sir."

"You really think Earle might be innocent?"

"That's what I'm going to find out, sir. But regardless, I think Shep Crawford is one dangerous man. And now it's getting personal."

"You're talking about a police detective—a respected police detective."

"I know, sir."

Tom leaned forward. "Look, I can't turn this into a bureau investigation, and you know that. I want clear-cut evidence of this man's innocence. I think that phone call to the governor better come from me. I want to check the evidence before I make the call."

"Sir, there's not a lot of time. Earle is scheduled to die in—"

Tom held up his hands. "Don't press me on this. Whatever happens, make sure you don't let this Lamberson thing slip. If it falls through the cracks, I might lethally inject you with a good dose of unpaid leave."

Mick started to leave the office.

"And, Kline, be careful."

"Yes, sir." Mick walked to his desk. If only he could've told Tom about the blood. But there was no way he could drag his supervisor in on that sort of thing. It was a delicate balance of sharing enough information to get permission to investigate while holding back things like the fact that he trespassed. He felt a hand on his shoulder.

"Hey, man."

"Reg, hey."

"You look terrible."

"Did you get Jenny to the airport?"

"Yeah. Her flight leaves in a couple of hours. She should be in Kansas City by this afternoon." Reggie sat down at his desk. "Are you okay?"

"Why?"

"Have you looked in the mirror this morning?"

"I'm tired. I didn't sleep last night. I spent the morning typing out some notes for you to review on the Lamberson case. Call Agent Lancaster—her number is in the folder— and tell her that I've been deterred for a few hours. Reggie, I think we're really close to cracking the Lamberson case. We just need someone to make a move and quickly. We'll put some more pressure on the Levilles to see what happens."

One of their white-collar-crime agents approached their desks. "Hey, guys."

"Hey. What's going on?"

"This just came through; thought you might be inter-ested in it. Sounds like it might be connected to the case you're working on."

"What is it?"

"It's an insurance company that suspects fraud. One of their buildings was burned down a few months ago. Not sure what prompted them to come forward, but they contacted our division."

Mick took the folder and opened it. He glanced at Reggie. "This is it. This is the first building that burned." Mick looked at the agent. "We're going to need to share this information with ATF."

"That's fine. Just don't make any moves without notify-ing us first. It takes a while to put these cases together, and

287

we're only in the beginning stages. If you've got information that could help it along, that would be great. But we still have to go through procedure."

"Thanks." Mick faced Reggie. "Go find Agent Lancaster. Get this to her as soon as possible."

"Where are you going?"

"You don't want to know."

A distinct, rubbery smell assaulted Mick as he opened the front door to the humble tire store. A few out-of-date posters of race-car drivers hung on the walls, and a cardboard prop with a smiling, waving celebrity stood by a stack of name-brand tires. In large gold lettering that seemed more appropriate for a law office than a tire store, the sign read Hume Tires. The desk was tidy like the store.

An older gentleman wearing a short-sleeve, cotton button-down and a skinny tie approached Mick. "Looking for a new set of tires today, sir?" He had that old-style salesman way about him. "I'd be happy to help you become a satisfied customer."

"Actually, I'm looking for Jay. Is he here?"

"Of course, but if you know Jay, he's going to be out getting his hands dirty, not in the store. I can get him if you'd like."

"That would be great."

"Can I give him your name?"

"Special Agent Mick Kline."

The salesman walked out a side door and after a minute reappeared with a man trailing him. The man wore a black bandanna wrapped around his head and had a string of tattoos up and down each bulging arm. The salesman needlessly pointed to Mick, since he was the only one in the store. Jay stepped up to him, wiping his hands on a rag.

"Jay Hume?"

"Yeah." He shook Mick's hand. "Who wants to know?"

"I'm Special Agent Mick Kline, but I'm not here on official FBI business. However, I was hoping you could help me out. I need some help identifying a couple of people you may have known in Vietnam."

Jay's curiosity was obviously piqued. "Vietnam. That was a long time ago."

"But never forgotten. Do you have an office where we can talk?"

Jay nodded and led the way out a different door and into a hallway that held several offices. He turned into the last one. Mick noticed a few black-and-white photos of soldier buddies lining his desk and bookshelf, which held more manuals than books. Jay explained his tour of duty with a lot of pride in his voice. Mick listened carefully and attentively.

Finally Jay looked at the folder in Mick's hands. "So, what can I help you with?"

"It's a little complicated, and I won't go into all the details, but I basically need some information on a few soldiers. Did you serve with a soldier named Howard Jefferson, Shepman Crawford, or Patrick Delano?"

Jay nodded. "I knew all of those men. Not well. But I knew them."

"So you knew the circumstances surrounding these men? That Jefferson and Crawford were killed?"

"Yes."

"Were you aware they were not killed by the enemy?"

Jay hesitated, then said, "There were rumors. They didn't tell us much. But everyone knew."

"Knew what, exactly?"

"That they had been killed by another soldier."

"Did you know who they suspected?"

"Not at the time. But later there was talk that it was Patrick Delano."

"How well did you know Delano?"

"I didn't spend much time with him. He wasn't a likable kind of guy. He was sort of abusive to his men. Didn't have much compassion for them, especially the young ones. He scared a lot of the guys."

"Do you think Delano was capable of murder?"

"I can't say. He was weird, yeah. But I don't see why he would murder another soldier. It doesn't make a lot of sense. It just means you're left with two less guys to fight with."

"Were you aware that Delano disappeared during his trial for killing Matthew Lassater?"

"My theory is that the government kidnapped him and took him away. I mean, they do stuff like that, you know? He's probably being held in some unnamed prison until he rots. Maybe he knew more than he was supposed to. Or maybe—just maybe—he was hired to kill Lassater for some reason, and he did his job, and now they're protecting him."

"What about Shepman Crawford? What do you know about him?"

"I talked to him a few times. We weren't friends. More like acquaintances."

"Did you find him strange?"

"Yeah. A little, I guess. He didn't really seem the soldier type."

"What do you mean?"

"He was real quiet. From Kentucky, if I remember right. Had a hard time hanging out with the other guys."

"Quiet. What else?"

"Shy too. Just one of those men who didn't seem to fit the profile of a soldier. He was likable. Really nice. But almost too nice. Some of the other soldiers took advantage of him. Broke his glasses a time or two. He was an easy target."

"What were you told about his disappearance?"

"Not much. One day he was there. The next day he was gone. That's all we knew."

"You think he went AWOL?"

Jay shrugged. "I don't know. He certainly had motive."

"But you were under the impression he was killed."

"There were rumors. But that's all. No one would tell us anything. They didn't want us to get distracted."

"But they found Private Jefferson's body."

"Yeah. I wasn't there, but we heard about it."

"But not Crawford's."

"Not that I know of."

"I have a theory that Crawford may have gone AWOL. Faked his own death and left."

"I have no idea. Interesting theory, though."

Mick flipped open his folder and showed a few pictures to Jay. The first one was of Private Jefferson and some other soldiers with Patrick Delano. "Yeah. There's Jefferson. There's me, to his left. And Delano. I can name off the other guys if you want."

"What about this picture?" It was the fuzzy picture that Travis had pulled off the Web.

"I can't really see the faces. It's hard to say."

Mick handed him a department picture of Shep Crawford that had been taken several years ago. He watched Jay as he looked at it carefully. He kept quiet. He wanted Jay's first reaction at seeing a soldier who was supposed to be dead possibly alive and walking around. A lot of time had passed, but he thought Jay might recognize him.

Jay studied the photo, then gave it back to Mick.

"You recognize that man?" Mick asked.

"Sure. I could never forget those eyes."

Mick glanced down at the picture. Crawford always did have that strange look in his eyes. "So you would agree this is Shepman Crawford?"

Jay shook his head. "Crawford? No, man. That's definitely Patrick Delano."

for the past ten years Sammy had been taking orders. It was a strange turn of events now to be granted his every request. Two guards stood on either side of him while he sat on the chair next to his bed. In front of him a third guard was on a small step stool, removing the white clock that hung on the wall. He'd found himself unable to stop watching it and had asked that it be removed.

He was being treated with respect—strangely the same way he used to be treated when he was practicing law. Instead of disregarding him, the guards now looked him in the eye, gave him assuring nods, acted as if he was about to die for something noble. Perhaps just the fact that he was getting ready to die against his will was reason enough to start treating him with dignity.

He had ninety-six hours to live, but now the only thing he had to mark time by was the shadows that crossed his room as the sun roamed from one end of the earth to the other, blessing the grimy walls with direct light for one and a half hours in the late afternoon.

Sammy ate quietly, tasting each bite of food, staring out the tiny window above him. Strange thoughts blossomed in his mind, pushing the darker thoughts to the side. He thought about *The Last Supper*. He'd noticed the painting on the wall of one of the rooms he'd been in. He'd seen it on coffee mugs, hanging crooked inside car-insurance offices, and even tattooed on one of his clients. But he'd never read the story of the Last Supper.

Curiosity, more than anything, had caused him to ask for a Bible. So this morning, with nothing better to do, he had read it. Surprisingly, the story of the Last Supper resonated with his own life. Not so much because he was a worshiper of Jesus Christ. In fact, he was not.

Now, though, it was as if the story were being spoken to him. He read the words over and over again, trying to understand how a man who was falsely accused could accept his death so readily.

Judas was a particularly fascinating character. He was, on one hand, despicable in his betrayal. Sammy had no problem equivocating him to the person who had betrayed him and led him to his own untimely death. Yet in the same breath, Judas found himself very aware of his own shortcomings, his all-consuming desire for money and fame that had probably sent him to this very spot, in the very least indirectly.

So Sammy had tried to get the story out of his mind, because there was this complex, nearly mesmerizing sense of guilt for identifying with a holy man, but he couldn't quite find it in himself to admit he was a Judas.

But it would not go away. As he ate his food, each bite reminded him of the story and how the Christ was nearing His own death yet willing to kneel and wash the feet of His friends, friends He knew would betray Him later.

"Hello, Sammy." Chaplain Barber stood in front of his cell.

Sammy set his fork down and shoved his food away.

"I heard you'd requested a Bible. I was hoping we could talk some more."

"I would like that," Sammy said, though it came out as a whisper.

The guard let the chaplain in and he sat in another

chair, only three feet from the bed. The two other guards left.

Sammy's hand found his face, and the words he wanted to speak burned in his throat. He hid his face and wept. The chaplain's hand, steady and warm, held Sammy's shoulder.

After there were no more tears, Sammy looked into the man's eyes. Calmness washed over him, and Sammy sat up straighter and took a deep breath.

"I am feeling guilty," Sammy finally said.

"For what?"

It was a hard thing to say, but his hours were short, and there was no use pretending anymore. "For relating to Him."

"Who?"

"Jesus. The Christ." Sammy stared at the Bible on his bed. "For understanding how He felt to be betrayed. I hate that I would even compare myself to such a man. And I know I would not be able to wash the feet of men who would eventually deny knowing me."

The chaplain smiled. "That is why Jesus came, Sammy. So you would know that the God of the universe understands what it is to be human. He lived a holy life so when He was sacrificed on the cross, your eternal punishment would be canceled."

"I read about the thief who was executed with Jesus. Jesus told him he would be with Him in paradise."

"It is never too late to believe in Him, to trust Him with your eternal destiny."

Sammy looked up at the clock but realized he'd asked that it be taken away. In its place was a pure white circle, where the wall had been shielded from all the years of grime. Sammy gazed at the circle, willing his soul to believe in the chance that he could be that unblemished. It seemed impossible, because the reality of his life was that in every minute he had lived, his soul had become darker, his life wasting away, receiving its only nourishment from fame and money.

"What are you thinking about, Sammy?" the chaplain asked.

His thumb rubbed the edge of the Bible on the bed. "That none of this is true."

The chaplain's expression changed from serene to startled.

"It can't be. Our whole life we are taught about reward and punishment, about consequences. So how can it all be changed? It's just a fairy tale. It's what people want to happen, so they've created religion to make it so."

The chaplain stared into Sammy's eyes. "No, Sammy. You're wrong about that."

"About what?"

"That's not what man wants. Man has always wanted to be in complete control of his own destiny, to be able to save himself . . . to have power and to become strong enough to be holy. So God gave man the choice—to become self-sufficient and in his own power try to cancel his own sins, or to become weak and humble and accept the immeasurable sacrifice of God's Son as payment for his own sins."

Sammy listened quietly, his hands limp in his lap and his back hunched. He wanted to believe it. But how could he? How could he believe in what was at its core, that one man would sacrifice his own life for another, less deserving man? He couldn't conceive of it.

"I'm tired," Sammy said. "Can you leave?"

The chaplain stood and shook Sammy's hand. It was good to feel the hand of another man grabbing his, firmly wrapping his fingers around his flesh.

Sammy shook it, then handed the chaplain the Bible.

"I don't want to read any more of it." He assumed the chaplain would tell him that he would be praying for him or to keep the Bible, just in case. At the very least, surely the man would remind him about the few hours he had remaining in his life.

Instead, the chaplain took the Bible and waited silently for the guard to unlock the door. Then he walked out and turned right, toward the exit, and he never looked back.

Mick finished his five-mile run, unusual for a Wednesday, and came to rest on a bench on the south side of the park by the playground. It was all he knew to do. Run and think. It was just before 2 p.m. when he finished.

"How'd you do?"

Mick turned to find Libby walking across the grass, cane plugging away at the ground. He stood and greeted her, kissing her on the cheek.

"You smell like you might've just run around the world."

He laughed. "Just five miles. Not even close to my best time. I'm a bit hampered by this cast."

"Wow. Anger jogging. It can do wonders."

"How do you know I'm angry?"

"I could hear it in your voice when you left the message on my voice mail to meet you here. You sounded like you had a lot weighing on your mind, so I thought I better come make sure you're okay."

They sat down on the bench, and Libby looked toward the sunset. "I used to run. Three miles a day. Then I'd do eight on the weekend. I loved it. I used to train for marathons too. But I couldn't ever win them so I quit." She laughed. "Yeah, that's right. I'm that kind of person."

Mick smiled. He wanted to brush her hair with his

fingers as it hung down across her shoulders. His fingers tickled the wood on the bench behind her, willing himself to keep his hands to himself.

She turned to him. "We got a huge break in the case today."

"The Lamberson case?"

"Yep."

"Did you get the stuff from Reggie? about the insurance company?"

"Yeah. And I decided to go with a gut feeling I had."

Mick laughed. "Your gut seems to have special powers."

"Indeed. I had Reggie ask your white-collar-crime agents to see if there had been a life insurance policy taken out on Nicole Leville or Ira Leville."

"And?"

"Neither."

"Well, that was a good idea, anyway."

"But there was a life insurance policy taken out on Mrs. Lamberson."

"You're kidding."

"No. Three months ago."

"That's significant. How does it play out in our scenario?"

"Guber thinks I've lost my mind. Maybe I have. But maybe we've been barking up the wrong tree, and so has Ira Leville."

"You think Mrs. Lamberson is involved in the fires?"

"I'm not sure. Guber says he doesn't believe we have enough evidence to justify an investigation into whether or not she was setting the fires. We do know Nicole Leville bought a gun today."

"And we're no closer to finding the documents."

"So we've got to keep Ira and Nicole from killing each

other while we figure out if Mrs. Lamberson was involved in all of this."

He groaned.

Libby said, "So your message sounded a little urgent. Why'd you want me to meet you out here at the park?"

"I stumbled upon a gigantic piece of the puzzle in the Sammy Earle case today."

"I can't imagine it's anything more shocking than your breaking into a homicide detective's house, but go ahead."

"I took a photograph to a former Vietnam soldier who lives in Dallas; he served with Crawford, Delano, and Jefferson. He identified Crawford."

"So?"

"But said it wasn't Crawford. He said it was Patrick Delano."

Libby's mouth fell open.

"I think Patrick Delano has been posing as Crawford all these years. He must've obtained his social security number and other IDs, then disappeared for a while. Since Crawford's case is classified, all of his military records show his service in Vietnam, but they don't reveal his death. And since he's still considered MIA, there is no death certificate. So Delano has been posing as a former soldier named Shep Crawford. And he was able to reenter society, living in Irving where few people had heard of the Vietnam case."

Libby stared at the sidewalk. "What are you going to do?"

"I'm not sure. I'm going to go home, write out the case as I know it up to now, and present everything to Tom in the morning."

"This guy sounds pretty psychotic. He marks everything he owns with blood, you suspect he murdered a fellow officer, and you've got evidence he's been posing as a dead soldier that he may or may not have murdered."

"With this kind of evidence, we may be able to turn this into a federal case, as long as we can keep the military out of it for now. The problem is that Crawford already knows we're onto him in some way. He visited my sister-in-law, and I think it was just a move to show me that he knows I know something. I sent Jenny to Kansas City. She should be there by now."

Libby stood as Mick did. "Be careful on this one, okay? I've got a bad feeling about it."

"Your gut?"

"Yeah."

Mick tried to smile, but there was something disconcerting about Libby's gut.

<hr />

Mick drove to his apartment complex, barely able to focus enough to drive safely. The run had helped with the adrenaline rush, but his mind still buzzed with scenario after possible scenario.

He sat in his truck for a few minutes, trying to unwind. There was a lot at stake here, and he didn't want to make a mistake by acting too soon or without enough information. The ominous tone of Crawford's showing up at Jenny's house continued to haunt Mick. It meant that Crawford was ready and willing to go to war.

He opened the door and got out. The air was thick and humid and still, with an occasional gust of wind. Hurricane Eve, in all her fury, was coming. He'd been chasing storms a long time, so long in fact that he could almost predict the coming weather by being outside. He was more often right than wrong. He'd feel the wind, watch the clouds draw together, notice the birds' and the animals' nervousness.

He walked toward his apartment. There would be no storm chasing today. His life was thoroughly wrapped up in two different cases. At least that meant he could spend more time with Libby. The more he knew her, the more he liked her, and there was a certain place in his heart that told him to hang on to her.

Marching up the stairs, he decided a shower was in order. Then it was time to go back through the box of stuff Jenny had brought over from Aaron's investigation. Maybe something new would pop out at him in light of the recent information he—

Mick stopped. All the breath in his body left him. He stumbled backward, almost falling down the flight of stairs behind him.

In the middle of his door was an *X*, marked in blood.

chapter thirty

mick reached for his gun but grabbed air. His gun was inside. He always left it in his apartment when jogging. He grabbed his T-shirt to check the doorknob. It turned, and his door slowly opened.

He moved to the outside wall of his apartment and listened for any movement. He heard nothing but his neighbor's music. With a quick motion, he peeked inside. The apartment was mostly dark, with a small ray of the evening's last light floating through the center of the living room.

If his gun was still there, it was in his desk drawer, which was about fifteen feet away. He knew the safety was on.

"Crawford!" Mick shouted. "Crawford! If you're in there, I'm coming after you!" The adrenaline that had disappeared after his run was now in full force again.

Mick rounded the corner of the front door and scanned the living room and kitchen. All looked quiet. He lunged for the desk and pulled out his gun, releasing the safety.

Everything was perfectly still.

"Crawford!" Mick yelled.

Silence.

He'd left the front door open, which let in enough light so he didn't stumble over the furniture. But the light switch was by the door, and Mick wasn't sure he wanted to move in that direction. He pointed his gun toward the hallway.

Passing by the coat closet, he opened it and almost shot holes through an unsuspecting umbrella.

"Crawford, you sick jerk. Get out here. Stop hiding." He inched down the hallway, each step calculated and slow. He opened the door to the bathroom. He quickly glanced in, but it was empty.

In front of him, the door to his bedroom was halfway open, revealing a dark room and two red, glowing eyes.

His alarm clock.

Behind him he heard a loud thud. He whipped around and aimed his gun toward the living room. He listened carefully, trying to control his breathing. He heard it again. It was the wind banging at his door.

His attention back on his bedroom, he walked forward, pushing the door open. He swiped the light switch, illuminating the room; it appeared very ordinary and serene. Everything seemed to be in place.

The closet. He stepped forward, grabbing the doorknob. With one swift yank, he swung it open and turned on the light. He pointed his gun forward, then left and right.

He couldn't believe what he saw.

His closet, normally plagued with dirty laundry lining the floor, was perfectly neat; all of his shirts and pants hung on their hangers. His closet had received a makeover.

He slammed the closet door shut, then went to his front door and slammed it shut too. Crawford had been here and was now playing mind games with him. He set his gun down and paced in circles near his kitchen. A cold sweat broke out over his skin.

He went to the bathroom to splash his face with water and try to get a grip. He flipped on the light switch and turned on the water. The cold water made his skin tingle, but he was still having a hard time thinking straight. After one more splash, he grabbed a towel and wiped it over his

face. He glanced in the mirror and froze. The mirror
showed something behind him on the bathroom wall. He
whirled around.

A message was scribbled on the white wall with what
looked like black permanent marker:

*Do you want her back alive? I have the woman you love.
She will drown at sea at midnight.*

Mick scrambled into the living room and grabbed his
gun. For the first time, he didn't know what to do. He
noticed that his answering-machine light was blinking.
He pushed Play.

"Mick . . . hi . . . this is Faith. Listen, this is going to
sound kind of weird, but . . . okay, maybe I shouldn't say
this over the phone. I need you to call me. Thanks. Bye."

Mick looked at his hands. They were trembling. His
gun had always stopped his hands from trembling. But now
the gun was no match for what was before him.

The woman you love. Who was Crawford talking about?
Jenny? Was that why he had visited her home? Could he
possibly know about Libby? If so, he would have had to get
Libby after they left the park. What about Faith? Was the
message she'd left an indication that something strange was
going on? Maybe Crawford had visited her too.

He gasped for breath, realizing he'd been holding it.
What was he supposed to do? It would take hours to explain
to the police or even to Tom what was going on. He didn't
have that much time. It was already fifteen minutes before
three.

A cold dread clutched him, and Mick fell to his knees.
Crawford was a madman, and Mick knew immediately
there was no logical solution to this. He fell forward, his
face mashed into the carpet. With barely the breath to utter

it, he prayed. For all the training he had, it was no match for this. He didn't know whether Crawford was bluffing or not. And if Crawford did have someone, which woman did he have?

Mick shut his eyes as tightly as he could, set his gun down, and put his hands over his ears, trying to block out the fear that screamed around him. He had to focus, not on the problem, but on the solution.

Drawing in a deep breath, he asked for God's help. He'd come face-to-face with evil. The chill in his bones was proof of that. But he knew he was going to have to fight this alone. There was no time to assemble a team.

His prayer wasn't much more than a few incoherent words strung together, and he begged more than asked. He wasn't scared for his own life. Mick hadn't feared death for a long time now, but what he feared was failure. He had to save her.

Her.

Who?

He jumped to his feet and took out a Texas map that was in his drawer. He also grabbed extra clips for his gun. After securing his gun in its holster, Mick snatched his cell phone and keys and ran downstairs.

First thing he needed to do was rule out who Crawford had. As he got on the highway, headed south, he called his parents. He knew Jenny would be there.

"Hello?"

"Hi, Mom. It's Mick."

"Mick! What is going on down there? Last night Jenny said you wanted her to leave town and come stay with us a few days. I'm thrilled to have her come visit—as you know she never did that quite enough even when Aaron was alive. But there was some panic in her voice, and she said she would explain when she got here. What's going on?"

"Jenny's not there? She should've been there hours ago."

"Her plane got delayed. The only flight she could take that early stopped off in Chicago, which is the one place you never want to have to go through."

"Have you talked to her? She called to say her plane was delayed?"

"No. This morning we talked before she got on her plane. She told your dad to make sure and check for delays before we came to get her at the airport. She said her cell phone was going dead, and she might not have enough battery to call us if there was a delay. Your father said that was no problem. So we called, and sure enough, there was a delay in Chicago. We checked about an hour ago, and it was still delayed. We tried to call Jenny on her cell phone, but she didn't answer."

"Let me talk to Dad."

"All right," his mother's fragile voice said with resignation.

There was a pause and then, "Hello? Son, what's wrong?"

"Dad, there's probably nothing wrong. Jenny probably turned off her cell to try to save her battery. But I need you to contact O'Hare and see if you can get ahold of Jenny. See if they'll page her. I need to know that she's in Chicago."

"Sure. We can do that."

"I'm on my cell. Call me back."

"Okay, Son. Are you all right?"

"I'm okay. Don't worry about me. Call me as soon as you can." Mick hung up and took a breath. He was pretty sure Jenny was in Chicago. Reggie had dropped her off at the airport this morning. He needed to turn to the second woman.

He dialed Faith's number. Her answering machine

picked up. "Faith, this is Mick. I got your message. I'm headed to south Texas right now. Will you call me on my cell phone as soon as possible? Thanks. And it doesn't matter how late. Just call me."

Mick looked for Port Mansfield on his map. That's where Crawford would be, and somehow Crawford knew Mick would know how to find it. Mick dialed Libby's cell phone but got no answer. He tried her office phone.

"Hello?" It was a male voice.

"I'm sorry. I thought I was dialing Agent Lancaster's office."

"Who's this?" Mick recognized the voice. It was Agent Guber.

"It's Mick. Is Libby there?"

"I can take a message."

"I need to know that she's there. Will you put her on the phone?"

"I said I can take a message."

"Can you at least tell me if she's in the office?"

He heard the man actually chuckle. "Look, I said I'll take a message. That's all I can do for you."

"Agent Guber, this is not a joke. Libby could be in danger. I need to know her whereabouts."

"First of all, Agent Kline, Libby is in no danger. We are monitoring Mr. and Mrs. Leville, and right now they're eating dinner. Chicken by the sound of it. So let me assure you that Agent Lancaster is not in danger."

"Is she there? I need to know if she's there."

"I think you've crossed the line here. It's pretty obvious you have feelings for her, but why don't you take a step back and use some professionalism, okay?"

"This is not about—" Mick wanted to reach through the phone line and punch this man—"this is of a professional nature."

"Great. Then I'm sure you can tell me why there is an urgency in talking to her."

"Why is this so hard for you? I need to know that she's safe. Just tell me if she's there at the office. That's all I need to know."

Guber chuckled again. "Look, Agent, I'm sure this is really important. I'll have Libby call you when she can." He hung up.

Mick quickly dialed another number.

Marnie answered the phone and didn't bother with hello, thanks to her caller ID. "Reggie's sulking. He's been sulking all night. He was ticked that you didn't call and check in with him."

"I'm calling now. Is he there?"

"Yeah. But it may take several minutes for him to get to the phone because he walks slower when he's sulking." There was a pause as he heard Marnie shouting for Reggie to get the phone.

"Yeah," Reggie said, picking up.

"Don't be mad."

With complete lack of enthusiasm Reggie said, "I'm really not that mad. I handled an entire investigation by myself today and had no idea where you were. But I'm not mad. That's why we have partners. So we can do everything by ourselves."

"Reg, I'm in trouble. Something's happened."

"What?"

"Go to my apartment. Seal it off and call the police. Crawford was there, and he's taken someone."

"Who?"

Mick sped around cars on the highway as he cradled the phone. "I don't know. He claims he has the woman I love."

He could hear Reggie breathing, wanting to ask, but pausing to ponder who that might be.

Mick answered for him. "I don't know who he's talking about. I can't confirm Jenny ever got on the airplane. I can't get ahold of Faith. And I can't get ahold of . . ."

"Of?"

Mick sighed. "Libby."

Thankfully Reggie was all business. "I'll get to your apartment. Where are you?"

"I'm headed to Port Mansfield. Crawford said he's going to drown her in the ocean, and I remember his beach house number from a photograph I saw. I'm sure Crawford knows we were in his house, and he probably realizes if I don't already know it, I'm on a fast track to realizing who he is."

"Who is he?"

"Patrick Delano."

"What? You're sure?"

"I had a soldier identify him today. Delano has been posing as Crawford for years."

"I'm going to contact the sheriff down there."

"No, not yet, Reg. Crawford is baiting me. If the police get involved, who knows what he might do."

"You're going down there by yourself?" Reggie wasn't hiding the resignation in his voice.

Mick sped past more cars. "Yeah. He can't be that much ahead of me. He may have an hour or so more, tops."

Ahead was a line of dark clouds, visible against the fading blue sky.

Eve. She was coming with a vengeance.

Mick was driving straight toward a Category 5 hurricane.

"Reg, I need you to do something else. Call Tom. Tell him what's going on. He needs to be on standby to call the governor."

"You think Crawford killed that DA ten years ago?"

"Delano. Yeah. I think he set Sammy up. He didn't want to kill him. He wanted to make him suffer. It's all coming together. Aaron was on the right track. He just didn't have enough of the pieces to the puzzle." Mick looked at the clock. "Reggie, how long does it take to get to Port Mansfield?"

"Port Mansfield? I think maybe nine hours."

Mick's stomach turned. It was after 3 p.m.

"Mick? You're breaking up. Can you hear me? Mick?"

The line went dead.

Mick stuck the cell phone in the front pocket of his T-shirt. The highway stretched long and straight in front of him, and hovering over it in the distance were threatening, black clouds.

Mick turned on the radio and tried to find a weather report. It wasn't hard. All the stations were saying the same thing.

The Texas coastline was being evacuated.

chapter thirty-one

Seven hours into the chase, Mick was growing weary. He'd encountered hard, pelting rain an hour back, and his windshield wipers were struggling to keep up. He'd had to slow down considerably. It was nothing short of disconcerting to see a line of cars coming from the opposite direction, piled bumper to bumper. Very few cars were traveling in his direction. Occasionally he would see a car in the distance, barely visible through the rain.

The clouds were ferocious, spewing wind-whipped rain, signaling warning after warning with intense lightning that splintered the dark sky.

The bars on his cell phone came and went, but he was not yet able to call out. His phone had rung once; it was Reggie, but when he answered it the phone was dead. Satellite phones were very handy in erasing roaming problems but useless in bad weather.

Mick tried his best to keep focused on the drive. His imagination wanted attention. It wanted to play out scenario after horrible scenario. But in reality there wasn't too much to play with. He didn't know who Crawford had, if anybody. Maybe Crawford was setting him up.

Mick remembered the fragile voice of Delano's former guard, Billy Wedestal, who had gravely insinuated that it was Delano's knack for exposing secrets that had perhaps been behind his mysterious disappearance from prison.

313

Perhaps Crawford had been watching Mick for much longer than Mick knew. Maybe since the first time Mick had visited him at his home.

Mick squinted, trying to see the road through the rain. How was he going to find the right house? And how insane was it to try to locate a beach house in the middle of a Category 5 hurricane?

The radio, fading in and out the closer Mick got to the ocean, was continuing to warn people to evacuate. Flooding was going to be a problem soon too. The eye of the storm was still a hundred miles off the coastline, but the storm surge would be catastrophic even now, reaching possibly twelve or more feet, maxing out at as high as eighteen feet. Mick knew the grim statistics—70 to 90 percent of all hurricane deaths are caused by storm surges.

On the side of the road, an electronic sign warned of the hurricane and flash flood. In blinking lights it instructed *Evacuate north now.*

Mick turned on the light in his truck and tried to manage the map and the torrential rain. He found Port Mansfield. Crawford's beach house should be pretty easy to find, with a small population and only a small amount of residential beach property.

Then again it was storming. It was going to be hard to see house numbers—assuming the houses were still standing when he got there.

The sky continued to glisten with golden white light. On an ordinary day, Mick would be out of his truck, pointing his camera toward the heavens, trying to capture that perfect photograph. But this was no ordinary day, and this was no ordinary storm. Mick had read a lot about hurricanes, observed Hurricane Gilbert in 1988, and recorded pictures of Hurricane Bret in 1999.

The highway narrowed to two lanes, and the north-bound lane was still gridlocked with hundreds of cars. He could see flashing lights ahead, probably state troopers warning people to turn around. Mick seemed to be the only person who wanted to go south.

He pulled up slowly to the roadblock. Several troopers were standing in rain gear holding flashlights. One approached Mick's window. As Mick rolled it down, rain blew into his truck and splashed against his face.

"Sir," the trooper shouted over the wind, "you need to turn around! There's a hurricane coming!"

Mick showed his identification to the trooper.

The trooper checked it and handed it back. "What's wrong?"

Mick shouted, "I'm in pursuit of a man who may have a hostage with him. He lives in Port Mansfield and is believed to be headed there now."

"Port Mansfield is right on the ocean."

"I know. This guy's armed and is wanted for multiple murders, most recently of a homicide detective. How far is Port Mansfield from here?"

"About twenty minutes."

Mick didn't know what kind of car Crawford was driving, so he asked, "Have you seen a male in his sixties with a young woman come through?"

"I don't know. We've had some traffic; most everyone has turned around. There are several other ways into Port Mansfield. This is just the main thoroughfare."

"What is the latest on the storm?"

"It's hedging between a Category 5 and a 4. It has weakened some, but it's still very dangerous."

Mick wiped the rain off his face. "All right. I've got to get this guy. Wish me luck."

The trooper pointed his flashlight south. "This will run

you right into it. There is a road called Front and that will lead you to the majority of beach houses."

"Thanks."

The trooper backed up and signaled for the other troopers to step aside.

Mick drove forward and rolled up his window. He was already soaking wet.

Front Road was nothing more than gravel. When Mick reached it, it was thirty minutes before midnight. His truck swerved against the wind. A semi with any height would be blown over. Mick estimated the winds to be at least one hundred miles an hour. They would only get stronger as the eye moved toward land.

In front of him he could see flickering lights and small beach houses. Some were trailers. The trees whipped and cracked and snapped. To get his bearings, Mick needed to find a house number. Then he could search for Crawford's.

He carefully stepped out of his truck, hanging on to the side. He could walk in this wind, but not very fast, and he had to hold on to something. Moving away from the truck, he tried to keep himself sheltered behind buildings and trees. A large piece of siding rolled across the street in front of him, clanging against structures, then floating to the sky as if weightless. The howling wind screamed as if all the devils in the world were being alerted to their final doom.

Struggling forward from tree to tree, Mick tried to reach the first house, which didn't look as stable as the tree he was holding on to. He decided he'd better crawl, so he lowered himself and moved toward the heavily boarded, square house on his stomach. Nearby the waves crashed into the darkness. The lightning had dimmed, and Mick was praying the electricity would hold.

He reached the house and stood at its back, finding

little relief from the stinging wind. He took in a deep
breath, suddenly realizing how alone he was. He also realized how easy it would be to drown someone. He couldn't
really see the water, but he could hear it and feel it.

Taking a deep breath, he moved around the side of the
house, trying to get to the front to see a house number.
Finally he saw three numbers hanging crookedly against the
wood. One number was missing. It read 11_4. He guessed
he was maybe five or six houses away, but it was hard to
know with the number missing.

He turned to return to the back of the house, and when
he did, he was looking right into the barrel of a gun.

Holding it was Crawford. "Hi, Mick."

Crawford's beach house was three houses down, and
they made their way along the backs of the other houses.
Crawford trailed Mick, his gun in Mick's back not-so-gently
reminding him to keep it moving.

Finally they got to Crawford's and went in. Mick's
clothes sagged against his body, and he began to shiver.
Crawford shoved him into the living room.

"Where is she?" Mick demanded as he fell into a
wooden chair near the center of the room. Crawford tied
Mick's arms to the chair with boating rope. "Where is she?"

Crawford smiled, wiping the water from his face with a
towel. "It's cold, isn't it? Out there, I mean? That water is
frigid."

Mick made himself stay calm. Crawford wanted to play
games; let him play games.

Crawford was silent for a while, wringing out his shirt.
The beach house rocked and creaked in the wind. Mick
looked at a clock on the wall. It was ten until midnight.
A gentle thunder, barely audible, rumbled in the raging
wind.

"You went to an awful lot of trouble to get her,"

317

Crawford finally said, standing across from Mick on the other side of the room.

Mick stayed silent. There was no need to bow to Crawford's demand for banter. Instead, he carefully eyed the overly tidy room. Crawford stood in front of a short hallway that most likely led to a bathroom and bedroom. Maybe someone was tied up there.

A couple of feet away was a small table, only big enough for two people to sit at. On top of the table was an open bottle of sherry and a glass half full.

The house seemed to lift and settle. Crawford held on to the wall. Mick's chair slid closer to the table.

Crawford looked out the front windows, which weren't boarded up. "It's all going to be destroyed. I spent years on this place. My private paradise. It's all going to be gone. I named her *Justice*. My sailboat. She's beautiful." Then he turned and walked down the hall and out of sight.

Mick heard the muffled scream of a woman. He tried to wiggle loose, but it was useless.

He glanced at the sherry again. If Crawford didn't kill him first, the storm would. He looked out the back door, which rattled in the wind. The rain blew in a straight, horizontal line.

The hallway was still dark and motionless. Mick raised one foot and with the tip of his shoe, knocked the bottle of sherry and the glass over. The sherry dripped into the carpet.

Mick scooted his chair away from the table.

A few moments later, Crawford emerged from the hallway with a woman, her face hidden in the shadows. Her hands were tied in front of her, and she had tape over her mouth. When she came into the dim light of the living room, Mick recognized her.

It was Taylor.

Mick addressed her. "Are you okay?"

She nodded, but her eyes were wide with terror. She looked out the front window then at Crawford as if wondering which thing was more dangerous.

"I paid her to be loyal." Crawford shoved her forward and pushed her to her knees in the middle of the room.

Through tangled hair, one eye peered up at Mick.

Mick was silent.

"But even that couldn't shut her up. She had to tell you." With his knee Crawford pushed her farther to the floor. "You couldn't stay silent, could you?" He smiled at Mick. "It's really all her fault. You're after me, thinking I'm the one that put Sammy where he is, but that's not the entire story, is it, Taylor?" Crawford ripped the tape off Taylor's mouth.

Taylor stared at the floor.

"You wanted Sammy to suffer just like I did. We made a pretty good team."

"What are you talking about?" Mick asked.

"I guess you know by now that I'm not who I say I am." Chills poured down Mick's already shivering body. "Sammy Earle deserved something worse than death. He betrayed me after I saved his life. And to give even less credibility to his already worthless life, he used this woman. Over and over again. So she helped me put Sammy into a place of tremendous suffering. Luckily for him, his suffering is just about over. But it was nice to know he was squirming for all these years."

"You made me do it!" Taylor screamed at Crawford. She looked at Mick. "He made me."

Crawford shook his head. "Taylor, that's been your excuse your whole life. When are you going to be accountable for your own actions?" He gazed out the front window, stilled by what seemed like distant memories. "She was supposed to disappear forever. And Sammy was supposed to go down for her murder. But then you and your brother got in the way."

Crawford faced Mick. "So I had to come up with a different plan. Worked pretty good too. I killed off a useless DA, and Sammy got framed for it. It was unfortunate that your brother found this woman the first time, but I decided to give her a second chance. She was supposed to disappear for good. But then you found her again. You just wouldn't give up."

Mick locked eyes with Crawford. "My brother knew, didn't he? He knew something was wrong with the entire investigation of the DA's murder."

"Aaron was something else. I admired him—I really did. I didn't think he was smart enough to put it all together. But I admired him." Crawford gestured at the air. "Doesn't matter. Sammy Earle is getting what he deserves, but unfortunately there're going to be casualties." He drew a knife from a sheath that rested on his hip bone.

Mick looked at the table, where the sherry was still dripping. Through the darkness it was hard to see, but as Mick's attention turned toward it, so did Crawford's.

"What's that?" he grumbled, leaving Taylor and marching over to the table.

Mick was hoping he was right, that Crawford's obsessive-compulsive neurosis wouldn't leave the mess undone. By the pained expression on Crawford's face, the idea of sherry dropping onto the carpet was more disturbing than the fact that he was about to spill blood onto it.

Without hesitation, Crawford grabbed a nearby towel and began sopping up the mess. And with one swift kick, Mick caught him under the chin, toppling him backward. Taylor was about to scream. "Run! Run!" Mick yelled.

She got up and stumbled forward and out the back of the house.

Mick kicked Crawford between the legs; Crawford rolled over and groaned. Then he moved away from Mick's reach and turned onto his belly before scraping himself off the floor.

Crawford looked out the back door. "I don't need her anyway. She's a weak woman and always will be." Then he took the sherry bottle and with one swipe knocked Mick across the head. A warm, thick stream of blood trickled down the side of Mick's face. Crawford hit him again.

When Mick opened his eyes, the room was blurry. The lights faded in and out; he couldn't decide if the house was losing electricity. He could hear the wind blowing, but he was getting dizzy.

Then the room went dark.

chapter thirty-two

mick opened his eyes. Blackness. But wind. It didn't roar. It was still strong, but not violent.

When he closed his eyes, he wanted to sleep. An enticing grogginess was outdone, however, by a searing pain on the right side of his head. And his left arm throbbed. He lifted his head and opened his eyes. He tried to stay awake. Images slowly came into view, but no clearer than bad reception on a television set.

He was still tied to the chair, still in the small living room. Outside, the ocean's unsettled tide continued to beat against the shore, but the rain pattered evenly against the roof. He could even hear the swishing of the trees. Lightning illuminated the room, but only every few minutes.

Where was Crawford?

There was an unidentifiable noise nearby. He couldn't place it. But it wasn't from the storm.

He tried to read the clock in front of him. He could barely see the hands. Was the hour hand near the five? No, that was the minute hand. He tried to find the hour hand, but everything was blurry. The more conscious he became, the more his head hurt.

And what was that sound? It sounded like scratching, like a cat or dog scratching at the door.

Focus on the clock. Seven. The hour hand was on

seven. It was 7:30 a.m.? He'd been unconscious that long? That was not good. That meant he had a pretty heavy concussion. His neck hurt too.

Mick took in a breath. He prayed. There was a feeling deep inside him that this was not supposed to be his time to die, but he also knew that Crawford had plans for him. He could've killed him hours ago, but instead he let him sleep.

He surmised that Crawford felt protected by the storm. Nobody was around. Law enforcement was busy. He had all the time in the world, assuming his house was left standing.

Mick looked out the window. Strangely, there was a hint of light, as if the sun was almost breaking through. How? Eve was a huge hurricane. Where would the light be coming from?

It seemed like the electricity was out. All the lightbulbs were dark. From where he sat Mick could see half of the back door banging against the frame. It was unlocked, left that way after Taylor fled. He prayed she'd escaped the storm, but she would have a hard time finding help.

Mick's attention turned back to the strange sound. It seemed to be coming from behind him, to the right. That was going to be tricky, because moving his head just a little was excruciating. But he did it inch by inch, slowly. Either his eyes were adjusting to the dark or more light was entering the house. Whatever the case, he could see things much more clearly now. He continued to turn his neck, and then he saw movement out of the corner of his eye. It looked like an arm about ten feet away near the wall.

Mick made himself turn even more, using his back to help. Then he saw the source of the noise.

Crawford.

Before him was a once white wall, now partially covered in black permanent marker. Crawford had his back to

Mick, not realizing Mick was awake, and he was scribbling all over the wall, almost as mechanically as a robot. He was mumbling, but Mick couldn't understand what he was saying.

Mick couldn't read any of the words. He could pick out letters, but every word was covered by another and another. In silence, with his pain as background, he watched with awe as Crawford's arm moved capriciously over the wall with the marker, as if it were his canvas on which a lifetime of derangement could spill.

A sickening feeling swelled in Mick's gut, and he finally realized what he was up against. Crawford had masqueraded as another man and had been able to disguise his insanity all these years. He was highly intelligent and full of vengeance. Nothing was going to stop Crawford's plan to frame Sammy Earle and watch him be marched to his death.

More light filtered into the house, and Mick knew instantly that it had to be the sun. But how? The storm couldn't have passed over this quickly. Had he been unconscious for more than a day? Things weren't making sense.

Before Mick could figure it out, his shadow fell against the wall that held Crawford's attention. A perfect silhouette of Mick's upright head appeared just inches from Crawford's hand.

The writing stopped. The marker dropped to the floor, and Crawford turned around. The expression on his face was unlike anything Mick had seen from him before. He looked as if he'd been caught naked. Redness flushed his cheeks and neck. And a terrifying rage swept through his eyes.

Mick wanted to raise his hands to protect himself as Crawford lunged for him, but his arms were still roped to the chair, and he was helpless to do anything except take what was coming. He squeezed his eyes shut and felt Crawford's fingers scrape across his cheek like the claws of a wild animal.

Mick winced and felt tears rush to his eyes. When he looked up, he saw Crawford standing over him. He'd grabbed something long and metal and raised it over his head with both hands. The sun's gentle rays glinted off it.

Suddenly Mick's cell phone rang. It was working again, thanks to a clearing sky.

Crawford froze, glaring at the phone in Mick's shirt pocket, which continued to melodically ring to the tune of the SportsCenter theme song. He lowered the bar he was holding and seized the phone, staring at it like he'd never seen one before. He looked at Mick and laughed. Then he shrugged and answered it, though he didn't say hello. He simply listened.

After a few seconds he said, "Who is this?"

He listened again, then looked at Mick. "I didn't realize so many women adored you."

"Who is it?" Mick asked.

Crawford didn't respond.

Mick could hear a female voice on the other end. He felt himself tremble from adrenaline. It was one thing to deal with Crawford himself, but now Crawford was engaging someone else's life, and Mick didn't like it.

Crawford looked amused as he listened, even smiling a time or two. Finally he said, "That's very interesting, but you'll never get here in time. I'm going to kill Mick. He thinks he's done a noble thing by trying to stop me, but it's too late. Everything has been set into motion, and unfortunately, he doesn't really understand the true meaning of nobility. Or sacrifice. He's never been to war to save this country from unspeakable evil. I have. And, like most soldiers, my sacrifice went unnoticed. Even judged as selfish. So, unfortunately for Mick, he is going to die for no good reason at all."

Crawford listened again to the female voice on the other end. He chuckled. "I'm not a fool. He has to die now. This is a satellite phone, and you're going to be able to trace this call to an exact location. But when you get here, I'll be long gone, across the Mexico border before you can get through all the red tape you'd have to get through to stop me. . . . I guess you'll just have to trust me that he's still alive."

Crawford turned to look out the front of his home. He shook his head and glanced at Mick. "She's crying. Can you believe that? The woman is crying."

His attention was back to the phone and then he said, "Why not?" He looked at Mick and shrugged. "I guess it's time for you to say your good-byes." Crawford held the phone up to Mick's ear.

The voice on the other end came through clearly. "Mick?"

"I'm here." It was Libby. His heart broke at the possibility of never seeing her again.

"Duck."

"What?"

"Duck."

It was his nature to ask why, but he didn't this time. Instead he closed his eyes and as best he could while tied to the chair, ducked his head and body. Then he heard shattering glass from the back door, something whiz over the top of his head, and a heavy *thump.*

He opened his eyes. He couldn't hear Libby's voice anymore. "Libby?"

He realized the phone wasn't to his ear, and when he glanced sideways, Crawford wasn't standing beside him anymore. He was lying on the floor, the phone a few inches from his fingers. A deep groan gurgled from his mouth, and there was blood soaking through his shirt by his left shoulder.

"Mick!"

Mick looked toward the sound and saw Libby coming through the back door, her gun aimed at Crawford on the floor. "Are you okay?" she said, kneeling beside him.

"Can you get me loose?"

After eyeing Crawford, who looked to have lost consciousness, Libby examined the rope. She worked to get it loose. His arms and hands were finally free.

Crawford groaned again and opened his eyes.

"Did he have a weapon?" Libby asked.

"A knife. I don't know where it is. And he has a gun somewhere too. Plus that metal bar."

Libby limped forward, keeping her gun pointed at Crawford.

Mick stood up, his entire body as wobbly as a newly born animal trying to stand. He was dehydrated, and every inch of his body ached.

Like a gigantic shadow had passed over the sun, the room went dark and then almost completely black. Mick could barely see Libby and he moved next to her.

"What's going on?" Libby asked.

Mick realized it immediately. The eye of the storm had passed directly over them, creating the illusion that the storm had vanished. But in fact, if the eye had passed over and was now gone, that meant the back end of the storm was coming, which would be more forceful than the front end.

They could hardly see Crawford on the floor. He was moving his legs. The wind's velocity picked up, and within seconds the trees were holding on for life. Mick could hear the water stirring and splashing outside.

Mick grabbed Libby's arm. "We have to get out of here. Now!"

The house creaked and swayed, and the front window shattered, spraying glass all over them and Crawford. The wind hit Mick and Libby, making them stumble backward. A heavy rain began to fall.

"What about him?" Libby hollered.

Mick hesitated. How could they get Crawford out of here? If they left him, he might be able to make it out and into Mexico. Mick needed Crawford in custody to make his case for saving Sammy Earle.

As if a huge bucket of water had been thrown against the house, a foot of water swelled at their feet, flooding the floors.

Crawford choked and sat up, disoriented. Then the house moved, as if it had been lifted off its foundation.

Libby screamed as she fell into the water. Mick took her arm and yanked her up. A large, crashing noise above them caused Mick to push Libby toward the back door. He stumbled behind her. A piece of wood fell onto his shoulder, but he managed to get outside. He glanced back. A huge tree had fallen into the middle of the living room. He could see Crawford's head, but it was too dark to see anything else.

He took Libby's hand. The rain was horizontal. She stopped, staring with horror at the scene.

A knocking and ripping sound caused Mick to look up. The roof to Crawford's house was coming off by the shingles. "Come on!"

For the first time since he'd known her, he could see the fear in Libby's eyes as she watched the beach house collapse further with each burst of wind.

He felt in his jeans for his keys. They were still there. "Let's go," he said, pulling her into the open terrain.

After they ran a few yards, Mick stopped.

"What's wrong?" Libby yelled.

"Where's my truck?"

They looked around; then Libby pointed to a grouping of trees. The truck had rolled and was upside down, smashed into a tree.

Mick turned, trying to swallow air instead of rain. None of the shelters along the beach would survive. Every minute that went by meant the storm was going to get stronger, and pretty soon the surge would be enough to drown them.

"How'd you get here?" he shouted over the noise.

"My motorcycle."

"Where?"

"Parked behind that garage," she said, motioning to the building about twenty yards away.

He couldn't believe that Libby had driven all this way on a motorcycle. In a storm! He took her hand and they moved toward it. Mick tried to pull her as fast as he could, because there was a good chance both of them could be struck by flying debris. But her bad leg made it hard for her to run fast.

Once they made it safely behind the garage, they found a little shelter and Libby's motorcycle, still standing.

"We can't stay here," Mick said. "This is the back end of at least a Category 4." He seized her helmet and put it on her.

She popped the visor down and took the key out of her pocket. She swung her good leg over and, with a trembling hand, put the key in the ignition. Mick got on and grabbed her waist with his good arm.

She started the motorcycle, then put her hand on her own shoulder. Mick took it and gave it a reassuring squeeze. She grasped the handlebars and revved the engine. She started it slow, and Mick could tell she was mentally calculating how to get into the line of wind without being blown over. She was going to have to enter it moving the same direction or they'd both be blown off.

She picked up speed across a patch of grass, and then with a quick maneuver, darted to the right and into the straight-line winds. The motorcycle swerved, but Libby maintained control, though the wind forced the motorcycle into a higher rate of speed.

Mick had to shut his eyes and put his face into Libby's shoulder. "Keep us alive."

There was only One who could hear a whisper through this storm.

i t seemed like years, but it was probably only thirty minutes until Mick and Libby had driven far enough north to be out of the worst part of the storm. They were both soaked and chilled. Libby decreased her speed as they drove along the wet highway. Gray clouds swirled, but the rain fell in soft sheets. Mick opened his eyes and glanced backward. In the distance, the black clouds suffocated the horizon.

They had gotten lucky. No, more than that. They were saved.

Libby slowed even more and Mick looked ahead. They were finally back to civilization. A traffic jam was evident by the long string of brake lights glowing from the vehicles ahead. Most likely the people evacuating at the last minute.

Libby pulled behind a yellow Volvo station wagon and stopped. She took off her helmet and turned around. "You need to get to a hospital. I think your head's going to need stitches."

Mick felt the side of his head. He winced and nodded. Stitches for sure. And maybe a Valium and a vacation. "How did you know where I was?"

"Reggie got ahold of me—no thanks to Guber—and told me what was going on. I had a gut feeling that you went after Crawford. I retrieved his address pretty easily. I tried to get backup, but everyone and their dog were busy dealing with the hurricane. So I just came alone. It was hard getting to you, though. It took me forever."

Mick wanted to kiss her, but instead he wiped her matted hair out of her face. Then he wrapped his good arm back around her waist, but this time, she laced her fingers between his.

She looked ahead at the standstill traffic. "We may be here a while."

"I could sit like this for a long time."

She laughed.

Her laughter was interrupted as a loud pop exploded beside them and her left mirror shattered.

Libby screamed, dropping her helmet.

Mick whirled around. A large red SUV—Crawford's—was only twenty yards away and gaining quickly. He held a gun out of his window.

Another shot, this time ricocheting off the fender of the car in front of them.

"Go!" Mick yelled.

Libby took off, around the right side of the Volvo and onto the side of the highway. She accelerated, and Mick pointed to the off-ramp ahead. He heard another shot, but it didn't hit them. When he looked back, Crawford was steering his vehicle to the side and barreling toward them, barely missing the cars to his left that were still stopped.

Libby raced up the ramp and turned east onto a two-lane road that looked to head into rural Texas. Crawford was still behind them, fishtailing as he tried to make the sharp right turn to follow them.

"Where is he?" Libby shouted.

"Right behind us!"

They were now doing eighty on the flat, rain-washed road, but the rain had stopped. Through his tearing eyes, Mick thought he could see flashing red and blue lights about a mile ahead. The wind had settled too, but the clouds still had a menacing look to them. A bright bolt of lightning stabbed the ground a few miles ahead.

Mick glanced back, and Crawford was still trailing but gaining on them. "Faster, Libby!"

"What about that?" she asked, pointing. Another stroke of lightning lit up the dark horizon. It was a severe storm, an offshoot from the hurricane.

As the flashing red and blue lights came into fuller view, Mick knew immediately what was going on. It was the sheriff's department closing the road. This storm was producing tornadoes. It fit perfectly into a normal weather pattern of a hurricane, which would typically spawn small storms at the right front quadrant of the hurricane.

The sheriff's car was blocking the center of the road, and as he saw them coming, he stepped out of his vehicle and waved.

"What are we doing?" Libby yelled.

"We have to keep going! Go around him!"

Mick could feel Libby breathing rapidly. She lowered her head, though, and pressed forward.

The sheriff yelled and waved frantically.

Libby raced around his car, leaving behind his panicked warnings. Mick looked back to see what Crawford would do. He didn't bother going around the car and plowed right through it. The sheriff's deputy jumped out of the way just in time, but his car was knocked to the side as if it were a plastic toy.

The sun was high enough in the sky to break through the scattered clouds behind them and illuminate the storm in front. Dipping below the heavy thunderstorm were wispier clouds, rotating in a circle at the edge of a wall cloud. It was hard to tell how far away it was, but Mick guessed about two miles.

"Keep going!"

She looked back at him.

"Trust me!" he said.

Libby sped forward.

Mick glanced back. Crawford was about a fourth of a mile behind but gaining speed. In front of them was a good-size hill.

"Mick!" Libby motioned ahead. A defined hook was lowering from the clouds. It spun into a cone shape and drifted toward the ground. "Mick!"

"Don't stop!"

"Are you crazy?"

"You have to trust me!"

He could feel the motorcycle slow. "Libby, go fast! Hurry! I've got a plan!"

The bike lurched forward and picked up speed. They were topping the hill, and the tornado was now on the ground, spinning up dirt. Mick estimated it was two hundred yards away. But only about thirty yards away was an overpass.

"Go under the pass and hang a right. We're going to hide behind the bridge. As quickly as you can!"

Libby raced forward, then slowed just enough to make the sharp right turn that would propel the bike up on the grassy hill that held the overpass. The bike tipped, but they both hopped off in time. Mick killed the engine and laid the bike all the way down, then dragged Libby up toward the bridge. He peeked over the bridge right as Crawford was coming over the hill.

"Give me your gun," Mick said.

Libby handed it over, but she was staring at the tornado behind them. Then she gasped. The tornado had separated, and now there were two. Twins. "Shouldn't we be under the overpass?" Libby yelled through the wind.

"Stay here. Do you hear me? Don't move. Don't go anywhere."

"Where are you going?"

Mick didn't have time to answer. He scooted back down the hill, still out of sight of Crawford's vehicle. All he could hear was a mighty rumbling as the wind blazed through the countryside. The twins crisscrossed paths over the road, swirling dirt and debris.

Mick waited. Then he heard a vehicle, and within seconds, Crawford's SUV sped under the bridge, but as soon as it did, it screeched to a halt.

Mick aimed the gun and shot out the back right tire. It exploded and caused the SUV to almost tip. He shot out the right front tire, and then it rolled twice, coming to rest on its side.

There was no time to waste. He ran to the SUV and hopped on top, breaking the few pieces of unbroken passenger-window glass with his foot. Crawford looked unconscious. Mick searched for the gun but couldn't see it in his hands or anywhere nearby.

He slid down the side of the SUV and went to the front, where the windshield was shattered. He surveyed the scene and still couldn't see Crawford's gun, but he could see his hands, which were bloody and resting on top of the steering wheel.

Stuffing Libby's gun into the belt of his jeans, he dragged Crawford out of the vehicle, dropping him onto the cement. He patted his pants and his shirt but didn't find a weapon.

Crawford opened his eyes.

"Don't move," Mick warned.

Crawford rolled over, and with a long groan managed to get onto his knees. He raised his head and looked at Mick, who immediately drew his gun. An entire side of

Crawford's shirt was bloodied from the bullet that Libby had fired back at the beach house.

. Behind him, Mick could hear the tornado. The wind gusts were whipping the back of his shirt away from his skin. He could see Libby, still by the bike. He prayed she would stay there.

Crawford wiped the blood from his face. "You're going to get us all killed out here. Are you willing to die just to get your man, Kline? And let the lady die too?" He looked behind Mick toward the tornado. Fear flashed in his eyes as he watched it move.

Mick wasn't about to glance around to see it. "There's only one person who doesn't have a good chance of getting out of here. And that's you." He kept his hands steady as he pointed the gun at Crawford.

Crawford shook his head. "You're going to get killed, you idiot. We all are. We're right in the path of two tornadoes, and you're standing here acting like it's a sunny day at the beach." He stood on shaky limbs.

Mick tightened his grip on the gun.

"You should run for it. Save yourself and her." Crawford motioned toward Libby.

"You even take a step and I'm pulling this trigger."

"Doesn't it go against your religion, Mick, to kill another human being?"

"Maybe. But I can blow your kneecap off without killing you."

"Is your God going to protect you from that tornado too?"

"Yes."

Crawford laughed. "I'd like to see that."

His smile faded as several vehicles with sirens and flashing lights topped the hill and sped toward them.

"This is the end," Mick said. "You've killed enough people and destroyed enough lives."

Within seconds, they were surrounded. Mick could see Libby close her cell phone and instruct the officers to take charge of Crawford. Soon Crawford was back on the ground, handcuffed, and then being led away.

"You need to leave here now!" one of the officers shouted at Mick before hurrying back to his car.

Libby came up next to Mick and pulled his arm.

But Mick turned and smiled at her. "It's okay. We're safe."

Mick watched the two tornadoes continue to spin and dance across the plains. For once, he didn't feel like snapping a picture.

"You are one crazy guy. I don't know why I trusted you to drive me straight into the path of a tornado, but something told me to do it."

"We had three things going for us. One, tornadoes almost always move from west to east. Two, tornadoes spawned from hurricanes are usually never stronger than an F1 or F2."

"Interesting," she said, watching them in the distance. "You were willing to bet your life on it, huh?"

"I was willing to bet your life on it, and that's a life I'd protect at all costs." He grabbed her hand and pulled her close.

"What's the third thing?"

"We're people of prayer."

She laughed. "Amen."

Mick watched as the officers put Crawford into the back of a deputy's car. Crawford looked up just in time to see Mick. He remained expressionless, and his face disappeared behind the backseat.

"I've got to make a phone call."

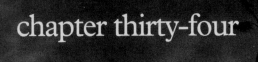

between the flashing lights, the media lights, the house lights, and the spotlight, the Leville house looked like a Broadway show. And there was plenty of drama to go with it.

An enormous bay window framed Ira and Nicole Leville holding each other at gunpoint. Nicole was dressed in a black strapless evening gown, complete with pearls. In one hand she was holding her evening bag. In the other, a handgun. Mr. Leville was dressed in a silk robe, his hair tousled on top. He sat in a big leather chair, also holding a handgun.

All of this was in plain sight of every law-enforcement agency that felt the need to get involved.

Reggie joined Mick and Libby, looking exhausted. "Unbelievable. How long has this been going on now?"

"Three hours," Mick replied.

"Why don't you say we all leave and see what happens? I have a date with my wife!" Reggie said. "Everyone knows these two people have no intention of really shooting each other."

An ATF agent approached Libby. "The hostage negotiator wants to know if you'd like him to try again."

"Maybe we should bring in a marriage counselor," Mick said.

Reggie and Libby laughed.

The agent didn't look amused.

"Tell Guber it's his call. I'm going to take a break. Mick, come with me."

Mick followed Libby through the mess of vehicles and to his brand-new car. "Let's take a drive."

"Now?"

"Oh, come on. The most exciting thing that's going to happen inside that house is the possibility that Nicole might break a nail."

Once inside the car, she said, "Nice car. I like it. Did you get a good insurance settlement on your truck?"

"Yeah."

"Decided to go with something more . . . grown up?"

Mick smiled. Yeah. Exactly. Everything felt right in his life. He'd called Faith, said his good-byes, and wished her a good life. And he'd received a heartfelt blessing from Jenny, who recognized that Libby was the perfect woman for him.

It had been five days since they'd arrested Crawford. Tom had called the governor, who had issued a stay of execution. The prosecutor was reviewing the evidence, but it looked very likely that Sammy Earle would be released soon, especially with Taylor Franks's testimony. She'd managed to escape, but not completely unharmed. She was going to need years of therapy, both mental and physical.

Crawford—or Patrick Delano—was facing murder charges that dated back decades. He refused to be psychologically evaluated and said he was as clearheaded as the day he was drafted for war.

Mick had spent an evening with Libby, telling her everything she meant to him. They talked long into the night about their future, and by the end of it, the only thing missing was a wedding ring and a formal proposal. That would come soon enough.

Finally, Mick had found her. And she was worth the wait.

"Where are we going?" he asked.

"I have a gut feeling."

"Oh no."

"Seriously. Get on the highway."

Mick groaned. "Is this going to be dangerous? I'm a week away from retirement, and I don't want to get killed. I finally got this stupid cast off my arm."

She laughed. "I'll handle the dangerous part."

"I don't want you getting killed either."

"This is the end of the line for us both," she said, smiling at him. "You're sure this is what you want to do? leave the FBI?"

"Positive. There's only room for one of us to be in a wacky profession like ours."

"As opposed to becoming a full-time storm chaser."

"Storms are more predictable than people."

She laughed. "I'll remember that when I'm having a hard day."

Libby had taken a job with ATF in profiling. Her body was still recovering, but it was her mind that was so brilliant at solving crime. She'd seemed immediately at peace with the decision.

Mick knew that peace. He'd felt it too when he decided to retire from the FBI, but Reggie had bawled like a baby.

"You finally get the girl and then you dump me?" he'd teased. Reggie knew it was the right decision though and was graciously throwing him a big retirement party this weekend.

"Where are we going?" Mick asked. "This isn't like you to not want to stay right in the middle of the action."

"I've been doing a lot of thinking."

"About me?"

"About the Lamberson case."

"Not about me?"

Libby smiled. "In my off time."

"Ah. Always the professional. So, are you going to tell me where we're going?"

"Get off on BeLoy Avenue."

Mick glanced at her. "Are we going where I think we're going?"

"There are two people in a house about to shoot each other because they think the other one is up to no good."

"And?"

"It got me to thinking."

Mick turned off of BeLoy and onto Carrie Street. They pulled into the Lambersons' driveway.

Libby stepped out of the car and surveyed the house. Mick got out on the other side of the car.

Together they walked toward the front door. "You want to have dinner tonight, Libby?"

"If this goes as planned, we're going to be working until midnight."

"I'll bring in the Chinese food."

She touched his hand. "You romantic, you. You know I can't resist a man who treats me to Chinese when I'm filling out booking sheets."

She knocked. After a few moments, the door opened. Libby cleared her throat and greeted Mrs. Lamberson with her badge.

"What's this about?" Mrs. Lamberson asked.

"We need to come in, ma'am."

Mrs. Lamberson stepped aside so Libby and Mick could enter. On the living-room television was the live shot of the Levilles' house. Mrs. Lamberson glanced at it.

"Mrs. Lamberson, we need to ask you a few questions."

"I've already answered every question there is to ask."

She avoided their eyes. A strange look of shame crossed her face.

"We have some new ones. We've recently found out some very interesting information. Mrs. Lamberson, were you not aware that your husband, Joel, had recently taken out a large insurance policy on you?"

She shook her head, but she didn't look convincing.

Libby said, "Mrs. Lamberson, we all understand what kind of man Joel was. Who could blame you, especially after he took out a life insurance policy with the intention of killing you, right?"

Mick looked at Mrs. Lamberson. Her bottom lip trembled, and a flood of tears rushed down her cheeks. She covered her mouth, shook her head, and slumped into a nearby chair. She cursed Joel's name, then said, "It wasn't enough that he had to do business that way. But then he wants me dead so he can pursue a woman who doesn't even want him!"

Mick and Libby exchanged glances. "Mrs. Leville?"

"He had such a fantasy about it. He thought once he had all that money, she would love him. I heard him on the phone to her one night, begging her. It was so pathetic. She didn't want him! I was good to him! I always looked the other way in everything he did and raised his daughters to love him anyway!" She tried to gather herself. "But all he cared about was money."

"So you stole the documents," Libby said.

"He didn't deserve my love!"

"And you killed him."

Mrs. Lamberson looked down. "You should've seen the look on his face. All these years he thought I was so weak and so lowly. You should've seen his face."

Thirty minutes later, Mick and Libby left the Lamberson home. Mrs. Lamberson was being led away in handcuffs by one officer, while another officer was trying to explain the situation to her two teenage daughters.

"So what gave it away for you?" Mick asked.

"The insurance policy and the acetone. I remembered that she'd mentioned working at a beauty salon. When we found out about the insurance policy, I knew she had motive. And it always bothered me that she didn't mention that Nicole Leville had been to her house. She was a woman scorned, and she hoped to see the two people she despised as much as her husband end their lives tragically."

"So Joel was responsible for the first three buildings. Mrs. Lamberson did the fourth building, and then Ira Leville, afraid that he would be found out, burned a random building to try to lead investigators on a rabbit trail."

"Ira better enjoy it while he can. Those documents are going to implement him."

"Hidden, of all places, under the mattress."

"The irony."

"And pretty savvy of her. She knew Ira would be our first suspect, and Mrs. Lamberson did a good job of steering us to him." She grabbed his hand as they walked to the car.

"I can't resist a woman with gut instincts."

She laughed. "My gut tells me I've found the perfect man, despite his tendency toward dangerous weather phenomena."

"Your gut is always right."

Despite being pale and out of shape, Sammy Earle walked proudly toward the door, swinging his arms just because he could. He opened the door himself, and the guard handed him a sack of all his belongings.

The warm sunshine delighted him, and he grinned at no one in particular. It didn't matter. He hadn't grinned in a long time. So he continued to grin.

One more gate, and he was free. The guard unlocked the chain-link gate and pushed it open. Freedom was only inches away. Three footsteps at the most. How could imprisonment and freedom be so close to one another? How could he reach from one to the other by barely moving his feet?

"Go on, Sammy" the guard said. "You're out of here."

Sammy thanked him. He wanted to shake his hand, but he just walked instead.

"Good luck," the guard said.

Sammy turned around. "Thank you."

From behind him he heard, "You need a ride?"

It was Chaplain Barber. Sammy hardly knew what to say.

"I can take you anywhere you need to go. Do you have a place to go?"

"The notoriety of this case has made me famous enough that some of my old law partners are speaking to me again. And offering me a place at their homes until I can get back on my feet."

"That's good."

"I thought you would come back."

"When?"

"The last time we talked. I figured you would come back, try to convince me one more time to believe what it says in the Bible. But you never did. Why didn't you? I was going to be executed. Wasn't that a good reason to keep trying in some way?"

"Sammy," the chaplain said, "I knew I wasn't going to be able to convince you. We'd come to a dead end, and there was nothing more I could say."

"So you just gave up?"

"I never gave up. I would've prayed until the last minute of your life."

"Prayed what?"

"I prayed that somehow God would show you what it means to receive something you don't deserve."

Sammy looked past the chaplain, toward the green fields. To breathe in fresh air, to be within walking distance of grass and water. He didn't have the words to explain what it felt like to receive it. "Do you still have that Bible you let me read?"

"Sure. It's in my car."

"Good." Sammy finally faced the chaplain, in one sense ashamed for rejecting the man's efforts, but also in awe of the fact that he could trust the eternal destiny of a man's soul to the power of God. "I heard that FBI agent almost died trying to prove Shep Crawford was Patrick Delano. Trying to save me."

"That's what I hear."

He shook the chaplain's outstretched hand and took a moment to find the words to express what he was feeling. Finally Sammy Earle said, "I never would've believed it. Before, I mean. And it's a hard thing to believe now. But I think I will believe it. Because it changes a man. It makes life have purpose."

"Believe what, Sammy?"

"That I am worth dying for."

acknowledgments

What fun I've had writing this series! I hope my readers have had as much fun reading it. Thanks to all of you who continue to read and enjoy my books. I will write as long as I am able! And thank you for all the kind letters you send me.

I'd also like to thank the wonderful people at Tyndale who are such a pleasure to work with—Jan Stob, Becky Nesbitt, Lorie Popp, Travis Thrasher, just to name a few. Thanks to all at Tyndale who contribute their hard work and their talent to make my books what they are. I couldn't do what I do without you!

I'd also like to thank Ron Wheatley for continuing his impressive work as my technical advisor. Ron, you know there is no way I could do this without you. Thanks also to you and Barb for your friendship.

I would like to thank my readers Nessie, Kaylea, Brenda, Kathie, and Ellie, who provided invaluable feedback in the early stages of this manuscript, and to Marc Rodriguez and Chris Short for additional technical help.

Thanks also to my agent Janet Kobobel Grant, who continues to keep me afloat!

And to my church, WCC, for your continuous, loving support.

And last but not least, "thanks" does not express how much my family means to me and how supportive they are at all times of my writing. Sean, John Caleb, and Cate, I love you!

Father God, thank You once again for letting me do this. It is a gift from You.